For the backbone of the theater,
Sam M, with best
regards;

Hugh Gilmore

Last Night on the Gorilla Tour

Last Night on the Gorilla Tour

When the famous explorer Richard L. Garner boards the train from Lynchburg in 1921, he is looking forward to a few hours of peace while he prepares the final speech of his fund-raising tour. After tonight's talk in Knoxville about "New Discoveries in Gorilla Family Life," he'll rest for a week and then go back to French Equatorial Africa.

Despite the care with which he has lived his life, Garner could never have anticipated the people who will intrude on him that day: A lovely young woman trying to leave her mistakes behind; a man stalking her who knows her secrets; the man's odd-but-artistic ten-year-old son, and a teenaged "travelin' traveler" who suffers from a rare disease. By the time the train arrives in Knoxville this little "family" of travelers will be so barbarously entangled only an emotional explosion can separate them.

The story opens in Greenville, Tennessee, in 1920 when the young woman, Clara Talbot, and her eventual stalker, Linder Charles, meet by chance in a grocery store. The strange love affair that evolves between them cannot be settled until Clara surrenders to Linder something no longer hers to give. Unfortunately for Professor Garner, their twisting trails have led them aboard his train. When Clara enters his cabin and asks him to help with "her little problem," the course of all their lives will change.

What follows involves thievery, an abduction, a daring leap from the train, an escape through a swamp, manslaughter, and a wild race along the Holston River to assure that everyone winds up in Knoxville at the same time and place. And at every stage: lies—lots of lies—until some final truths are revealed in a way that helps no one.

Funny, gripping, sexy and intelligent, *Last Night on the Gorilla Tour* is a quirky and entertaining novel about love, family and the animal in us all.

Last Night on the Gorilla Tour

A Novel

Hugh Gilmore

SoundStars Press
Chestnut Hill, Philadelphia
2013

NOTICE

Last Night on the Gorilla Tour is a work of fiction loosely set in the region between Lynchburg, VA, and Knoxville, TN, in the years 1920/1921. With one exception, all characters depicted are entirely fictional and any resemblance to actual persons, living or dead, is entirely coincidental.

The one exception is the character of Richard Lynch Garner (1848–1920), of Abingdon, VA, one of the pioneers of early primate field studies. While the essence of Garner's research efforts is portrayed accurately in this book, many of the plot details are purely inventions of mine. Both I and "Professor" Garner were doing fine with this book until certain characters like Clara Talbot and Linder and Eddie Charles crawled into the story. All hell broke loose after that.

Hugh Gilmore
hughmore@Yahoo.com

Cover design & photo by Hugh Gilmore

Copyright © 2013 Hugh Gilmore

ISBN-13: 978-1481849685
ISBN-10: 1481849689

Dedication

To Bill Pinkerton, Brother Damian Luke and Loren C. Eiseley, three men who were kind to me in my youth, while guiding me onto Nature's path.

Other Works by Hugh Gilmore

Local Humor: An Anthology.
With Janet Gilmore, Jim Harris & Mike Todd
iUniverse. 2009.

Malcolm's Wine: A Noir Crime Novel.
SoundStars Press. 2011

Scenes From A Bookshop: A Short Story Collection
SoundStars Press. 2012

Redneck Noir: A Personal Journey
Amazon Kindle eBoook. 2012

A Remembrance of Loren Eiseley.
Amazon Kindle eBook. 2012

Juan Belmonte's 'Killer of Bulls' as an Existential tale.
Amazon Kindle eBook. 2012

Part 1
May, 1920 Greenville, Tennessee

Blue chalk for Eddie

One warm afternoon Linder Charles stepped into Hobson's General Store to steal art supplies for his ten-year-old son, Eddie. Eddie's medium lately was blue chalk, which he used to draw what Linder called "jungle pictures" on the debarked trees and stumps in the fields around his mother's house. Snakes and birds, mostly, sometimes a cat-looking creature. Triangles, too. Sometimes he went up and drew on the floor boards of the porch, though Honeybunch, his Ma, always erased them. Then she'd tell Linder to keep a better eye on Eddie while she did all the work around there. That was the least Linder could do, she'd say, being the boy's father and so on. Linder didn't mind helping Eddie keep busy, so he encouraged him. Keeping Eddie happy might also get him in good with Honeybunch, which occasionally led upstairs for an afternoon—other than that she didn't let him in her home anymore.

So that's all he wanted from Hobson's store: some fat blue sticks of carpenter's chalk, because school chalk snapped too easy. That's all Linder was thinking about as he stepped up into Hobson's and saw Clara Talbot for the first time.

Clara's back was turned when he went in and at first she just looked like a young lady in a nice floral day dress standing at the counter pointing at a large Crisco on the shelf. Mrs. Hobson shot Linder a squinty look and her tongue slipped over her lower lip, as though she wanted to say something like, "Take a look at the thief and liar who just came in." But instead she turned and grabbed the can for the young lady, who Linder reckoned, being a newcomer, must be somebody's visiting niece.

Linder figured that moment with Mrs. Hobson's back turned was a good chance to get his shop done. He headed up the last aisle, the darkest one, where the afternoon sun didn't quite reach, and pocketed three nice fat pieces of blue carpenter's chalk. He needed string too. When he looked over to see how vigilant Mrs. Hobson was being, he saw her staring at him. He moved his eyes away, knowing his face had reddened. He barely managed to suppress the brazen smile he wanted to give her. Might as well wear a sign saying Shoplifter at Work. Not easy being the provider to an odd, but talented boy, he thought.

With his head still bent down like he was browsing, he thought he heard the young woman ask for peaches. Maybe she was just commenting on things, but one word he clearly heard her say was "peaches." So, that would be the word he later on would always associate with first hearing her voice: "peaches." And proof that "peaches" was the first word was when he looked up again and saw Mrs. Hobson putting a peck of peaches on the counter. First of the early crop. A moment to be remembered forever, because that was when the gal turned around and he got his first look at her—the pretty-but-ordinary, plump young girl he'd later sit in a jail cell and remember as a cold-hearted bitch.

But just then, fair as a summer's day, her ample arms bare in a short-sleeved dress, she was a comely young woman in town for an hour, buying some flour and shortening and peaches and other goods

Linder often later wished he'd had a Kodak of that moment so he could study her and look for some detail that might have served as a warning. But, really, truly, there was nothing to see but a young lady with pretty eyes and flushed cheeks, a small enough waist, full up top—ripe as a fruit you'd like to squeeze.

She, meanwhile, didn't even look at him. Her gaze swept by him like a searchlight ignoring a stump, and he felt a little foolish standing ready to smile a greeting. She turned around again. She had pretty shoulders.

Later on, he'd have more than enough time to think about the finer details while lying on the steel shelf the prison called a bed, hearing train whistles taunt him at night. Sometimes, if it made him feel better, he told himself that when her eyes nearly met his that first time, he practically forgot to breathe. Other times he'd explain his first reaction away by saying he couldn't breathe then because of the thickness of the fruit smell in the store. Underneath though, there was always the same truth: the sight of her young, full body and shining hair, combined with the way she ignored him, drove home the truth of his greatest dread: there was a finer side to life he was never going to know. That's how highly he thought of her that day. And then a train whistle would call from somewhere out in the darkness, and he'd wish he was back home, which only went to twist his sorry-ass soul all the more by reminding him he'd never known such a place.

As much as he was mooning about that young lady that afternoon, he was also feeling uneasy about the stolen chalk and string in his overalls. You didn't have to be a genius to know Mrs. Hobson was on to him about the thefts. And that she also didn't like the light in his eye when he looked at that young lady. He should have ushered himself out of the store at that moment. Everything would have turned out different. But he just froze in flight at the sight of this especially bright flower in an otherwise dull field.

The young lady shut her purse and began signing the receipt. Linder felt like he was about to lose something he didn't want to bear the memory of losing. It felt to him like she had already started sliding away. To do nothing would be to *have* nothing. Forever.

He shifted his eyes from the girl to Mrs. Hobson, who was staring hard at him now, but he didn't care. A kind of determination came into him. This time he did wink at her old prune face and followed that with a full-bore smile. She drew up like a salted snail. He figured he'd go outside and wait and see what the girl would do if he tried to talk to her.

But then he got a better idea.

He walked up to the front of the store and swooped over to the counter and said, "Here, I'll give you a hand with these, Miss." She turned only her head, barely looking at him with beautiful, indifferent hazel eyes, and before she could say yes or no, he'd lifted a heavy sack of flour onto his shoulder. His knees gave just a little. He didn't realize these bags were so heavy. But one bag didn't seem impressive, since he'd just seen Mrs. Hobson lift one, so he grabbed another and humphed it onto the other shoulder and started for the door. Knowing they were watching him, he walked easily up to the screen door and pushed through in one easy motion.

Once outside, he felt she'd be obliged to at least say thanks and the rest was up to him. He walked onto the wooden sidewalk a few paces and turned around for her to tell him which way her carriage waited. But she hadn't come out yet. He refreshed the bags' positions on his shoulders with some shrugs and brightened up his posture and stood ready for her, trying to look fresh and casual. But still she didn't come out. All too quickly: the bags felt too heavy, the day was too hot and the sun was too much in his eyes. He wanted to look in the store window to see if she was coming yet, but he didn't want to be thought weak. The left bag started putting a painful crick in his neck and shoulder blade.

Clara

She saw him out there all right, and she knew what he was up to. She walked around the store wondering if there was something else she could buy, just to wear him down. There were a few things she might like, but she'd already spent what Aunt Polly had sent her to town with. Mrs. Hobson had been told not to give her credit, even if she said something was for Aunt Polly.

She walked down the fabric aisle and stopped to browse the small stack of dress pattern envelopes again. These old Buttericks bored her, but Mrs. Hobson would be suspicious of her if she just pranced out after that man. And she couldn't ask Mrs. Hobson who he was. That would be like saying she was curious about him, which she neither was nor wasn't. He was just a field hand or some day laborer. And probably a lazy one too, in her estimation. Who else would be loafing around when all the men his age were working during the day?

She'd already paid her bill, so she knew Mrs. Hobson was wondering why she was lingering. And everything she did in town, or didn't do, got told to Aunt Polly, sometimes even before Clara got home. Still, she was enjoying making Mrs. Hobson work hard at pretending to be busy while she really was just spying. She hardly thought she was so interesting she was worth being spied on.

And that man in the overalls. What did he think he was up to? This was the oldest game in the world and not one she cared to play, certainly not with someone so very local and uncouth.

She'd only turned around before and let him get a good look at her because she was curious to see who Mrs. Hobson was shooting daggers at with her eyes. She took in that it was a grown man, but didn't give him the satisfaction of noticing him. Now she was enjoying keeping him waiting while she trailed her finger along the long table of goods. She took her time advancing toward the front window.

Now look at him, she thought. Hot and sweaty. Serves him right for being so forward. He's trying to appear casual, like those bags were actually epaulettes he wore on his shoulders. Maybe he was a returning soldier and that was why he didn't have work to do. Some of them were still getting back from Europe. This one didn't look it though. There was nothing crisp about him. She could practically smell the barn on him when he brushed past her. She went to the window and looked at him again.

Okay, he looked bushed enough. He wasn't even smart enough to stand under the store awning while he waited.

"Good bye, Mrs. Hobson. Thank you. I'll say hello to Aunt Polly for you," she called as she went out the door, not giving Mrs. Hobson the chance to send her off with a thousand pieces of advice. She shut the screen door behind her, thinking I hope I never am an old widow like that, running a store and nothing better to do than pushing my nose in the duff, looking for other people's truffles. The man stood with his back turned to her, his hands at his sides, the two bags bookending his head.

"Thank you for carrying my flour sacks," she said.

Putting his hands up to steady the sacks, he turned and said, "Where you want 'em put?"

"My carriage is over there," she said, pointing to where she'd hitched the pony carriage in the shade. He went over and eased the bags from his shoulders into the small cart. He stretched his arms and bent his neck side-to-side before he turned to look at her from under his flat cap.

She was caught off-guard by his light brown eyes and long eye lashes, enough to say, "I'm sorry, I thought you knew which cart was mine."

"No ma'am, I never had the pleasure of seein' you before, but I knew that was Miz Wooton's cart and pony. So I guess she's your auntie or somethin' like that?"

She decided to ignore his attempt to get personal.

She said, "Is that so?" She lifted her handbag and took out her change purse and snapped it open. "Well, the way you swooped up my bags in your 'take charge' manner, I knew you were Hobson's delivery boy and I do appreciate the service."

She offered him a dime. She knew he didn't work for Mrs. Hobson, and he certainly wasn't a boy, but she didn't like his being fresh.

He took off his cap with one hand and held it against his hip and put his other hand in his jeans pocket and looked away from her for a second while he ran his tongue over his teeth with his mouth closed. Clara thought he actually looked like his feelings were hurt. He must have felt she'd been impulsive and mean. She'd just meant to be funny. Not to his point of view, but funny later, in another scene where she could imagine telling a friend about how she'd handled this big local oaf who'd tried his rooster strut on her.

All sincerity, he said, "No miss, don't work here. Just like to be helpful when I can. Don't feel right standin' around doin' nothin' when I see a woman burdened."

She sensed right away he was lying. He'd finished his speech with a polite smile that emphasized how cute he was. His shoulders were wide, his hips were small, his hair was dark and thick, as were his eyebrows, his nose was large and bumped, but his lips were full. He was what other girls at the seminary she used to attend called "ugly handsome." But devious, a liar. About what she didn't know, and she didn't care to know the details. You don't have to count the scales on a snake to know to step aside.

"Well. You are a gentleman, and quite helpful, too," she said. She decided to work him some more and send him on his way. She didn't like manipulators. He'd be begging for the dime by the time she was through with him.

She said, "If you're not too worn out, there are some more things I need to have brought to the wagon."

He trotted after her back into Hobson's. "Have brought," he thought. Uppity, and annoying. But then said softly to himself, as though wanting to learn a school exercise, "have brought," "have brought."

She pointed at two more bags, heavy ones he maybe should barrow because he still had sharp pains between his shoulder blades from the first load. But he carried them. From here on until he finished she just waited inside. Each time he came back she pointed at more things. On it went. Canned goods, chicken feed, rice and beans, his sore shoulders now carrying just one sack each trip. Finally, she said, "That's the last one, thank you," and followed him out of the store.

As he loaded that last sack, she stood on the wooden sidewalk watching him. He readjusted the pile of sacks, gave the top one a pat, and then turned to look at her. At that moment, she would tell him later, when she knew him better, she wanted to laugh because he looked like he was waiting for her to throw a stick he could run and fetch with his teeth.

That wasn't what he was thinking though. He might have been just a cur dog to her right then but he'd picked up the scent and begun his cast.

"You look like you're fixin' to do some baking," he said.

She startled momentarily as though a wooden Indian had begun talking, but she came back at him with exaggerated wide eyes and said, "Why, yes I am. But how on earth did you ever guess that?"

He started to mention the flour sacks, and shortening cans, and fruit, but caught the twinkle in her eyes. She got him, but what she didn't really suss, he could tell, was that she'd joined the game. She might be the sly fox, but she'd opened the pursuit.

He said, "Must have been a lucky guess, I reckon. You a good cook?" Let her swing her little fists all she wanted, he wasn't coming away from this empty handed. She was unhitching her pony, but she turned and said, "Some people think so. Occasional dyspepsia, but I haven't poisoned anyone yet ... as far as I know."

Disspepsia, huh? Everyone of these little superiority darts she shot at him he was gonna catch and bend into a chain link. He pressed on: "You any good at making pies?"

For the first time she took her time looking at him. "What kind of pies are you talking about? And what's your name?"

"Linder Charles. Folks call me Linder. I'm talkin' peach pie."

She was quiet for a minute as though trying to decide something. Linder didn't want her to finish her thought in case she decided against him, so he rushed her, "Why you askin'? You just curious, or you sharin'?"

She smiled her concession. He figured she must have felt a little guilty for working him so hard and trying to humiliate him with Websterisms, because she said, "Okay, I guess you earned a pie. This time next week I'll bring you a peach pie."

"What's your name?"

"Clara Talbot."

He knew who that was. The Talbots hailed from somewhere along the Holston, north of Knoxville. Damned near the whole family died to Spanish Flu two-three years ago. Polly Wooton, just out a town a ways, was her aunt. She's an orphan girl. Polly's ward.

He saw no sense mentioning any of that now. He might maybe use that later. He said, "Well, yes, Miz Talbot, thank you for your offer of a peach pie, but I have a small problem from that. You see, I get lonely when I eat somethin' good as peach pie all by myself."

"Lonely?"

"Yes, and if I get lonely, I get indigestive and can't enjoy the pie. So, I wonder if you'd do me a favor?" She asked what that would be. And he said, "Could you help me eat some of that pie next week? That way the juices wouldn't disagree with me."

She asked him to clarify what he was talking about, so he came out with it and said, "We could sort of have a peach-pie picnic." She said it was generous of him to include her in his digestive plans, but she wouldn't have time to do anything more than deliver the pie as promised.

"That's okay," he said, figuring he could work on her some more next time, the pie being at least a start.

"Okay," she repeated, but in a different tone, one he couldn't figure, as though she had taken the word and held it at arm's length. Then she thanked him for helping her, climbed aboard, and gave the reins a crisp snap. The little horse set into a quick walk.

"Be seein' ya," Linder said as he leaned, one hand on the hitching post, watching the little carriage go up the dusty street, turn the corner, and disappear. He was glad she agreed to see him again, but irked by her taking him for a delivery boy and thinking big words would put him in his place. He went back into Hobson's. No one was behind the counter. He swiped a new Barlow knife and left right away, feeling a little better compensated for his hard work.

Twenty-five minutes later, after a long and dusty tramp with plenty to think about. Linder arrived back to what, for better or worse, he called home, his pockets full of presents. He gave the chalk to Eddie and told him to go give the string to Honeybunch. He kept the pocket knife for himself. His mood was certainly better than when he'd set out looking for day work this morning. Thoughts of Clara filled his mind. His mood improved with every step as he returned to his tent set in the woods back of Eddie's mother's house, where he'd lived since she'd kicked him out a couple of years ago.

Pie making

Back at Aunt Polly's, Clara had little time to think about that strange man from town. The minute she changed from her town clothes Aunt Polly made her pay for those few hours off by sending her out to clean the henhouses. Plenty more chores lay ahead. Clara resisted complaining. She was determined not to be broken by her sour old aunt, much as she knew Polly meant well for her.

In bits and pieces, whenever her chore was monotonous enough, she tried to make sense of what happened between her and that strange town man. She felt some small urgency to figure out that peach pie business, because in one way she'd been please to make a sort of conquest of a male suitor, even someone as inappropriate as a farm laborer, and in another way she felt like she'd been beaten at her own game.

Feeding the geese later she thought some more on the topic. Though she was hungry to learn more about men, nothing about him seemed right. For one, she would prefer a somewhat younger man. Linder's face had too much by way of manly creases around his mouth and crows' feet at the edges of his eyes. And though he was good-looking, it was in a hillbilly way. In his favor, he was lean and strong in a way the schoolboys she'd known were not, though you didn't notice his strength till he used it.

But picking up her bags like he did, when he first met her, that was showing off. It seemed like it would be fun to fix him for being so pushy, so work him she did. She might even have felt sorry for him, if it didn't seem the whole time like he was looking for a weakness in her to exploit. When she finished working him, she let him talk a little ... well, not exactly let him ... just suddenly he had her talking.

As for his talk, his way was slow and easy, but with more wit than she expected, enough to be a little challenging. Though he certainly didn't give any of her favorites from the Smart Set magazine a run for his money. But why compare Mr. Mencken and Mr. Nathan to a man with Greenville, Tennessee, dirt on his scuffed farm shoes?

Anyway, seduction of the innocent was obvious behind his joking, just like at those Chicago parties the magazine stories described. But why'd she say she'd bake him a pie?

Maybe it was the sad eyes, kind of dreamy with a touch of self pity, that did it. Not that she felt like nurturing him, or anybody else, for that matter, but maybe, just maybe, she did owe him a little something.

That night, up in her room, she stood at her bedroom window resting her forehead against the cool glass and looked down at the moonlit yard. Her aunt's biting voice still hurt her ears. "You're not in Baltimore, girl. We don't live in Godless Baltimore, we're in Greeneville, we don't do things like that here." Someone sent word to Aunt Polly that Clara had stood on the sidewalk talking and laughing with that man this afternoon, that awful man who had nothing better to do than hang around town when everyone else was working, that low-life who worked a stem of grass in one side of his mouth and talked nonsense to girls out the other

It had amused Clara when she first came back from town to have found such an effective means of animating her lifeless old aunt. But the old lady wouldn't stop. Aunt Polly followed Clara everywhere she went—around the house, out to the porch, back into the kitchen—all the while piercing Clara with her shrill questions. In the early evening Clara ran to the bathroom and shut the door and ran the water loud. She sat on the edge of the tub holding her ears. It didn't work. Her aunt's voice reached around, up, over, under, through the door to attack her. "You'll find out soon enough who cares about what in these parts. You may be new around here but you ought to have more common sense." And so on. Whenever there was a pause, it was only so Aunt Polly could move the Victrola needle back to the edge of the record and start replaying the same tedious song.

After a while the cool blue moonlight in the yard below began to soothe her and her eyes no longer needed to restrain tears. In bed, she remembering falling asleep with her hands warming her lower belly. A frosty week between her and Polly followed, but fortunately there were no more scenes. The quiet gave Clara a chance to think about that funny man.

On one hand, he was uncouth—including dirty fingernails—and quite undereducated. There would be no sparkling dialogue between them, no cocktail party battle of the wits prior to "shacking up" as people called it nowadays. On the other, he was a good physical specimen and looked quite virile. If his eyes were to be believed, he'd know how to get her experienced before she went off to join the literary circles of the Jazz Age, another phrase she liked.

Most positive, he didn't count. He didn't seem to have any feelings, only animal desires, and she'd never see him again after she left Tennessee. Men like him were interested only in huffing away at women's bodies. Otherwise, they were incapable of forming a sentence that did not have the words "soil" or "rain" in it.

Her aunt was driving her crazy. She wouldn't come into her inheritance for two more years and had to live here in Greeneville until then. Unless she ran away. But what would she live on? She had no skills. All she'd bothered to learn at seminary were literature classes and French. She was going to be stuck here a while, but at least she had a chance to experiment with life a bit before she left. She decided to keep her promise to that man about the pie, deliver it to him personally, and see how he'd react, see if he'd come after her, know what it was like to have a pursuer. The thought had a delightful tension, like a schoolyard game with naughty overtones.

Unfortunately, the day before the pie was to be given, Aunt Polly's last female cousin over in Greene county, near the town of Chuckey, died and Clara would have to go to the funeral with her aunt.

Clara's disappointment about not seeing Linder tomorrow soon changed to worry that he would take her absence as rejection and not come around anymore. She wanted him to keep on the chase. A solution presented itself when Aunt Polly told her she had to go to

Greeneville to pick up funeral foods from two older women who knew Polly's cousin but whose ailing constitutions would not allow them to make the trip. Clara cheerfully agreed to do that and set about baking some funeral goods herself, ignoring the occasional suspicious glances coming from Aunt Polly whenever she walked by and saw her baking voluntarily. It wasn't hard at all to make an extra peach pie, peaches were just coming in season then.

The simplicity she'd imagined took another twist, however, when she wondered how Linder might interpret being handed a pie by Mrs. Hobson and not by herself. He'd very likely think she intended it as payment for services rendered and that was that, and he'd not be back. She decided the presentation of the pie deserved a little personal note to go with it.

Putting words to paper though, despite her insincerity, was nerve-wracking. Confident while writing the first words, she felt desperate as she wrote the last. She considered tearing up the note, but the prospect of emptying her life of an experiment she wanted to try, a sample perhaps of what awaited her when she finally left this backwater, was terrible.

She wrote:

> *Dear Linder Charles:*
>
> > *As promised, here is the peach pie I made for you.*
> > *I hope you enjoy it. I'm very sorry that the funeral*
> > *of an old and dear cousin kept me from giving it to you*
> > *personally. If you ever feel inclined to issue another*
> > *pie-eating picnic invitation, I might consider making*
> > *myself available to accept.*
>
> *Sincerely yours,*
> *Clara L. Talbot*

She put the note on top of the pie itself (not wanting Mrs. Hobson to see she had written him a note), wrapped the pie, and left it at Hobson's for him in the course of making her charitable rounds.

Peach pie surprise

The morning he was supposed to get the peach pie from Clara, Linder got up early and washed his face and slicked back his hair. It was barely daylight, but Eddie was up already, out in the field of burnt-out trees and stumps behind his mother's house, drawing blue chalk triangles and squiggly lines on the barkless gray trunks and branches. None of it made any sense in the usual ways, but the straight lines were straight and the circles were perfect and you could see he had a confident, talented hand. And the boy loved doing it. He sensed the boy liked him to watch, and he did sometimes, but he wished the boy would balance it with some hunting, or fishing, things a father and son could do together.

During the walk to town he had time to figure where he should wait until she came with the pie. He needed a place where he could keep an eye on Hobson's, but not be seen hanging around like he was waiting for someone. Livezy's stables across the street seemed the best bet.

When he got there he went in the back door and up the ladder to the loft and cocked the hay door open. After that, all he had to do was just lay on his stomach, watch and wait.

The morning slowly became midday. Noon became afternoon. It wasn't working out. He climbed down the ladder and walked through the stable without saying anything to the hay men who paused at the sight of him. He went out the back door without bothering to close it and walked around the block. When he got to Hobson's, Clara's pony cart still hadn't arrived yet. He stood there wondering what to do. Finally he put his face to the screen door and looked in.

Mrs. Hobson yelled, "Somebody left something here for you, Linder."

He went in at once and waited while she took a package from a shelf behind the counter. "It's from Clara Talbot," she said.

She put the string-tied brown paper package down before him. She eyeballed him and said, "Smells like a peach pie."

That was annoying, her not minding her own business, but his feelings were too hurt from getting the pie in this third-party way, so he just said, "I should thank Miz Talbot. She gonna be around later?"

"No, she's not," Mrs. Hobson said, "Her aunt's cousin, Florrie Stedman, over in Chuckey, died and she went to the funeral. She brought that package for you last night before they left."

He swiped a piece of chalk to get even with her on the way out. While he walked away he began to notice how hard he was taking this. All that waiting for nothing. He didn't care about the pie, it was the chance to talk to her again he'd wanted. Walking toward his own long afternoon shadow, holding the pie daintily by the string, he decided he might as well eat the pie because it smelled good. And then he reckoned the pie would smell and taste even better warmed up, so he headed to Eddie's mother's house, smoothing his cover story as he walked.

It was now late afternoon and Eddie was still out in the field, inscribing a stump with the new Barlow knife Linder shared with him, but the boy got up and came forward when he saw him, his eyes examining his pockets for bulges or lumps. He asked the boy, "You still got any of the chalk I give ya last week?" Eddie said no, so he told him, "Well, I got some more, but don't use it up so fast. When you're down to one piece, like now, make it last till you're sure more's comin'." He gave him the chalk and the boy sidled over to a large stone and started chalking it again.

He watched Eddie for a few minutes, unsure as always, whether he should encourage the boy by bringing him a wagon full of chalk or normalize him by dynamiting this field and never giving him chalk again.

Then he walked around to the front of the house, up the steps, across the wooden porch, and sat in the rocker so the package was prominent to notice in his lap. He knew she'd probably peeped him come out of the fields and talk to Eddie and seen the parcel and wondered its contents. He sat waiting. Curiosity would overcome her. That's the nature of the female beast.

After a while, though, she had not come out. He sat there jiggling his foot. He gave up. She could always outwait him. Darned if he could figger that out. He got up and knuckled three quick, loud raps and hurried back to the chair, legs crossed, package on his lap. Very casual.

The curtains parted and her pretty, but tired, face appeared against the glass panel in the upper part of the door and then she came out and spoke with sarcasm right away, "My, my, Linder, wonders never cease. Yesterday I saw you at the back of the house. Today I see you at the front. You sure do get around."

"Yes, I do, Honeybunch, thank you for noticing. I surely do. And here's proof, should you want it. A special treat. A surprise."

Her blonde hair, as always, looked like it was one hair brushing and a ribbon short of beauty. She refused to look at the package, just said, "Biggest treat I could think of would be for you to get a job and stop moping around."

"Well I got a peace offering here, something for us ... and Eddie, too." Her eyes slipped for a moment to the package and he said, "You're curious, ain't ya?"

She refused to answer.

"What's here's a treat for our whole family to enjoy."

She eyeballed him some more. "I can tell you're a little leery, so I'll tell you what. You do not like the deal, I'll leave the whole thing right here with you and the boy and I'll clear out."

"What's in there?"

"What is in here, did you say?"

"I'm going in," she said heading for the door.

"Okay, okay, I heard you. What's in here is a peach pie, is what."

She turned around, "Where'd you get a peach pie?"

"Don't sound so surprised. I got my ways."

"So does that skunk you won't trap out for me."

"We'll deal with that later. Things're gonna be different 'round here soon. I got a job helpin' out down at Hobson's lately and it might turn into a reg'lar thing."

"You working at Hobson's? That's a laugh. Everybody down there knows you got sticky fingers."

"You laugh all you want, but Hobson's knows that ain't true."

"Really?" she said in a mocking tone.

"Yeah, really," he said imitating her tone, "that's how come I got this little present to share with you. I was workin' in the store and some lady needed a bunch a supplies hauled out to her wagon ..."

"What lady was that?"

"Don't know her name, just a rich lady. New 'round here, I 'magine. Miz Hobson knows, if you want me to find out for you. I just work there."

"So you volunteered to help this rich old lady?"

"More or less. Nobody else at Hobson's strong enough to carry, so I got the job."

"So this customer sent you a peach pie?"

"To thank me for helping out."

"Wasn't that nice of her?"

"I guess so."

"Wonder how she knew to make your favorite?"

"Just lucky, I guess."

"Was this old lady real old, or just old?"

"I forgot to ask, Honeybunch. I see her again I'll check her teeth, okay?" Silence. She was thinking it over. He asked, "You gonna give it a try, eat some?" More silence. Linder spoke again, "I could just leave it here for you and the boy. First of many, you might say, given this new job 'n' all. But I figured it might make you lonely to eat a nice pie like this all by yerself, so I'm willin' to stay a while, keep ya company, make it social, ye know, share a piece."

Finally, she said, "Okay, Linder, you win. You want it like this or you want it warm?"

"Warm would taste better maybe. Bring up the smell some."

"Okay, wait here, I'll go in and warm it up. When it's warm, I'll bring it out and we can eat it."

He resented not being invited in, but thought one step at a time was better. He slid into the rocking chair, closed his eyes and rocked gently while he waited. He sat there on the porch, in the rocker, eyes closed, stomach eager, acids erupting at the back of his tongue as he pictured warm peach pie sliding through his mouth and gullet down to his craving tummy.

And then:

There she was.

Honeybunch.

Right there, coming through the door, but coming too fast, faster than could be good. Something bad was about to happen.

"I lost my appetite, Linder, but that shouldn't stop you from enjoying yourself. Here's your pie back." It was out of the brown paper wrapper, snugly filling a tin pie plate. Before he could say anything, she put the pie on the slatted porch floor next to his feet and stomped it hard in one sure, swift motion.

Linder looked down reflexively at the pie and then back at her again. She wore her calm face as she stepped back and leaned against the doorway in order to tug her pie-soiled shoe off and throw it past Linder's head so fast he wouldn't have had time to duck if she was a better thrower.

"Get out of here," she said, "you lyin' dog you."

Before he could blink she had one-shoed through the door and slammed it. He heard the lock click. He blinked. Then he looked down. The pie was crushed flat in the middle. But it didn't look too bad around the edges. There was a small juice-soaked paper in the middle of the collapsed crater. He bent down and looked. The paper had writing on it, female writing. Linder carefully lifted one edge of the note and peeled it away from the pie. There was too much juice and crushed peach on it for him to be able to read it, so he licked the fruit and juice from the paper as gently as he could. It tasted sweet, sweeter than anything he ever tasted before, sweeter, even, than he knew a pie could taste.

He walked to the edge of the porch, blowing on the note softly, anxious for it to dry so he could read it.

Eddie had come around from the other side of the house and up on the porch to sit beside the peach pie. He told the boy it was okay if he ate it, so Eddie began eating Honeybunch's Special Day-Old, Smashed-Peach Pie Surprise with his hands. In the yard right below, the dog had found Honeybunch's shoe and lay on his side holding it between his paws, licking the sticky peach juice off it.

Linder went down the steps without looking and walked along the path to his tent, alternately blowing on his note and looking at it, hoping the words would magically reappear.

The picnics

Clara was only nineteen and exceptionally inexperienced. She'd just put herself on a path to learn, the hard way, that writing notes can lead to trouble. Though Linder could read, he'd hardly ever had had cause to, and the personal note she sent to him, simple as it was, was the first and only hand-written note he'd ever received. It overpowered him more than a bookish person, especially a glibly literate person like Clara, could ever imagine. He saw the personal letter as a wondrous marriage of thought and paper, come together in a way that was fixed and binding forever. Why else take up a pen, or the expense of a good piece of blank writing paper?

Polly and Clara had stayed on two days at Polly's cousin's home after the funeral. By the time Clara next came to town she'd nearly forgotten Linder. She certainly didn't expect to see him, coming in as she was, on a different day of the week than usual.

He hadn't forgotten her, though. The moment she stopped her buggy, Linder was beside the pony, taking its reins. His frayed overalls and beat-up flat cap, only her second time seeing him, made her feel embarrassed by his familiarity and then mortified that she'd sent this grubby man a note—on purple stationery!

When she stepped down from the carriage, he presented three irises to her (swiped from Alma Rieser's garden, she learned later), which she accepted while wondering how to shoo him away without hurting his feelings. The occasion might for other girls have been an opportunity for one of those happy "firsts' by which girls measure their progress in Love's Great Contest—first flowers, first love note, first kiss, first "I love you," first marriage proposal, first night together, and so on. Though 'first baby' was certainly not on Clara's list, the others might have been, had the swain been more suitable to her tastes. Linder's presence was thoroughly embarrassing and not worth the trouble that would follow if Aunt Polly's spies were marking this scene. She thanked him for the flowers and placed them on the floor of her carriage where she hoped no one would see them.

Right away he suggested a picnic, which seemed forward, especially since he didn't have a picnic basket with him and seemed to assume she did. She started to tell him no, but then for the first of many times (until she later grew sick of it), she noticed and remembered the enchanting sadness of his eyes and how his smile and wisecracking ways lived just below as protection. A Dorothy Parker review in Vanity Fair magazine had described such a vulnerable man, and here she was noticing the same thing herself. How touching.

His face said he was expecting disappointment, was used to it, had been born to it, and his sad and desperate look so contrasted with his impressive height and strength it struck her as residing there only in the way it comes to dwell in a horse or a dog: it must have been beaten into him.

It struck her heart that some terrible injustice lay behind his sadness and that she could be the one to right it, to heal him, and thus for the first time in her life, possibly be useful to another human being. Perhaps it is love itself that dwells behind such tenderness—the need to soothe another's bruises. This feeling came to Clara only as a flicker, but with enough pulse to make her change her mind and tepidly agree to his request.

He surprised her again, this time by giving her directions to a picnic spot he'd picked out. Then, to her even further surprise, while she still considered the commonsense notion that she should get away from him now, once and forever, he loped down an alley as though racing her there. He seemed so childlike and genuine.

Then the alley was empty. The influence of his sad eyes attenuated and she again considered turning the pony around and going home, but that seemed ruder than she could muster. She trotted her pony through several streets till she'd gone down a dusty lane to the isolated grove near a small creek back of town where he said he'd be waiting.

A half-minute later she saw him standing on a grassy slope under one of the willows, one arm straight out against the trunk, the other cocked on his hip, his upstage foot crossed over the other. Away from town, seen through the swaying willow tendrils, he looked good to her, a picture of casual manhood.

Neither of them had brought food. He beckoned her to sit down in the soft grass and then surprised her by sitting at a respectful distance, something she had wondered about on the way here. All they did was talk, and almost none of what he said was flirtatious, which in a way was mildly disappointing since this was the first time she'd been alone in this fashion with a male, a man, actually, and some part of her was a bit giddy with the anticipation of fighting off an advance.

At one point he said, "That was the best peach pie I ever tasted, that pie you brought me."

She said, "Thank you," and then, to tease him, "But what about the note I sent you, didn't you like the note?"

He looked at her in exaggerated confusion and said, "Note? No, I don't remember any note." Then, as if he just remembered a gaff he'd made, "Say, one part of that pie tasted extra chewy. Was that a note? What it say?" For a second she started to believe him, but the spark in his eyes gave him away, so she said, "Oh, nothing, it was just directions for heating up the pie."

His conversation, even his voice, was more gentle and considerate than she could have guessed. By the end of this picnic she'd enjoyed herself enough to agree to meet him again the next week, and then the next, and they soon fell into a routine of meeting once a week for as long a time together as Clara felt she could hide from Aunt Polly.

He seemed harmless enough, though a little spooky sometimes. It wasn't anything he overtly did, it was just that he was so different from her. Much of that difference started with his simply being a man. His maleness drifted along under their conversation, and no matter how witty or friendly they both were, she felt some very elementary, very primitive contest happening. Though she felt superior to him in just about every way, she felt the lurking presence of barnyard sex, something crude and real, and far removed from the naughty, witty sophistication of a Jazz Age speakeasy, or the raucous Baltimore or Chicago apartment parties she read about. She and Linder were meeting at the back edge of a rural southern town in a grove of willow trees on a grassy creek bank she constantly worried would stain her dress with evidence. And all through their conversations one or the other of them had to brush away or pick off flies and beetles and ants and centipedes and worms that treated the two of them as though they were merely detritus intruding on the insect landscape.

Linder was never aggressive, always polite, ready to be helpful. But male like an farm animal, a creature bred to taking and giving blows without complaint, unoffended by thoughtlessness, indifferent to weather or rough textures, accustomed to responding to what his body wanted. It was repulsive in a way, especially to think it could be used against her. Attractive if it could be used to make her safe, or satisfy her needs.

While he seemed content to lie there on his side forever, a grass stem at the corner of his mouth, grinning at the funny things she said, she also noticed that beneath his muscles' dumb needs he had inside him infantile hurts that his manhood had encapsulated in the way trees will absorb an iron fence as they grow.

Their early conversations contained, barely disguised, everything they'd ever need to know about each other. She told him she was selfish. Linder replied that, well, everyone had to look out for himself in this world. She said she always needed to throw herself completely into whatever it was she was working on. Linder allowed that was better than going around doing things half-ways. She said she was going to get out of the country and move to a city, any city, one day. Linder declared that's where the opportunities were. She said she'd never marry. Linder said "never say never." She said that even if she did find a man to settle down with, she most definitely would never have children. Linder said well, they are a big responsibility, people got to think twice, and if they aren't ready they shouldn't have them. Children were a gift, he said. Someday he hoped to settle down and have a family.

Not me, she said. They were sitting side by side at the time and she remembered that Linder's eyes stayed on her for a while after she spoke. He didn't say anything, but she went away wondering if she'd offended him.

They fell into a pleasant rhythm of meeting, talking, eating, wondering and waiting to meet again. And then the kissing began. Their first kiss was made memorable by happening at the end of an otherwise flat afternoon.

When she said she had to go, he got up first and helped her up but didn't let go of her hand. She knew what was coming next. Then he took her other hand. She was surprised that his hands weren't calloused and that his hold was gentle as he pulled her to him, very close. He held her like that briefly and then leaned forward a little, bent down, and gave her a tender kiss on the lips. It was nice, her lips tingled. He held the kiss for a few seconds, then started to slacken.

Something went off in her. She didn't want the kissing to stop. Before he could take his lips away, she mashed her lips against his and held him tight, rubbing her half-open mouth against his, then mashed some more. He was caught off guard and that excited her, made her feel she'd gained an edge on him in a contest, made her keep going. She squeezed tighter, making a low throbbing hum go through her. He seemed overwhelmed, was having trouble breathing, seemed to be hanging on so he could assert who the man was here. Their kiss had become a lip-crushing contest that lasted until she stopped and let go of him.

Her emotions intensified after that day and in future meetings the time spent eating and talking diminished as the kissing and hugging got hotter. Soon most of their picnic time was spent moaning and sighing, their bodies flushed, wisps of wet hair stuck to their faces. It was glorious, though sometimes terribly unsatisfying. Then, one day, they discovered what she came to privately think of as her special gift.

It happened the afternoon she first let him rub the place between her legs. She was breathing hard and moaning, nothing new, but she also felt something happening inside her which she wanted to keep happening. Linder, though, kept changing the way he moved his hand. Each time he did, the feeling started to back down. Finally, desperate, she felt she could tolerate his erratic touching no longer. She grabbed the back of his wrist and held it tight and still against her while she began hunching her hips to rub herself against his hand until she threw her head back and muffled a scream as she felt a new pleasure convulse inside her and blossom out through her body. Her blood was pounding as she caught her breath. She needed to squeeze her legs together and did, crushing his hand. She wanted to do it again, and was about to, but when she opened her eyes he was grinning ear to ear as though all that could be done, had been done. She looked away to the quiet brook and let the tingling subside.

That tingling became everything to her. The next time they met under the willow she climaxed again but didn't let go of his wrist and didn't open her eyes. When it was clear he would let her do this her way, she moved again, and went again. And then she went again. And went again. Once she opened her eyes and saw him gaping like he was at a sideshow.

Linder could only imagine what she was experiencing but it got him aroused him enough to undo his buttons and put his 'boner'—as he called it—on display for the first time. She enjoyed having aroused him so, but she didn't like the assumption he was making. Part of her believed he'd already been amply rewarded by being allowed to help bring on her pleasure. Besides, she had no idea what she was supposed to do with that thing sticking out from between his buttons.

She remembered that moment as an opportunity to learn some things she'd need to know about men. She couldn't be going to the city and drinking bathtub gin and having acerbically funny conversations and then not know what to do when it was time to be alone with a man-about-town kind of man. She didn't want to come across as provincial, or seem to be a naïf.

Linder would be her education, far away from prying eyes, a safe man because he'd never be part of her social circle (once she had one). In short, he didn't count, not as a friend and never as a potential husband. He jogged his anxious tool closer to her.

It must have been obvious that she didn't know what to do, because he reached out and put her hand on him. After some guidance, including how to use the drool from his thing for lubrication, she brought Linder to his own paralyzing conclusion. As he spurted she was at first awed, but then frightened as the viscous hot flow pulsed over the backs of her fingers and down her wrist, heedless and indifferent as it surged, as though given enough volume it would bury everything in its path.

She felt childish, as though she'd played with something she didn't know was dangerous and had escaped simply by good luck.

She shelved her misgivings and kept seeing him, but made it clear there would be no progression: He could not go under her clothes. She wanted to save what she'd been led by her reading to think of as the better, the deeper, the more intimate part of herself, for someone she admired more, someone maybe she could even love.

Toward the end of the summer she felt she'd learned as much as she could about men, or at least maleness, from Linder and began to lose interest in him. She daydreamed of ways to end their relationship. She probably would have too, if Aunt Polly hadn't started to end it herself.

When the rains came

Clara was in the pantry replacing the shelf paper when Aunt Polly walked in and said, "Clara, you needn't go into town today."

Clara willed herself not to turn around as she said, "Oh?" She knew not to say more. Polly would be listening for her tone.

"Yes," her aunt said, deliberately brief, trying to force her to ask why, but all she said was, "Okay, Aunt Polly. I'll just busy myself around here."

Polly then relented and explained that she had some errands to run herself and there was no need for two of them to waste an afternoon. It was obviously a lie, and spoken while she knew Polly's cold gray eyes waited for her to turn around so she could search Clara's face. Besides, their tacit agreement was that Clara's trips to town were meant to ease the boredom of her being the only young person living on this immaculate, isolated farm.

Clara turned and said, "I understand, Aunt Polly," trying to match Polly look for look until she felt her face flush. Polly's tight lips leaked the merest smirk before she turned and left.

Clara forced herself to keep busy to stay ahead of the pain she knew would rush her if she stood still. At the hour when she knew she should have been meeting Linder she went out and swept around the chicken coop with such violence that the hens were still complaining hours later. She wondered how he felt when he saw the carriage at a distance and then saw Aunt Polly driving. She wondered how she could last an entire week before she could go to town and see him again. Not once through this deprivation did she wonder how she'd gone from planning to cast off Linder to missing him with all her young heart.

As the week went by, time quietly heightened her desire to see Linder, so it was a shock when the following Thursday came around and her aunt again said she'd do the drive to town. Polly had declared war, the kind of sneaky, sniping war she excelled at. After her aunt rode away, Clara went out behind the barn and sat with her back to the wall. She vowed to fight back, willed herself to do her chores as though steadfastness would bring her back to Linder, but the friction of the passing minutes wore away the pretense. When she noticed that the shadows had moved beneath the trees, like they must have at the willow grove, she went into the house, up to her bedroom, closed the door and lay squeezing a pillow against her. She wanted to cry but was afraid Aunt Polly would see from her face later that she had broken down. She smoldered there like that until she heard her aunt's pony coming, and then rose and smoothed her indentation from the bed and was downstairs peeling potatoes when Aunt Polly came into the kitchen.

It took a while to get to sleep that night, her body was so tight, but eventually she did, though lightly.

She awakened when she thought she heard a crunch on the gravel below the window. She lifted her head from the bed and listened. Someone was approaching the house. She got up and went over to the dresser next to the window and began brushing the sleep tangles from her hair, listening as she heard the trellis beside her window being ascended. His climb was neither quiet nor quick, each loud clunk against the wall being followed by a long silence. She waited. Delighted.

Then, "Pssst. It's me."

"I'm right here." And then, as though she hadn't been planning to jilt him before Aunt Polly interfered, out of her mouth came, "Oh, Linder, I missed you."

"Me, too. Could you hear me coming up?"

"A little. I don't think Aunt Polly heard or she'd be shooting you by now."

"She what stopped ya from comin' to see me?"

"Yes, she thinks I'm up to something."

"You are. Follow me."

She fetched her shoes and came back to the window and climbed down using the trellis and porch column. She felt exposed being in a flannel nightgown in the yard at night, a man beside her. Every sound was heightened by the night's silence. Even the whip-poor-wills had gone quiet. He took her hand and went ahead, sticking to the shadows. He seemed rather practiced at this and she wondered whether it was just him or if this was simply something men knew how to do. As soon as they'd left the yard he pulled her up to his side so they could walk together holding hands. It struck her as odd that this was their first time doing something so old-fashioned even though they'd done more intimate things. She wasn't sure she liked the equality implied by holding hands.

Linder led her toward the peach orchard where he'd already spread a large blue blanket on the ground. She felt flattered. They lay down facing one another and started kissing right away. To mark the specialness of the occasion, she let Linder's hand go under her clothes. It was nice, a bit invasive and raw, but nice, though it didn't take her personal sensations much farther along than their previous way.

He walked her back. When they were beneath her window, she felt the pain of what it would be like to miss him. Or, more poignantly, the pain of returning to the emptiness of farm life. She kissed small kisses all over his face, which amused him, then said she had to go up. He stopped her and said he had a plan for from now on. He'd wait for her in town each week as usual at the willows, but if she didn't show up, he'd know why, so he'd meet her in the orchard, exactly at midnight.

The sneakiness and desperation required to get around Aunt Polly enhanced Clara's romantic fervor, enough to make her care again for Linder. "The highway man came riding, riding ..." she whispered, in the same voice she prayed with, as she lay in bed till it was time to climb down and see him each Thursday night. Despite the care she took to disguise her new happiness from Polly, she doubted her aunt was fooled. But, until Polly declared war openly, Clara would hide behind her polite smile. In the battle of unspoken accusations only physical evidence would count.

On Sunday of that week, a late afternoon rain started and continued through the night. When she awoke on Monday morning, it looked to be over, but by mid-afternoon, rain clouds came racing in low from behind the hills, bringing big drops that held steady for a while and then, all at once, fell so fast and thick you couldn't see across the yard. Coming back from tending the animals, she stepped into a puddle that wasn't there earlier and the water went over the ankles of her boots, down into her socks. All through dinner the wind blew the heavy rain against the south side of the house and by the time she said good night to Aunt Polly and went up to her room, her nerves were bad. The room was chilly and smelled damp. She noticed that she'd left the window open a few inches this morning and went over to pull it closed, but it was swollen from the rain and wouldn't budge. She jiggled it. Then thumped it. Then pushed against it. She grabbed the frame and hung from it, giving occasional jerks with all her weight and finally worked it shut.

Tuesday and Wednesday it rained new gullies and ponds into every low spot. Wild ducks and geese flew in by the dozens to dabble away the afternoon. The rain gradually tailed off and by Wednesday night, it had stopped.

Thursday morning she awoke and went to the window. The sun was shining and the pale sky promised a pleasant day. Her spirit lifted. It felt good to see the sun and crisp shadows again. She'd be seeing Linder that night.

Downstairs, she granted Aunt Polly a brief flicker of eye contact as she greeted her, made up two pieces of butter and jelly bread and ate them quickly before going about her chores with great energy.

She knew Aunt Polly would not say which of them was going to town until the carriage was ready, but it didn't matter, Aunt Polly could do whatever she pleased. She and Linder had their counter-plan ready.

At noon her aunt announced her departure, not bothering to explain why she alone was going. After watching the carriage disappear, Clara stepped down from the porch and looked up. The sky was cloud free, bright and pretty, but the rest of the world was still damp, on the verge of mildew, and would take days to dry. She walked over to the henhouse. It took several pulls before she could yank the door open. After that it wouldn't shut right.

Her aunt looked like she had a lot she could say when she returned, but didn't talk except to give orders in her neat, clipped, only-semi-requesting way. Dinner was peaceful, surprisingly free of tension. When they'd finished cleaning up, they sat in the parlor while Aunt Polly read aloud her daily Bible passage. On her way upstairs afterward, Clara thought the banister felt unpleasantly sticky

An unexpected breakthrough

Clara was nervous and midnight seemed far away. She lay down on her side, her back to the window, with one hand on each side of the pillow under her cheek. Right away she allowed into her mind a thought she'd been pushing away: did she want to have intercourse with Linder? He wasn't the kind of man she'd ever pictured "giving" herself to, but wasn't that where all the petting they'd been doing was leading? No girl she'd ever known well enough to talk to had ever admitted to having sex that way with a man.

The way people talked, no decent man would ever want her for a wife if she wasn't a virgin, but she suspected that wasn't true, especially in a city. And besides, she wasn't sure she wanted to be married. Certainly not to a country man. Maybe if she met a sophisticated men who read books and went to the theater, someone who could banter. There was more to life than picture shows. Linder might be good to practice with before such a time came. She couldn't decide, but let the subject drift away knowing that when the time came she'd do whatever felt right. That might be as early as tonight.

She rested her eyes for what was intended to be a minute and awakened in confusion to see that it was 12:17. He was waiting. He'd wonder where she was. He'd think something had gone wrong. Worse, he'd make a fuss asking if her lateness said something about her feelings for him. She pulled her shoes on and went to the window. When she went to open the window it was stuck, swollen from the week's rain. She yanked again. There may as well not have been a window there. The window was as stuck as a brick in a wall.

She looked to see if he was down there waiting, but saw only the gentle sway of the willows in the soft night breeze. Like a silent language. She considered trying to creep down the hall and down the stairs and out. But everything was squeaky—probably deliberately on her aunt's part—and her aunt slept with her door open nowadays. No, she'd try the window again.

She bent her knees and got the heels of her hands under the edge of the frame and pushed up as hard as she could. Nothing. Not even the start of something. She stood up and grabbed the handles and pulled. No. She bent her knees and tried pulling with her arms as she pushed with her legs. No.

Oh, Linder, she practiced thinking, I tried. I really tried.

But she kept going. She jerked abruptly with all her might. Her fingers hurt terribly from the thin metal handles. She grabbed a stocking from her drawer and cushioned her fingers with it and pulled again and again. She felt like crying, but knew that would cross into rage the moment she started. Was he still waiting?

She put her forehead against the cool glass and stood as close as she could to the window so her leverage would be straight up and she gave a fast, mighty pull.

In an instant she felt glass scrape her nose and cheek and stab her in the neck as she heard the crazy tinkle of glass breaking on the gable below. She'd recoiled and still stood inside her warm, safe bedroom. She knew she was about to find out something terrible. She let go of the window handles, grasped the jambs for a second, and then sat down hard on her bottom. She wondered on the way down if anyone had heard the noise and if she'd be in trouble.

Sitting in the dark room in the pale moonlight, she touched her face because it felt scratched. It was wet and it hurt to touch it. Her neck hurt too and it was pulsing hard and she reached to see how much she'd been hurt. Her neck was very wet. So was her hand now.

She decided she should get back in bed. What was wrong was that she should not have gotten out of bed before. Before she could move though, she got cold and sick to her stomach and vomited onto her nightshirt. Her arms and legs were too weak and she couldn't get them aligned to crawl back to bed. But she had to. Her stomach heaved again. The floor was very wet and slippery. There's blood on the floor, that's why, she thought. I should get help.

As soon as she felt a little stronger, she decided, she would call for help. The cool breeze coming through the window made her hands feel cold and sticky. "I'm going to be in trouble for this." She heard footsteps running down the hall to her room, thought, I'm going to be in trouble. Her door opened suddenly and the light went on and Aunt Polly was kneeling beside her saying in the kindest voice she'd ever heard her aunt use, "Oh Clara, Clara, what have you done girl?" Polly's worker's, Missu and Thomas, were there too, Missu coming forward with towels. That's all Clara remembered from just then.

She remembered her neck hurting and being told to not fall asleep whenever she started to wash over into a drowsy and peaceful resolution to all this fussing that was keeping her awake.

And she remembered when Doctor Deakins arrived, smelling of pipe tobacco, breathless from the stairs. He lifted the tea towel Missu was holding to her neck, saying, "Let's see what we've got here." He put the towel down again and pressed harder than Aunt Polly had down. With his other hand he pulled her chin to one side and then the other, looking at the smaller cuts the glass had made.

"Well," he said, 'her face is mostly just scrapes, maybe a stitch here near her cheek 'n' ear. The only bad one's on her neck. We gotta close that up. But she's a very lucky girl, all things considered. How'd she do this?"

"She didn't say," said Aunt Polly. But Clara knew, even in her pain and hazy humiliation that Polly knew.

He turned to Clara. "How'd you do this girl?"

"The hwindow…"

He said nothing.

"Hih hwoudn open," Clara added, feeling that would explain more.

Still later, Clara opened her eyes and wondered why everyone had gathered in her room. Her neck throbbed. The pain was sharp.

Her face felt wind burned. Doctor Deakins had been hovering about her neck, but now he stood up and unbent his back slowly, putting a hand on each hip as he slowly straightened. He twisted his hips side to side and then he stopped moving and looked hard in her direction. She couldn't read his expression. He stepped forward again and extended his hand toward her head. She warmed at the thought of a kind touch but instead his hand reached into her hair and pulled out her ribbon. Purple and bloodstained. He ceremoniously let it fall on top of the bloodstained linens and towels near the side of the bed. Then he went to the foot of the bed and unlaced Clara's shoes.

"New style I guess. Young women going to sleep at night wearing ribbons and shoes with their night robes."

She felt so battered from all she'd been through she could only make herself a promise through swollen eyelids to start hating him forever as soon as she got her strength back. A few seconds of silence accumulated, during which she supposed she was expected to apologize. She closed her eyes instead. He said, "You're lucky, young woman. It could have been much worse."

"Amen," Aunt Polly and Missu said almost simultaneously.

He went on, "I've never seen anyone do what she did and sustain so little damage."

Clara stayed quiet and listened, content to remain in the third person now. Doctor Deakins added, "She'll heal. It'll hurt for a while, but she'll heal. Probably be a few weeks before she can resume normal activity."

He hesitated, then said, "One last thing. I did the best I could. This isn't a hospital and I'm not a plastic surgeon. Your neck is going to scar up a bit. Nothing anyone can do about it. Wear high collars I suppose."

Her eyes still shut, Clara had to restrain the small smile she felt wanting to form. Almost at once she was eager to see her scar. Done for daring to try to go out the window to meet a midnight lover.

And immediately she wanted Linder to see it, so he'd know she tried. He'd be proud of her. She wondered if he was still waiting for her in the orchard. She fell asleep. In the middle of what had to be a dream, she heard the steady, insistent tapping of nails into wood. A coffin being made was what it sounded like.

There was a board over her window when she woke up late into the next day.

Outside and down below, it must be Thomas, someone was dropping pieces of broken glass into a barrel.

Tea without sympathy

Three weeks later the parlor was designated as the place for a necessary conversation. Clara sensed Aunt Polly would use every trick she knew to get information from her. She'd tell her nothing. And as soon as she was able to sneak out again, she'd see Linder and tell him what happened. And show him the scar she'd earned. She doubted she'd be able to say, "for love," or "for the right to meet my lover by moonlight," though the latter was closer to the truth than the former. In the meantime, she would volunteer nothing to Aunt Polly.

Her aunt poured tea. Clara sugared and creamed for both of them. They each took a small sip from their delicate cups and sat back. Aunt Polly began with the conversational equivalent of a slap to the face.

"Do you know that man you're seeing is married?"

"What man?"

"Is this how you're going to conduct this conversation, evasive and deceitful still?"

"I simply asked you what man you are talking about."

"Very well: The man you're seeing is the one who stole Mrs. Eisenreich's blue blanket and left it to rot in our apple grove."

The words "man" and "married" had practically knocked her off her seat, but she kept what she could of her poise, hoping all the time she'd not started to blush, and managed to say, "Who is Mrs. Eisenreich?"

"You are being bold, aren't you? Who is Mrs. Eisenreich? She's a member of our church, a widow, and the former owner of a blue blanket that was stolen from her wash line by your night visitor."

"My 'night visitor'?" Clara shrieked, almost laughing at what she saw as terribly old-fashioned speech.

"Yes, the man you climb out the window to see at night. The one you left a pie at Mrs. Hobson's for. The one you spend time with back of town near the creek."

"Aunt Polly, I can ..." She stopped, finally mortified.

"I thought you might be interested to know," Aunt Polly went on, "that he is married, at least by common-law, to a woman who lives in Clearfield. They have a son about ten years old, whose name is Eddie."

"Aunt Polly. I don't think I even know one Eddie from around here."

"I can believe that. Why would a married man who's taking advantage of a young girl want to reveal the names of his children?"

"Aunt Polly, why are you saying these things to me?"

"Clara, I'm not blind. Don't you think there's a very obvious interpretation of why a young woman has ribbons in her hair in the middle of the night? And has her shoes on? Or when Thomas and Missu see a man in the apple orchard at midnight and later find a blanket spread out on the ground?"

Clara blinked.

Polly went on, "Have you ever asked yourself, Clara, why this man only comes to see you in the sneaking way that he does? Why doesn't he come to the front door? Why doesn't he walk with you in public when he meets you in town? Is he ashamed to make his feelings for you known? Or is he afraid of being caught doing something he shouldn't be doing?"

Clara had never really wondered about those things herself. That was just Linder's way—everything was either backwards or sideways with him. And that was fine with her. It was fun being on the sneak to see a lover. Much more fun than having him come to the front door. Which Aunt Polly would never tolerate. And which Clara doubted she'd ever want—being publicly associated with the likes of Linder.

"That's all I'm going to say for now, Clara. I've got no need to embarrass you further. Lord knows, I've tried my best to raise you right. I promised your mother, my sister, I'd try. And I have. You do know that, don't you?"

"Yes, Aunt Polly."

"But I also want to say one more thing to you before I leave you to think about all this. I want to make it clear. This nonsense with that man has got to stop. And it will stop. I'll put every fiber of my being into making it stop."

With that, she stood up, brushed the creases from her skirt, picked up the tea service and left Clara embedded in the soft chair. Clara fought the urge to curl up and cry. She sat until she collected enough strength to go upstairs and lie in bed.

Thinking it over, she was surprised by the protectiveness implied by her aunt's speech. She had thought of Aunt Polly as a jailer and critic for so long that she'd forgotten that her aunt was also her caretaker, out of kindness to both her and her mother. It couldn't have been easy for her.

As for Linder, she wasn't crushed to hear that he was married. It fit in with what she already knew about him and would make it easier to get rid of him. Doctor Deakins' predictions about how she'd heal were right except for one thing: it looked like her neck would not scar up "a bit," but a lot. His eyes were weak and he sewed her from an awkward angle and he'd sewed up too many farmers and lumberman and other people who weren't overly concerned with preserving beauty or symmetry. The scar was long, thick and raised.

By arrangement, Polly and Clara had a second parlor chat the next day. Missu brought the tea, set the tray with the teapot and cups before them and left the room. Then Polly spoke.

"Linder Charles has been in the county jail for the past three weeks."

"Yes?"

"Yes," said Aunt Polly. "Among other things, he was arrested for stealing from Mrs. Hobson's store."

"Why are you telling me this?"

"He gets released from jail three days from now."

"And?"

Aunt Polly leaned forward and carefully poured the thin warm tea into the delicate porcelain cups. She lifted her cup with one hand while holding the saucer an inch below with the other. Soft steam rose from the tea. "Very well, then. I'll ask you straight out—do you want to talk to me about yourself and this man?"

"There's nothing to talk about."

"Suit yourself, girl, if you won't talk with me about this, I'll just have to say what I must say and be done with it."

"Please do."

"Please do ..." her aunt muttered. "For the past few weeks I've done little other than worry about you and what's to become of you. And all that worrying and thinking has led up to this: A decision must be made, Clara, and you must make it. Either you will abide by the rules of this house and stop carrying on this business, or you will leave this house and take your shame with you."

Clara wanted to laugh at the word "shame"—such an old-fashioned notion, but she'd already decided to endure this session so she worked her jaw and waited numbly for Aunt Polly to finish.

Until she heard, "As you know, your parents left you some money which I've been holding for you. I haven't told you this before, but that money can be released whenever I judge that you are of sufficient age and maturity of judgment to manage your own affairs. Perhaps I should have told you sooner, but I didn't."

The anger Clara felt at hearing that she'd been held in check so long by what she regarded as her aunt's whim, gave way almost immediately to a surge of fear. Who would take care of her? How would she behave if her external restraints were lifted?

"You're too old now for a tired old lady like me to try to control. Take some time to think about it. A few days, a week, whatever you need."

Her anger returned. Clara wanted to kick over the tea table. She started to jiggle her foot, but stopped. Her aunt was being gentle and considerate—and was probably right. She should take her time and think through what was best to do. But having been stripped and exposed, feeling so powerless and worthless, she needed to strike back.

"I'll be leaving, Aunt Polly."

Polly sat up, braced.

"As soon as it's possible to transfer my parents' money to my account, I'll leave."

Polly was not without her own pride: "I'll do that this afternoon, Clara. Your money will be available by the end of the day."

"Thank you, Aunt Polly. In that case, I'll leave first thing tomorrow morning. May I be excused now?"

"Yes, you may," said Aunt Polly.

Late the following morning Thomas carried Clara's trunk and her bags downstairs. Aunt Polly did not show her face, but had left a canvas tote bag for Clara at the foot of the stairs. It contained hardboiled eggs and other lunch foods. On top of the bag lay a brief, handwritten note.

Good luck, Clara.
God bless you.
Aunt Polly

Clara left a note of her own on the dining room table.

Aunt Polly:
Thank you for taking me in
and taking care of me.
Sincerely, Clara.

Part 2
Knoxville, Tennessee, 1920–1921

A new start for Clara

Thomas drove Clara to the train station after she'd left her note to Polly. Last night she had decided that she certainly could not reside in Greeneville any longer, not with her aunt's shadow already thrown across any possible path she'd want to tread. Linder, too, was as rooted to Greeneville in her mind as that willow tree they'd laid under. So that was the end of Linder too. She regretted not getting to show him the scar he'd made her get, but somebody, someday, would be sure to appreciate the deliciously sordid story of its making. Somebody far from here though.

She decided to make her transition to city life in small increments till she felt confident about the bigger places she could go. Definitely a city, not a country town, but which one? New York seemed overwhelming from this distance, as did Chicago and St. Louis. So she chose to buy a one-way ticket to Knoxville. Once she got accustomed to life there, she could move on to Baltimore, maybe,—where Mr. Mencken lived—and thence, perhaps with an introduction from someone from his set, she could go to New York and meet Mrs. Edith Wharton, or Henry James. They'd surely be kind to her once she acquired the right wardrobe and achieved some distance between herself and Tennessee. But for now, for her apprenticeship: Knoxville.

She found a ladies' rooming house without much effort and that same afternoon began walking the streets to look for a job. She tried several clothing shops, a few millineries, jewelry stores and even a restaurant—as a hostess only—before she charmed her way (in her assessment) into a job in a book store that sold mostly used books. Such luck, she thought. She'd be able to read and acquire a bookish education while she earned her keep.

Unfortunately the owner, Mr. Lucretius Allen, could not offer anything but the basest pay, but money was not a strong motive now that she had her inheritance. Mr. Allen did tell her she could have an apartment upstairs, above the shop, an advantage she immediately accepted. The owner of the rooming house, however, would not refund her week-in-advance payment. That marked the first time Clara felt taken advantage of by big city ways (already! so she made a note of it as a baseline in her future progress upward from squalor). But the landlady did have the porter send over Clara's trunk and bags, no charge.

In her new apartment: There, Clara thought, moving a small green lamp from one side of the sofa to the other. Only a few days ago Aunt Polly was trying to stop her from seeing "That man," as she called him, and she'd already fixed the situation herself. No more Aunt Polly, no more Linder, and a step closer to her real life.

Knoxville was noisy. Too noisy most times. But nobody here was trying to stow her in a little bug jar with only a small breathing hole punched in the lid.

She began to flourish. She worked in a bookstore for a genuinely kind and educated man (though she was surprised at the trashy romance and suspense books that seemed to form the bulk of most people's purchases). She read authors like Willa Cather and Dorothy Canfield Fisher at night, ate meals she learned to cook thanks to a cookbook she'd found in the kitchen cupboard, and stayed away from men. At least for now. She certainly was not going into any speakeasies, though there sure were a lot of them. And folks were pretty open about it too, even though Prohibition was supposed to have put an end to all that.

She worked hard in the bookshop. She surprised herself by doing so, since Mr. Allen was not a pushy boss, nor particular about the shop's tendency to grow piles of books in unexpected places, almost like mushrooms popping up after a spring rain. He didn't seem to mind her propensity towards neatness. He never complimented her, nor did he ever criticize. If he wanted anything different from how she did it, he'd just redo it his own way, nearly always when she wasn't looking. In that way, in her eagerness to please, she learned what he wanted. He seemed almost to be like a character from a book himself. One with a sweet, innocent grin under a balding, bespectacled head.

She felt certain that by working in a bookshop she'd taken a step up the ladder toward life among the literate, the sophisticated, and the witty, but not necessarily toward what she was also curious about, the wicked. Three months of catering to the intellectual needs of normal citizens did not leave her feeling any closer to being part of the Jazz Age.

One night, partly from boredom, partly from loneliness, she wrote Aunt Polly a brief note that was neither effusive nor interesting and after she posted it she worried that Aunt Polly would guess correctly that she had reached a state of stagnation without acquiring any magical memories along the way. She imagined Aunt Polly telling Mrs. Hobson, "At least she's working in a bookstore." And Mrs. Hobson would tell Mrs. Eisenreich, "Imagine, Clara Talbot working in a bookstore." And so on, until in the way of a small town, everyone would learn that she was working in an old bookshop in Knoxville, even the people who lived in crevices.

Which in a way is what happened.

Back in Greenville

The day Linder got out of Greene County, the fat jailer with the pig nose made a point to tell him, "You needn't be in such a hurry, man. That gal you was after done left Greenville." That was like a kick in the heart to him ... if it was true.

But it was.

Through the rest of the summer he went on the hunt for her. He didn't dare let folks know his intentions by asking about her directly. People like Mrs. Hobson—she didn't tolerate him in the store anymore, for one, so he went and hung out just about anywhere people let him, and were likely to gab and give something away. He made the rounds in town. It wasn't easy to be still and passive about something so important to himself. He had a very strong urge telling him, Just go. Just go get her! But, the rude question, Go where?, stopped him. The earth's a mighty big place, he told himself. All's he knew was she was big city-bound, but he tried to remain confident he'd find her by saying, "Love will find a way." That was a line from a poems book she'd read him once.

He'd sat there under the willow whenever she read, hardly listening, because he just liked the sound of her voice and liked to watch her lips move, but he remembered that one, because she lowered the book and looked at him and smiled like a choir singer when she repeated, from memory: "Love will find a way."

A way to what? he thought at the time. But now he knew. She'd sent him a message in a way. Imagine. He couldn't get over the thrill of a fancy gal like her being with him. Not quite too high-class, but that was good. She was just enough over him to be quite a compliment, but not so far as to be out of reach. Her being younger was also a compliment to him too. It's not like she was poor and willing to overlook his maturity because she needed money. No, this was a lot cleaner than that. Why she went away without sneaking him a note though, he didn't know. He'd ask her to explain when he caught up to her.

He'd got in the habit of stopping by for checkers at Winand Drug Store after the mail train dropped the incoming sack at 2:15 p.m., more or less, every day. One day, sitting playing checkers with Old Louis Marshall in the post office, which in Greenville was just a counter and window in the back of the store, he heard something he wasn't supposed to hear.

Mrs.Winand said, while sorting the newly arrived mail, "Well, what do ye know? Polly Wooton's niece has finally writ her."

Mrs. Mortimer was at the counter picking up some photo post-cards she'd just ordered made. And she said across the room, "Where from?"

And before Mrs. Winand could curb her tongue in Linder's presence, "Knoxville, using a book store's stationery," was out of her mouth. Linder knew nobody was likely to tell him what book store it was, and he knew he was headed back to county jail if he did what he wanted to do right then: Go through the swing gate and take that piece of mail from Mrs. Winand. So, he just stared at the checkerboard and stopped any smiles that wanted to come into his face.

A long second or two of silence sprung up behind him which suggested that the ladies behind him must have pointed at him while making sssh mouths.

He moved one of his checker pieces dead center, like dangling bacon to a hound, and Old Louis reached over to jump it, then stopped and looked at Linder—who did not return his look—leaned forward— probably to be sure he saw what he thought he saw—and then reached out with his big left hand that didn't have neither the pinkie finger nor its pal, thanks to not paying enough attention at Peedee's Sawmill one long-ago day, and jumped just about every checker on the board.

Game to Old Louis. Linder shoved forward his currency, all three of his remaining crimp-top bottle caps, and said, "You outfoxed me again, Old Louis. I'll try you again sometime, but I have to go home now." Old Louis put the bottle caps with the others in his hat on the table and shrugged and sighed at the empty chair across from himself. Linder heard the conspiring silence behind him as he walked through the drug store and out the door.

He walked the dusty path back to his tent thinking of what he'd pack and how he'd get to Knoxville. His plans felt flimsy, so he tried saying "love will find a way." The saying failed to inspire confidence, however. He felt about as sturdy as paper ash just then.

In his tent he started stuffing an army knapsack a veteran had given him. He packed his shaving kit—also ex-army—and a blanket and some extra clothes. In fifteen minutes he was ready and he paused to say to himself again, "love will find a way," before he stepped out of the tent into the sunshine, ready to reclaim his woman.

There stood Honeybunch at the tent flap.

Answered prayers

"Joining the army?" Honeybunch said.

He stepped to the side, squinting too hard from the sun directly behind her. "How's that?" he said.

"Well, you got your army bag there and I guess you got your army shavin' kit and blanket roll inside, so I guessed you were goin' off to join General Pershing."

"I don't even know who that is, but no I am not," he said.

"Good thing. War's been over two years."

She looked fierce beneath her mocking eyes and grin. Wrung out too, he thought, like a mop pulled from a water pail.

He said, "Anything I can do for you before I hit the road?"

"Take your son with you."

"Don't think I can do that just now."

"You have to."

"Can't. I got important business to attend to."

"I'm sick. I'm goin' to hospital. One of my woman's organs ain't right."

"I'm truly sorry to hear that, but can't it wait till I'm done my business?"

"No. I'm leaving tomorrow. Every day is almost too late, they tell me."

The bag was heavy. He put it down and opened and closed his hand where the strap had dug into his palm. "Can't your sister take Eddie?"

"No, she's takin' me to the hospital and stayin' with me there. This ain't a bent fingernail, ya know. My whole system's corrupted."

"Oh man. Thing's are happenin'. What would ya do if I hadn't come back here today?"

"God answered my first prayer."

"You must be real hard up, 'cause I ain't ever been the answer to nobody's prayers."

"Amen, but that's how the Lord works, Linder. Now if you have to go somewhere, you go. But you take your son with you. Little Eddie deserves carin', same's any child brought into the world. He won't be no trouble to you."

"Never said he was." Then, licking his lips, antsy to get going, he said, "Okay, but hurry up 'n' pack his bag. You could ask ahead next time."

"Lord willin', there won't be a next time. His bag's right here." And it was.

When he thought about all this later, from prison, he said to himself, Once again the female spider at the edge of the web got me to come forward and touch a string.

And what further proof should he have needed that day than: lo and behold, little Eddie, right on cue, stepped around the edge of the tent, picked up his already-packed bag, and walked over to the opening in the tall grass where the way out began. He stopped there and stood with his back turned to them, waiting.

Linder was so anxious to get on the trail of Clara he took the deal. He put a hand on Honeybunch's shoulder and said, "You gonna be okay?"

"I should be, if what the doctors say is right."

"Well good luck. How long you gonna be anyway?"

"Don't know, just keep checking."

"Okay. I gotta get goin'."

"Yeah, I know. Peach pie don't keep long."

He looked at her. Yeah, that's what she meant, he thought, taking his hand off her small shoulder. Just how it sounded is how she meant it.

She gave him a quick stretch of the lips for a smile and then pointed her finger at him and said, "Watch out for Eddie with all those motor cars in Knoxville."

For the first fifteen minutes walking behind Eddie, he had his head down, his mouth pursed, shaking his head in anger and wonder. How's she do it? he wondered. Was he that obvious? Maybe she was more privy to town gossip than he knew.

Then he got over it and walked up to Eddie and clapped him on the shoulder. He said, "Here, you take this one, Eddie," pointing to the heavy duffle bag, taller than the boy. Eddie put his own bag down and walked up to the big bag and tried to lift it. He couldn't.

Linder laughed. "I was just joshin' you, Eddie. Here we go." And he lifted both his and Eddie's bags and they went on till they reached the road where they might catch a ride to Knoxville.

Linder shows up at the bookstore

A few weeks later, Clara was at the front counter of the bookstore, wrapping a customer's purchase, when she looked out the window and saw Linder. The sight of him immediately repulsed her, which was a reassuring reaction to her since she worried sometimes that a re-acquaintance might revive her primitive attraction to him. So that revulsion was good; she did not want to take a step backward in life by even letting on she knew him. But she did begrudgingly admire whatever craftiness and pluck on his part had led him to travel what must have been, for him, half the length of the earth to see her.

He was pretending to browse the five-cent table. Mister Allen mustn't know she knew him; that might get her in trouble. She decided to keep Linder from coming in by going out to shoo him. Mister Allen was in the back of the store on the typewriter, tapping away at his catalog cards. She called back, "Mister Allen, I'm going to put some more books out front."

His continued clacking meant he had no objection, so she gathered an armful of cheap books and went outside, determined to keep Linder from entering the store and acting familiar with her in front of Mister Allen.

She worked the books into the gaps on the table, not looking up, until she was close enough to say, "Didn't know you liked books so much." He kept an open book in front of him, as though he were reading, and didn't speak. "You're not welcome here," she said, and then went back inside. When she looked through the window again a few seconds later, he was gone. She went out and looked at the table for the book he'd picked up, out of curiosity. It was gone, of course.

That night, she got in bed and turned out the light, wondering what his next move would be. With Linder there was bound to be a next move. She guessed he'd come to the bookstall again, probably tomorrow.

She was wrong.

Three faint taps at the kitchen door made her prop up on one elbow and listen. After a brief silence she heard it again. She went to the doorway and looked across the kitchen. He stood outside on the fire escape, his face at the window, his hands shielding his eyes like blinkers as he looked in. She stood in the shadows hoping he'd go away, but he saw her, and smiled and then bobbed his head and pointed his finger at the handle. She went to the door and pulled the shade down in his face.

He immediately started knocking, lightly at first. But louder when she didn't answer and she had no choice if she wanted to avoid advertising to the world that she had a night visitor, but to go over and raise the shade again.

He smiled, like he was friendly, but she could see he was annoyed and only pretending to be happy to see her. She stepped up to the door and softly said the word "No" while exaggerating her mouth movements so he got the message. Then she pulled the curtain again.

He knocked the soft knock again immediately. Up again with the shade. She made a stern face and said "No" louder and "Go Away." Shaking her head no.

He leaned back against the railing and gave her his number one beaten-dog-in-the-rain look and shook his head, like, How unbelievable. How unkind can the world be?

She wasn't falling for it.

"Go Away," she mouthed, lips tight, hands folded across her chest, head shaking no after no.

He put his cap back on, stepped forward and shook the handle. She stepped back. He turned and put his shoulder to the door and bumped it. Not too hard, but letting her know he was ready to do it again harder. She stepped out of his vision.

"Boom," went the first of his shoulder slams. Then a kick with the back of his heel at the bottom of the door. A pause. Then "Boom" again and a steady heel kicking.

"God damn him," she said. She knew she could outlast him anywhere but here, not with other people on a city street, people who were worse in a way than country neighbors. Everybody would know she'd had a ruckus with a man tonight.

She went over and unlocked the door. "Leave the lights off," she said.

He said, "Long time no see, huh?" and sidled in.

Clara thought she saw a blond-haired boy get up off the bottom step of the fire escape and go around the edge of the building, out of sight.

All the Little Linders

She said, "Was that your son sitting down there?"

"Might a been."

At least he didn't lie about having a son. But the boy had looked pathetic sitting down there in the dark. "What's he doing out at this hour of the night. Why's he with you in the first place?"

"He's with me here in the city for a little bit. His ma took sick."

"What's he doing here? How can you leave him outside there?"

"He must a followed me. He likes to walk around at night, same as back home."

"You can't let a child go around at night like that. This is a city."

"Oh, it's okay, he's got his own key. He's prob'ly heading back t' where we're stayin' by now."

She said, "Well, what are you doing here at this hour?"

"Come to see you. Couldn't come no earlier. You don't come up here till late."

He'd been spying on her. For a day? Weeks? She said, "What are you doing here at all?"

"You gonna ask me to sit down ?"

"No. I want you to leave and never come back. What's done is done."

"Maybe so, far's you're concerned, but I got questions."

"I don't want to answer them."

"Now see, that's an example. I got a side a this story too."

"There is no story. Get out."

He patted his shirt pocket and said, "No. Not yet. I got a letter right here that says there is a story. So we can't go from having a story, to there bein' no story, not when there's contrary evidence on the positive side."

My god, how long did it take him to think that up, she thought. She said, "What letter are you talking about?"

He meant the peach pie note, but chose to be more mysterious and say, "You'll find out soon enough. I got feelin's too you know."

"I don't want to hear about it. I want you to go. Am I not making myself clear?"

"I'm not leavin' without answers."

She was tired after working all day. "To what? What could you possibly not understand?"

He paused.

She guessed he was looking for a place he could pretend was getting straight to the point, but he surprised her with "Last time I seen you was in the orchard that night. Then the next time we was supposed to get together you didn't show up."

"As though you don't know why."

"Can I sit down please? My feet're killin' me."

She said nothing, probably because now that they'd started she hoped she could limit him to a brief statement or two and then insist he leave. He pulled back a chair and sat at the kitchen table in the dark. She remained standing.

He said, "I heard some things and guessed some others, but that ain't the same as hearing it from you."

"I guess it isn't, but I don't really have anything to say. Whatever relationship we had is over so there's really no need to talk."

"You know, just because you don't want to talk, doesn't mean I don't have some things to say. I've traveled a ways and gone to some trouble to find you, so ... would you mind sitting down so's I can see you?" She started to pull out the other chair but felt manipulated, and offered her own initiative.

"In here," she said, walking into her small living room. He followed her in, waiting in the dark while she pulled the shades and closed the two curtains. Then she turned on a small, dim lamp and pointed to the chair next to it. He walked over and sat down needing to shift around to get comfortable because it was a lady's sewing chair and almost too small for him. She sat across the room in a reading chair, out of the light.

He put one leg over across the other, obviously uncomfortable, and said, "Maybe I should start by asking you what you wanna know?"

She'd imagined this conversation many times and though he was here uninvited and unwelcomed, she may as well ask him. With mock enthusiasm she said, "Okay, Linder, why don't you tell me all about Mrs. Linder. And all the little Linders, however many they may be. And how they all fit in with what you were doing with me?"

"I knew it!" he said, standing up and clapping his hands together once. He sat down again right away and said, "I figured that's what put the bee in your bonnet. I got a answer for you, but I ain't one for talking private matters from across the room."

He went to the kitchen and grabbed the maple chair he'd sat in and brought it to about three feet from her, turned it backwards and straddled it, resting his arms across the top and his chin on his hands.

"First thing I got to straighten you out about, Miss Talbot, is your sense of humor. My name is Linder Charles. First name Linder. Second name Charles. So, there is no 'Mrs. Linder' and no 'Little Linders', as you call them. You may be mad at me, but you got no right to disrespect my name or belittle people who never done nothin' to you."

Here he goes again, she thought, seizing a minor mistake and using it to grab the high ground.

"If we can't get that straight, I might's well leave," he said, "We can't patch things up without mutual respect. Without that, I have to walk out a here."

She wanted to scream. Who wants things patched up? I don't. Once again, he'd driven his wedge in and was trying to split her wide open. She felt off-balance, afraid that if she gave in to anger, Linder would topple her.

"Okay, Linder, I can respect that," she said calmly. "Tell me about Mrs. Charles and your son Edward Charles."

"Oh, you know his name, huh? Well, he's the only one, in case you're wondering."

"Just the one, then?"

"Yeah, that's right. And another thing," he said, "She ain't Mrs. Charles. We ain't married."

"Not married, eh?"

"No. She's a widow. Her husband died from a thresher accident when they was married only a year. The farm was too much for her. She needed money so she sold parcels till all that's left is the iddy bit she lives on now. That's the story." He sat back.

"Well, that was certainly a thorough biography, Linder. Are you sure you didn't leave anything out?"

"Not much. I worked for her old man when the farm was big and I kept on helpin' after he died, though she didn't have much to pay. Some days all she'd do was sit on the porch steps pettin' the dog and cryin'. It was hard to watch. Just before she was gonna have Eddie, she asked me did I wanna move in. So I did, but after a while she asked me to move out again. I sleep in a shed out in the woods back a her place. Summer times, I put a tent up back there."

"You kind of skipped over something there Linder. Are you Eddie's father?"

"Yeh, I am, I reckon. Couldn't be anyone else."

Clara was quiet for a little while as she came to terms with this information. Then, figuring this would be her last conversation ever with Linder, she allowed herself some curiosity. "Is she pretty?"

"She's okay. Country pretty."

"Do you still have relations with her?"

"Beg pardon?"

"Do you still go to bed with her?"

"Not really, no."

"Not really? What does that mean?"

"Well, once in a while she gets sick a bein' alone and calls me inta the house." Linder looked up as though he was going to reveal a great, but little-known truth. He said off-handedly, "Sometimes a woman needs to be with a man as much as a man needs to be with them."

"Oh really?" she said in mock astonishment. "Could you say that again? I'm not sure I followed all that."

Linder's eyes narrowed and he puckered his mouth for a second in suspicion, but went on anyway, probably because he seemed proud of this special insight. "Okay, I'll say it again so you can get it clear in your pretty little head. What I said was sometimes a woman needs a man, you know, to be beside her, as much as a man needs them."

"Them?" she said, "A man needs *them*?"

"Yeah. You don't think so?"

"You're saying 'A' woman needs 'A' man, but 'A' man needs 'Them.' Would you mean 'All' of them, Linder? Or just me and Mrs. Charles and ... whatever other pearls are on your strand?"

"Ah, now, I didn't mean it that way, honeybee ..."

She shot him a fierce look.

"I mean 'Clara.' My words got twisted. It's my bad grammar. You got it all wrong if you think me and Eddie's mother are like you 'n' me."

"I didn't follow that declaration, Linder."

"Okay, I'll try it again. Watta ya want first, 'you 'n' me,' or 'her'?"

"Start with 'her 'n' you' please."

"Okay. Her. It started as sympathy sort of. She was always sittin' around mopin' on the porch steps. I felt sorry for her, so I started going up to her. I'd pat her on the shoulder or the head, or put my arms around her. She even asked me to hold her while she cried. So that got to be the habit 'round there. Part a being there at that place, at that time. Just a habit."

He seemed to be looking at something over her shoulder when he paused. Clara was tempted to turn to see where he was looking, his stare was so miserable and intense.

"And then?" she said.

"And then, well, things happened, like they would with any man and woman finds themselves like that. You know, one thing leads to another and so on. Just happens." He looked over her shoulder again and this time she wondered if he was recalling anything pleasurable. To her surprise, it bothered her to think so.

"And Eddie?" Clara said.

"Eddie. Well, Eddie's a good kid. Peculiar in some ways, but who ain't? Me and him always gets along. He got talent for drawin' pictures."

Clara interrupted: "I mean how does Eddie fit into the family picture here?"

"Ain't no family picture, Clara," he snapped at her. "Watta ya sayin' somethin' like that for? If there was a family picture, I'd never a taken up with you. No, nothin's back there for me when Eddie's mama comes back from the hospital. That's why I got such strong feelings for you. I want a family, that's for sure, and I want it t' start with you 'n' me."

"If you mean a mamma bear, papa bear, and baby bear, Linder, I've already told you I don't want a family. Besides, what do you mean there is no family picture? You live with a woman in the same place and the two of you are raising your child together. Isn't that a family?"

"Not really," he said, "since Eddie's been born we all kind a go our own ways. Loneliness sticks us together. Sometimes she and I get in bed together, but it ain't for love." He looked over at her, "And it ain't for what you're thinkin' either." He stood up, turned his chair and moved it closer so it touched hers, all in the same movement.

"What are you doing?" she said.

"I'm tellin' you that the whole *world* isn't as big as the feelin's I have for you. You're everything a man could hope for in this world. You're beautiful, you smell nice, you feel good, and I can't stop wantin' you."

Linder's nearness had been accomplished so neatly, so smoothly, so suddenly that Clara didn't try to stop him. She'd read such words before, but never actually had them spoken to her before. She felt vulnerable. She'd been lonely. Linder seemed to sense this as he went on talking, never pausing, never allowing a space for decision. As he talked, he put his hand near hers, as if in invitation. She sat still, saying neither yes nor no, just being the beach as the tide moved slowly, inexorably in. His hand softly covered hers and he talked sweetly of his need for her. Her arms were being gently caressed, little chills arose on her skin, and then she felt his lips at the base of her neck.

But that made her remember something, and suddenly the mood changed. Her body calmed like the surface of a quivering pond when the wind suddenly dies. He paused, befuddled. He pulled his face back enough to look at her. "What is it?"

Like a coy Southern flirt from the hellish city of Baltimore she said, "I'm thinking you haven't mentioned one word about this scar on my neck."

Clara, poor Clara

She could not have given Linder a more wide open invitation. The one true mark of passion on her young life, the brand of romance, her single point of pride, and the indicator that she leaned toward the head-spinning world of witty wickedness, that scar on her neck pulsed with the need to be known. Showed off—even to an oaf just off the farm.

"I seen it," he said, "and I heard how you got it, but ... well, to tell the truth, I've been workin' so hard just getting my foot in the door I figured we'd get to that later."

"Well, your foot's in the door, so start asking."

"Yeah, okay. Let me remember." Until this moment he had been leaning toward her, but now he straightened up in the chair and positioned himself to look at her while he told his side of the story. "I was waiting for you in the orchard that night. It was still pretty wet, so I brung a ground cloth and dry blanket for us. I was happy I'd be seeing you again. Then midnight came, and you didn't show up. That made me a little nervous. It got later and later. I walked up to the house to see if your light was on or anything, but there was a lot of commotion, people yellin' and running around and all the lights were on. Then I saw Doc Deakins arrive. I was hoping yer auntie had a heart attack, to tell the truth."

Clara laughed. "No it was me Doctor Deakins came to see, not Aunt Polly."

"Whoever it was, I figured I better get out of there."

"Did you find out what happened to me?"

"Just that you got hurt and got some stitches. What happened?"

"From the window. I was trying to open the window so I could get out to see you that night. Only the window was swollen shut from all that rain. I had my head pressed against the glass while I was trying to pull up on the handles, and then the window broke and my head pushed through a little. I got some cuts on my face, but they hardly show anymore and I also got this."

She reached to turn on the reading lamp and bent her neck so he could see her scar.

"Holy cow," he said, "that is some scar."

"The doctor says I got it from one of the bottom pieces of glass that didn't fall out of the frame. When I pulled my head back in, one of them cut me."

"You're sure lucky it wasn't worse."

"That's what they tell me."

She had the feeling from the glint in Linder's eyes that this scar thrilled him, that it was his mark on her, got from knowing him. He knew that now she'd always remember him. A passion scar. She felt that way about it too. Life had dramatically emblazoned on her neck forever a souvenir of daring deeds done for love and passion. That scar was an open sign of who she was. Her only regret was that a more dramatic or worthy man did not lie behind her story.

"You okay now?" he said.

"Yes. It's healed as much as it's going to."

"Can I see it again?" he said. Clara leaned into the light again, her head sideways showing the side of her neck. Linder leaned over, gently touched her jaw, positioning it so the lamplight would shine directly on it. With two fingers of his other hand he slowly began to trace the scar's path down her neck, stopping at the barrier of her collar.

"Look," he said "it squiggles along here like a big old worm."

She laughed and tried to flex her head against her shoulder to make him stop. It was ticklish. His grip was firm though, so she couldn't move much.

"Now you're the one squiggling. Cut it out. Doc Linder here needs to do his 'zamination. Hold still. I see somethin'. Okay, I was right—a big old worm's crawling on your neck." She giggled again and pulled away a little, slightly flushed. "It tickles," she said.

"That's 'cause you're squirmin'. Hold still. I wanna see it again."

"No, that's enough."

"Okay. Tell ya what. I'll give ya a nickel t' see it again."

Though she'd never actually been drunk, she felt like this is what it must be like. She felt so pleasantly silly, after all this time alone in Knoxville, she didn't want the mood to end.

"Let's see the nickel," she said. He stretched out his leg, reached in his pocket, and pulled out a nickel, the whole action done as smoothly as if it had been scripted and rehearsed. "I was gonna buy you candy and flowers and a new red dress with this thing, but heck, here it is." She took it, giggling, and held it in her curled fist.

"Hey, you know what?" he said, "I'll bet nobody's done the scar initiation."

"What's that?"

"It's a ceremony. It makes the scar good luck."

"Yeah? Will it really?"

"Sure will."

"What do I have to do?"

"Nothin'," I'll take care of it. Just keep your head still and I'll do the rest."

"Okay." She remembered tingling before he started. She sat still, her head erect. He gently tilted her head again, exposing her neck. She could feel him looking there with tender lust. It made her neck heat up, her skin wanted his lips. Linder leaned forward, descending slowly until his cheek rested against her neck. After a few long seconds, he quarter-turned his head in a slow arc and nuzzled her. Clara sighed and relaxed, almost went limp between his big gentle hands. Then he slowly, almost daintily, kissed her scar. He kissed the length of it in little kisses, over and again, up and down, gradually increasing the pressure until he was doing big hot kisses against her glowing neck.

Clara was breathing hard and her body was hot. She felt herself swelling and beginning to seep. Linder paused and looked at the side of her face.

He put his mouth close to her ear and said, "Poor little Clara. I'm sorry you got hurt."

He kissed her neck more, gently, up and down the scar. She shivered, was speechless, was on the verge of moaning.

"Poor Clara," he whispered again, "I wanna make it better for you, all better. Every bit of it. Make it better." He paused with his mouth close enough to her neck so she could feel his warm breath. He leaned up to her ear and spoke again. "Where's it hurt? Here? Where's this go?"

Her lips, barely parted, were humming a low moan as she put her finger to her neck and traced a feeble line along the scar to the collar of her night gown which she pulled down to follow the track of the scar across her clavicle and down onto her breast. She closed her eyes and opened her mouth in anticipation.

Linder said, "Poor Clara. Poor, poor Clara. You poor little thing. We're gonna make it better. Gonna make it all better. Make the hurt go away." He kissed her neck some more, down over her collar bone and onto her breast. As he did this, he circled his hands under her and lifted her and still talking sweetly and kissing her, carried her smoothly across the room. Clara held his strong upper arm, felt like she was lighter than the air. He never jostled her, not once, never did anything to bump the dreamy feeling of floating to her bed, where he undid her night dress, kissing each button as he freed it, until he peeled the robe away and lay beside her, one hand gently roaming the contours of her exposed body, the other held under her head as he kissed her long scar.

Deep in her trance, the fleeting thought came to Clara that Linder must have planned this at some point, that it couldn't possibly be as spontaneous as it felt. But she made no attempt to hold that thought, just let it glide by like a carousel pony. If he'd planned this, she thought, it was a good plan. A very good plan. Bold. And smooth. So exciting to be the object of someone's plans. No one else cared if she lived or died. He's a scoundrel, she thought. Very good. Very good at it. She was beyond caring.

Clara is late

Clara let Linder stay in her bed awhile after he took her virginity that night, but made him leave before sunrise. She locked the door when he left and went back to bed, taking comfort in the way her soft quilt enwrapped her body.

She needed some sleep, having been unable to sleep with Linder there. First she wasn't comfortable with another person, especially Linder, lying beside her, maybe watching anything funny she did while sleeping. Second, he kept at it all night—not all night actually, since they'd started late, but from after midnight till near sunrise he just didn't let up on what he'd been after since the day he'd carried the flour sacks for her. As far as she was concerned she didn't know what all the fuss was about—the actual intercourse itself, that is. If she had to tell, she'd say the best part was seeing how pleased he was and that her body—she—was what got him both so riled and so pleased. In that respect she felt she now was in on the big secret everyone was always whispering about. For her own satisfaction she didn't need anyone, and that triple-plus included someone so musky smelling, lying on top of her and concentrating so hard you'd think he was praying. When his prayers were already being answered! She fell asleep thinking that thought.

Of course he came back that night and the following night, and soon, too soon, whatever this was had become a habit. She looked for his boy each time, but did not see him again and assumed the boy was back wherever the two of them were staying. Or maybe gone home to his mama already. She didn't ask, it not being a favorite subject. Her problems arose from the father, not the son.

For a while she might now and then feel a mild affection for Linder when he relaxed for a moment and wasn't pushing an agenda. But, now that the issues of anger and jealousy had been brushed aside and she could think more clearly, she realized that she had lost whatever feeling she'd ever had for him. More than anything, her problem was that she was lonely in a city where she did not know how to make friends. Friendship had seemed so easy back in her school days.

Even so, at some point every day, usually while shelving books at the store, she rehearsed telling Linder that he should not come back anymore. There was no future in their knowing one another and it would be better if they did not grow too attached (meaning: he should not).

Though she'd decided what to say, she couldn't find a time to say it. Once he came over, there never seemed to be a spare moment suitable to tell him any of this. She wondered once or twice if that was the purpose of his non-stop chatter and/or pawing at her. And lately he'd begun talking and acting as though their bond grew deeper every day.

That didn't mean she stopped taking pleasure from their time in bed. She did, but in what seemed to Linder (from his initial puzzlement) to be a strange way. One of the girls in seminary had told her about a way to perform intercourse that "favored the female." Clara was curious and tried it one night. She had Linder lie on his back and keep his hands by his sides or behind his head and she sat on him and inserted him and then did her own moving. A marriage manual would probably claim that position as a form of intercourse, but to her it was closer to the self pleasuring she'd learned under the willow tree back home. It satisfied her though. It was quite nice. The independence also helped her begin feeling the distance from him she'd need for the final scene she was building up to. She needed to be free of him.

But, of course, as was the case with all things involving Linder, she was a beat behind when she finally got the nerve. She was sure she was pregnant.

She felt like such a fool. Why had she thought that being a virgin immunized her from a man's seed?

As he came through the kitchen door that night, she told him to sit down, she had to tell him something. He smiled and sat down, but his eyes got a worried look.

"I didn't get my monthly," she said, "I'm five days late."

The wariness left his eyes and they brightened at once as he smiled and said, "I'll be danged. Ye sure?"

She tried to stay poised and calm as she said, "Absolutely. Women keep track of these things."

"I'll be durned," he said, "Ain't that somethin'?" His smile stayed put as he bobbed his head up and down in confirmation.

"I'm not happy about it," she said.

He said, taking off his cap and leaning forward. "It's just the surprise. Don't worry. I'll take care of you. And I'll do the right thing, too."

"I don't need being taken care of, and if you mean marriage, it's out of the question. I'm not marrying you or anyone else, either."

"A baby needs a family," he said, his voice high-pitched.

"Maybe it does, but not with you and me as the parents."

"But we are the parents." Something in the way he was looking at her said this is what he wanted, that he'd wanted her to get pregnant so she couldn't leave him, that this had been his plan all along.

He said, "What gives you the right to make such a decision? We're both involved here. That baby's mine too."

"Yours?," she said, "Your contribution to this baby would fit in a spoon."

He glared at her, his jaw muscles working the sides of his cheeks. Clara regretted her words, but had to fight to keep from being crushed by the weight of his plans. Finally, he drooped his head and slumped his shoulders. Not to lead us in prayer, she hoped.

She went on, "Im not going to be this baby's mother and I'm not getting married. And that's final."

Speaking toward his knees he said, "Watta ya mean, you're not going to be his mother?"

"I'm not going to be this baby's mother. I'm not going to be anybody's mother."

"Are you sayin' you're adoptin' out this child?"

"No, I'm not saying anything. It's none of your business."

"How can it not be my business? I don't get no say in this? That ain't right."

"Well, not to be critical of something I know so little about, but I don't see you as very involved in raising the boy you already have."

"He's his mother's baby. I don't get along with her and I didn't want no baby with her."

"But you had one."

"Just a accident. I planted the seed without meaning to … out of loneliness, not from no wish to family-up with her. She wanted a baby and she squeezed one out of me. Them two are like peas in a pod. I'm the outsider there."

"Well, I hate to say it like this, but it seems like you have a knack for putting your seed in the wrong woman."

"That ain't funny."

"It's true."

"I told you it was an accident."

"I don't want an accident to change my entire life."

"Not the same 'tween you and me. This ain't no accident, Clara. We care about each other. It was meant to be."

She started to challenge him, so he quickly added, "Why else would we be getting under the blanket together every night? Ya can't do that and then say an 'accident' happened. We made it happen."

They sat in silence for a while. Then she said, "Did you ever think you might get me pregnant?"

"Sure was possible, but that's life. You gonna get in bed together, sooner or later there's gonna be a baby. That's the way things are. Get married, raise the baby, you know."

"Having pleasure in bed together doesn't mean a man and a woman need to get married or become a family."

"It don't, no, but why would a woman do it so often if she wasn't thinking along those lines ?"

Clara opened her mouth to answer and stopped. Then to her surprise, dismay filled Linder's face, as though he'd just read a "Danger" sign at the same moment the earth began trembling.

"Look, Clara, maybe I'm not expressing myself right."

"No, Linder."

"Look, I'm gettin' down on my knee before you."

"Don't, I don't want you to."

"I'm doin' it right. I'm gonna ask ya proper ...."

"Don't. Please, Linder. Please don't. I don't want to hear it." At the edge of angry tears, she sat back, with her elbows on the table and the heels of her hands supporting her chin while her fingers covered her eyes, bracing herself to endure his proposal.

"Clara, I want you for my wife."

There was a long silence. Through her fingers, looking past Linder, Clara saw a jumble of books in the living room. She'd brought them up from the shop yesterday. They needed to be priced and taken back down to the store tomorrow. More than anything in the world right now she wished she had the freedom to go arrange those books in neat piles and price them.

But he said it again, "Will you be my wife?"

Her tears came out in a continuous roll as she held back her anger. Linder was trying to roll over her. If his being pitiful didn't work, he'd cast her as the ogre, the destroyer of dreams, the mean one. She could see in his gleaming, hopeful, doggie eyes, that he thought she was crying because she was flattered and touched by his proposal.

She went to speak, but couldn't, just shook her head "no" a few times in a slow rhythm she didn't want to stop doing. He got up from his proposal posture and sat beside her. She was sniffing hard to keep her nose from running and her shoulders made little convulsions. He gently touched her back as though to reassure her. She shook it off and stood up.

"No, Linder. The answer is 'no.'"

He looked crushed for a second, but a look came into his eyes that said she'd just satisfied a suspicion he held about her. The look scared her enough to make her say, "Please excuse me. I mean 'No, thank you,' Linder."

He looked down, his elbows on his knees.

"It was very sweet of you Linder. Thank you. But I do not wish to be married."

Finally after a long sigh, he lifted his head and spoke. She thought his eyes were watery when he said, "Well, then, what we gonna do?"

"I think you should leave now."

He surprised her. He stood and picked up his cap and went to the fire escape door without a word. She followed, wanting to lock the door as soon as he left.

He stepped through the doorway, but turned around, his face half in darkness. The wind lifted the shadows of some branches and exposed his profile momentarily. His hands were in his pockets and his shoulders were slightly hunched as though he were about to walk into the rain.

"When should I come back?"

"Not anytime soon."

"What's that mean?"

"It means I don't think we should see one another anymore."

He stood there, then put his thumb nail flat to his lower lip and looked down so he could bite the nail a little. While doing that, he brought his eyes up from his fist to meet hers and said, "Don't do nothing to my kid."

Then he descended the wooden staircase quietly and turned the corner of her building without looking back.

Baby vs. pregnant

Clara locked the door as soon as he went out of sight. A swirl of gratitude and fear left her nearly dizzy. He'd left too easily. That wasn't his way. He'd be back. Only a question of when and how. She forced herself to walk calmly through her dark apartment and check that the windows were locked and then draw the curtains. She did not even turn the light on when she eased into bed and burrowed into her comforter. Lying there she felt like a small animal waiting for the return of some creature that had been snuffling about up above.

That image caused her to sympathize with the unwelcome little thing growing inside her. She felt invaded. Linder had planted a parasite inside her through the devious course of sexual pleasure. But the little creature itself was innocent of any motive other than wanting to go on living now that its time to be had come.

In the morning she hesitated before opening the curtain, but then threw it open anyway, deciding she would not live in fear of Linder or any other man. If he tried to come back, she would not let him in. She'd never let him embarrass her again. If he made a racket, she'd open the window and call for help until the neighbors joined the fuss. Linder was a private bully, but a public coward. He'd give it up.

If he came to the shop she would tell Mr. Allen he was a nuisance. They'd call the police. If he stopped her on the street, she'd yell as if attacked. He'd get the message.

At noon of the first day she had to walk to the postal station with two wrapped books Mr. Allen needed mailed to a catalog customer. Going down the street, she sensed Linder stalking her.

While she stood in line in the post office, she refused to look around for him. She told herself he didn't really want her, not as herself. He liked what she represented to him: someone who was a cut above the farm girls he knew, in terms of her clothes and education. That flattered his image of himself since he'd never accomplished anything on his own. Her leaving him attacked his self esteem. He probably felt she gave him the boot because she was a snob who thought she was too good for a hillbilly. She'd never called anybody a hillbilly in her life. That wasn't how she was raised.

She spent the rest of the day maintaining her poise, imagining herself watched, but determined to seem normal and indifferent. That did not mean she was not upset. When she wasn't conquering her fear of him, she sometimes missed Linder, or at least she missed having a companion. Her seeming indifference was not an easy pose to maintain.

But what was she to do? she thought as she rearranged the books out front of the store. If she looked sorrowful, he'd use her slumped shoulders as an excuse to come forward and console her. If she did anything out of the ordinary to betray her internal thoughts, he'd be watching and noting. He was very good at sliding his fingers over the surface of things till he found that slight raise that betrayed a crack. First a fingernail, and then his fingers, and then he'd be inside quicker than you could notice.

She made it through that first day and finally said good night to Mr. Allen and went upstairs to cook and eat and read by herself. The entire day she'd felt watched. She didn't know where he watched from, but she was sure he was out there following her. She felt sure he was watching the house right now, alone in the dark. Once or twice she almost felt sorry for him, disappointed and lonely in the dark all by himself. But why feel sorry for a stalking wolf because his ribs are showing? Better to stay wary.

All night she'd had the apartment lights on in defiance of the fear that tried to tighten her skin. Now, in the last moments of the day, all lights off except her bedside reading lamp, she tried to uplift her thoughts by reading from John Ruskin's *Sesame and Lilies* for a while.

But she felt sleepy. The nerve-wracking nature of the day had tired her. She couldn't concentrate. She turned off the light and snuggled down, hoping sleep would overcome her.

But it didn't. Lying in the dark she couldn't help but face the question she'd avoided thinking about all day: *the baby.*

No, not the *baby.* That word was too strong. It implied a human being. Her *pregnancy* was the problem. No need to talk of an *other.* Her problem was merely her own physical condition. Something inside her. A condition of her body, a new conformation of her organs, like a health problem that needed tending.

Dammit. She and that man had their pleasure in bed together. They both enjoyed themselves equally. And then he had to go and leave his calling card. And she carried the result. That was so unfair, another sign that the world wanted women to be little more than beasts of burden, serving at man's leisure. Well, damn it all. She'd find a way.

But then it was back to thinking of *the baby.* What was inside her was *a baby.* Maybe she should let herself say the word *baby.* It was kind of a miracle. She'd take care of this little dependent creature, and she wouldn't be alone anymore.

But that thought was revolting. It was not a baby, it was *a growth,* a parasite like the eggs a wasp would lay in a caterpillar. She hadn't got any further from Greenville than Knoxville and she was determined to live out her dreams and not be stuck somewhere in the backwoods of America, in the greatest era ever, without having lived.

No *baby* talk. She stopped that line of thought immediately. It would not serve her well, or help her decide what was best for herself.

Baby. Pregnant. One of those words needed to dominate her thoughts, and subsequent actions, and soon.

She willed herself to sleep, not caring as she let go of the day, that the house was being watched by someone who felt he owned half her problem and held the only possible definition of it.

When Linder went down the steps

When Linder went down the steps, like she'd demanded, he did not go lightly. He knew she'd watch to be sure he left, so he kept his shoulders squared. He came out of the alley and turned the opposite of the way home, even though it obliged him to walk clear around the block, just so she would not know in which direction he lived.

As he walked he fought the urge to go back and break a window or two. He only didn't because he knew such behavior gives folks the excuse they need to keep you away for good. He didn't need to get locked up again when his child needed rescuing.

He'd never known his own mama, and his daddy didn't stick around, and he made up his mind early on that he'd be damned before he ever let that happen to some other little kid. It's not a kid's fault if its his turn to be born.

When she was telling him all this and turning down his marriage proposal, he thought she'd looked pretty as ever, her hair swept back like it was. But inside she was harder than that plaster statue of Beauty he'd seen in the pool parlor window he just walked past.

It wasn't hard to back off tonight, 'cause he'd be back. A child deserves to have parents. Things were tough enough on this orphan question, between the War killing so many people overseas and the Influenza killing so many Americans back home. That and Prohibition getting passed because so many broke-down drunk parents weren't minding their kids. You couldn't go ten steps down any Tennessee road without an orphan stepping up, cap in hand. No sir, he thought, not with what I've been through, I will not abandon this child.

He paused across the street from a closed cafe where a single light bulb shined onto its sign. He watched the milkman deliver some bottles to the doorstep. The man's horse shook his collar and then returned to his slump-shouldered loll, patient and tired in the eternal way of the cart horse. Linder slipped behind a bush and waited.

Of course, strictly speaking, he never really was an orphan, but his mama did get sick when he was five and his daddy was always so lickered-up he couldn't even get harvest work. Mama sent him off to live with his granny. Then he got sent over to his Uncle Aygee. Then Auntie Jennie, Uncle's sister. Three years of, "You behave boy. You sit there on the porch or your momma won't ever come see you no more."

Wait and wait, hours-to-days-to-weeks till mama might come and divide her attention between him and his brother, or him and his sister, and a bunch of kinfolk who were as mean as dirt when they weren't drinking and meaner than dirt when they were. A little pat on the head from Mama and a gentle squeeze and she'd be gone again, her frail self diminishing in size as her little cart carried her down the road and away till maybe a next time.

So that was about the same as being an orphan, in Linder's opinion. He stepped out from the shadow, and watched the gray horse and the milkman plod quietly down the street, the horse so used to the routine his steps almost silent as he moved away.

Linder casually crossed the street to the cafe's stoop and picked two pint bottles of milk, which he maneuvered into his pants pockets, and one half pint of cream that he hid in his palm. He walked the rest of the way home with the back of his milk-toting hand forward so it couldn't be seen.

At the rooming house he saw that Eddie still had the light on in their room. He'd have to say something to him about not wasting electricity before showing him the milk. Then he'd show the cream as an award to him, for not following him over to Clara's again.

Days turned into weeks

And so the days turned into weeks, with Clara trying to decide what to do about her "problem," and Linder stalking and waiting, planning counters to every move he could imagine her making.

Most worrisome to him was, What if she wants to call it quits with the whole thing? How could he know ahead of time so he could change her mind? He hoped maybe he'd notice some change in her activities. Like, she might go back and forth talking to some folks first. Maybe doctor visits, to get advised. Or could be she'd go out carrying an overnight bag. If he saw such as that, he'd rush over and make a fuss until she retreated and thought better of such negative actions. Meaning, convince her not to harm the baby. He wasn't sure how long he'd need to be ready against her doing that. Until the baby got too big, he guessed. Then she'd have to birth it. And then probably put it out for adoption.

Clara obviously had the first-move advantage, which is also the advantage of time. She could act on her decision in a moment and be done with it. She needed to be watched.

For a few days Linder showed up, unseen, to see if she arrived at the bookstore on time, which she did. Then he'd send Eddie by once or twice a day to look in the window and be sure she was still there. Which she was. And then he'd come back himself to make sure she went home after work. Once or twice a night, at first, he'd go by at night to be sure her light was on. Every now and then he'd see her move around up there, or some shape he assumed was hers, and the sight pleased him. One time seeing her reminded him of a poem line she'd once read him, "All's right with the world."

On the way back home, though, he felt bad for being made happy by such a slight thing. Like that was all he deserved, a little glance, a suggested shape. All at a distance, too much like a fading memory with nothing physical to keep it going. Just memory feeding on itself. But he couldn't stop coming by because at least he had that much. If he stopped, he'd have nothing. And besides, his looking in on her was not all just a matter of keeping the love lamp lit. He was also working on behalf of the unborn child.

Man may not live by bread alone, but he sure does need bread. When he first came to town Linder was going to get a job unloading down at the freight depot, but now he couldn't afford time away from watching Clara.

Not only that, from what he heard from teamsters and such who came in from Greenville, Honeybunch wasn't yet back home from her medical treatment. Different men said different things about where they heard she was staying now, but they all agreed she wasn't back yet. It looked like Eddie would be with him for a while.

If he could snap his fingers and order up a dream, he and Eddie would be partners in a fishing guide business. Rich men came from all over to try the clean waters and beautiful bass they might catch down here and they paid plenty for guides to take them to the best spots. That's what he would do.

But for now, he and Eddie settled on stealing things from people's bags whenever people were dumb enough to put them down. What was sweet about how they did it was that there was something about Eddie that people didn't know how to respond to if they caught him. Eddie could just walk up to a bag and open it and take out a choice item or two and walk away. If someone stopped him, he just stared at the person with no expression, so blankly they let him go, like he was only a dog that nosed their bag. Worse came to worse, the kid could run like hell and not get caught by someone carrying a bag. And if they did leave the bag to give chase, Linder was on the other side of the action. He'd just walk up and help himself. Whatever they stole Linder pawned or sold to a couple of resell men long on cash and short on questions.

Clara every once in a while thought she saw Linder out of the side of her eye, but never actually caught him. She knew he was out there watching her though. As for her decision: she was a big gal, and strong, and once her body made the initial adjustment to her physical condition, she tried not to think about it. Something reminded her every day, but since she felt no physical urgency, she delayed her decision.

Eventually it was too late to stop the pregnancy. Most of her clothing was too tight. She was showing a little. She took to wearing an apron in the shop. Her thoughts turned to finding a place out of town where the baby could be born and adopted right away. She asked Mr. Allen for a leave of absence, saying only that she needed to attend to family matters. From near the top of his shelving ladder, he said yes, he'd hold her job.

Linder, in the meantime, wondered now and then if she'd made up the pregnancy story as an excuse to get rid of him. He told Eddie he'd do the mid-day walk-bys himself. Just notice with his own eyes for a while. He knew she'd taken to walking around during her lunchtime. She didn't look pregnant, but he knew it took a while with some women. Then one February day, from across the street, he saw her come out of the bookshop. It was windy, and one look at her belly with her skirt blown against it told him it was true: she was carrying.

Despite everything wrong with the situation, he felt a twinge of pride. And a renewed sense of hope. Maybe if he could find a way to get her to listen, she'd believe she needed him now. It was just a matter of convincing her she could depend on him.

And then something happened that he'd never even considered before. A man walked up behind Clara, hurrying the last few steps to catch up. And as soon as he did, he turned and greeted her. Lifted his hat, even. Both of them were then all smiles. They talked a long minute and then strolled up the street, together.

He'd never got sick to the stomach over a woman before, but this came close. She'd always acted so independent towards him—if not downright ornery—Linder had never before thought of her being happy with another man. He stood inside the shoe store across the street watching as they floated out of sight as easily as two dandelion puffs.

He went back to the rooming house by way of the alley behind the building and opened the tall gate fence. He saw Eddie in the yard sitting in a corner looking at something. Linder walked over to see what. Eddie was watching a hop toad. It just sat still in front of him, brown and lump-ridden, bulging its throat, like they were sharing confidences. He left them and went up to their room and lay on the cot.

He started thinking about her as a woman then and not just the incubator of his coming child. Because she'd been a virgin, he'd always thought she had no sexual appetite other than what he'd created in her. He didn't see how she could just switch over to another man. The man didn't look that well off to Linder, either, just dressed for town was all.

He took his shoes off and put them under the cot and lay back down again. She was different, more exciting than any country gal he'd known, especially the way she saw things and talked about them. Sex wasn't so hot though, she moved around too much and made a lot of noise, and whatever she was up to didn't seem to have much to do with him. It's a wonder they connected enough to make a baby.

It wasn't right she wanted to get rid of the baby, but it sure was typical of her. It reminded him how she'd go crazy if his juice got on anything of hers. That's what she was doing with the baby, getting rid of a stain he put on her. *In* her.

He closed his eyes and saw that suggestive, bulging lower belly and imagined the unwanted baby in there, locked away from the father who *did* want him by a woman who *didn't*. It took a while to explain it to himself, but what he came up with was that maybe that man on the street was her new lover and came to see her at night. The two of them might want to start fresh by putting the baby up for adoption—by a stranger. With all the real orphans walking around in Tennessee, what sense was there in creating an artificial one?

He and Eddie moved to a room closer to Clara's apartment, one that belonged to a man he knew from county jail who just got sent back. It made it easier to keep tabs on her during the day. One night he got a pencil and a calendar and worked out her likely due date. He started thinking about where she might go to have the baby. He developed a strong urge to go up her steps and look in through the kitchen window. Half the time he pictured her sitting and reading, holding her hands over her belly. The other half he imagined her kissing some new man. Or pullin' the man's rod to keep him patient till she delivered.

One February night he woke in the dark because everything sounded too quiet outside. He went to the window and saw snow on the ground. That was a strange sight for Knoxville. Right away he got the idea to go over to Clara's place and look for a man's footprints on her fire escape steps. Footprints seemed so real and definite compared to the labor of thinking and wondering all the time. He knew it was a ridiculous, dangerous idea, but he couldn't stop himself.

He dressed and went out, surprised he could see his own breath turn to thick smoke. He didn't expect it to be so cold. But he'd finally have proof one way or another about her and this man, so there was no turning back from the peace he hoped the truth would bring him.

When he got there, after much slipping as he walked, he looked on the fire escape steps and the other side entrance to her apartment and all around the sidewalks out front and he saw no footprints anywhere. Not even tire tracks in the street. That satisfied him at first, but walking over here in the cold had riled up his mind. The need to know for sure wasn't satisfied. Maybe he'd arrived too soon. He might leave just before the other man arrived. He should be sure.

He sidled to the corner and looked up and down the street. No one was out. Then he looked through the bookshop windows, which he knew was ridiculous, but he did so anyway so he could stop thinking about it. Then he figured he should wait a while as long as he was here anyway. He hid behind the steps, but a minute later thought he'd be less obvious if he stood across the street, so he went over there. But the snow was now coming down so hard it made Clara's side of the street too fuzzy. He hurried back and hid in the bushes next to the alley.

He blew on his cold hands. Being here wasn't working out. Even his brain felt cold. His mind drifted. He almost forgot what he'd come here for, when he suddenly looked over to the pavement near the bookshop and was startled to see dozens of foot prints. Right away he wondered how people had managed to come and go unseen while he was hiding here. He stood up and came out from behind the bush.

Footprints lay around the staircase, and on the first few steps, and under the fire escape. They looked like they were from just one person, a man his size. There were more near the garbage cans, and beneath the hedges, and at the windows, and across the street and back again.

And then, even when he realized the footprints were his own, he yet was curious about them, as though they had a tale to tell him.

And yes they did, he realized: he was acting crazy, if not become crazy. What the hell was he doing out here in such cold? He felt humiliated at seeing what he'd created here, what he'd revealed about the workings of his mind. A crazed self-portrait. He attacked the footprints, kicking at them. He broke some branches off the shrubbery and swept away every print he'd made. He looked at the tracks going across the street and back. Them too? How like a crazy, chained-up dog he'd been. He threw the made-up broom behind the hedge and walked quickly away. He turned once, tormented to see how the tracks followed him home.

When the sun came out again

On Thursday, March 1, 1921, the temperature was back up to 60 degrees and sunny, evaporating any evidence that Linder had ever driven himself half crazy last night trying to decode his own footprints in the snow.

Soon as they woke up that morning, Linder and Eddie both ate two biscuits each after dipping them in bacon grease. Linder sent the still-sleepy Eddie over to the train station to hustle up some merchandise to sell later. He himself hurried over to the bookshop to make sure Clara had opened up for Mr. Allen.

But the shop was closed.

Now what's goin' on? he thought. Sleepin' late, maybe. Gettin' a bit slowed down carrying that extra weight around. He guessed she was now in her sixth month.

He felt he should go over to the train station and make sure Eddie was okay. But if he did, he knew he'd be nervous till he checked on her again. He wouldn't be able to concentrate. He told himself Eddie would be alright. He decided to wait a little longer for Clara.

He started feeling conspicuous standing in one place so he walked around the block, stretching it out to almost fifteen minutes. He did that four times. But the store hadn't opened yet. And there was no excuse note on the shop door. Linder decided to come back again later. He hoped she probably was at the doctor's and her boss took her there. He went across town to catch up with Eddie.

The boy already had found a pocket watch and a cameo brooch. Linder patted him on the head. "You're the original million-dollar baby, Eddie," he said. Eddie looked up at him for a long second. Linder wondered if he was trying to figure out how a baby could cost a million dollars.

"Come on," Linder said, "Let's go down to Greenie's right now. Get some lunch money for these things. You need anything?"

Linder kept the mood light all afternoon, even though he felt like he was carrying a cold stone in his stomach—not for the first time since Clara Talbot had entered his life.

Twice he walked across town to that bookshop, barely keeping himself from breaking into a run at times. On the third trip, at five in the afternoon, Eddie with him this time, he saw with relief that the Open sign had been flipped. But the sidewalk display of cheap books had not been put out.

He told Eddie to go in there and look for her. The boy went in and came out after only a few seconds shaking his head No.

Now Linder was worried. He sent Eddie home and started wandering the streets, stopping at intervals to check the shop and her apartment after dark. The lights went on at the bookstore, but he couldn't see Clara. The lights did not go on at her apartment. Linder even went up the fire stairs to peep in, the second time not bothering to be quiet about it. He shielded his eyes and looked through the glass window of the kitchen door but it was dark as a witch's cave in there.

Later that night he tried to talk himself into believing that maybe she had to stay in the hospital overnight because of medical complications, but he didn't find the thought convincing.

He couldn't think of anything to do the next day other than to repeat yesterday's spying routine. But he did not see her anywhere.

And the next day.

And the next.

Until Eddie, told to go in the bookstore, finally said, "Linder, I don't wanna go in there no more."

"I don't want to hear back talk, Eddie. Just go in there. It don't take but a minute."

"The lady's not gonna be in there, Linder."

"How you mean that?"

"She's on vacation."

"What's that mean?"

"I seen her."

"Seen her where?"

"Train station."

"When's this yer talkin' about?"

"Day I got that brooch we bought pork chops with."

"Three days ago?"

"I reckon."

"Well, Eddie, godammit, I sure wanna know why you didn't mention this sooner, like right away. I sure do wanna know that, but I know what you're gonna say. You're gonna say, 'You didn't ask,' ain't you?"

"You didn't, Linder."

"Well, godammit, Eddie, didn't you think it was the least bit odd to be walkin' into a bookstore, lookin' for a bookstore lady, when you know you saw that same lady go on 'vacation' down at the depot. Ain't it odd, godammit?"

"You didn't ask."

"That's zackly what I knew you'd say. Three little words. How to balls up your old man, and business partner, with three little words. Godammit ta hell: 'You didn't ask.'"

"You didn't."

Linder marched Eddie in silence back across town to the train station and made Eddie reenact his sighting of Clara. Where he was. Where she was. "Vacation" Eddie had assumed because she had two handbags and a trunk.

"Which platform did she go to?" Eddie walked him over and pointed. Northbound.

"Did the conductor call out a destination?" No.

"Was she with anybody?" No ... maybe.

"Maybe?" Someone helped her on with her luggage.

"What he look like?" Wore a suit. Had a mustache. Some gray hair.

Linder got a flash of inspiration: What exact time did the northbound train leave?

Eddie said, 8:15 in the morning, according to the watch he'd just lifted a few minutes before that.

Linder grabbed Eddie's shoulder and turned him around and together they went into the station. Linder looked for a Schedule of Northbound Trains and found one. He turned Eddie's shoulder around and pushed him gently to start the walk home.

He'd find her, he vowed. And the child she'd carried off with her. He had three months.

Part 3

Southern Railway Company's Lynchburg Station, Virginia. May 13, 1921. 7 a.m.

Human Audacity

Almost everyone on the platform stepped back as the train for Knoxville rolled into Lynchburg Station. It was simply too big to take in up close. One old gent even took off his cap in respect. And why not? That train was a testament to human audacity: tons of explosion-craving power willed back only by iron bolts and rivets. The wheels themselves stood taller than the average man. At the end of the platform the engine chuffed one last time and eased to a stop, sending a wave of small lurches and bumps down the line.

Among the folks who'd been impatiently waiting was Richard Lynch Garner. He was a well-dressed, slightly gray-haired and fully mustached man. He got up from the bench where he'd sat for the past hour and approached a sooty crewman climbing down from the coal tender. Garner was a Virginian, from Abingdon, and a man of the world compared to most western Virginians. He was an explorer, in fact, who'd written books about his exploits studying apes in the West African Jungles. He was on tour now, raising money to supplement his latest grant from the Smithsonian Institution. He had to be in Knoxville and on the stage by 8 p.m. tonight.

"This the train for Knoxville?" he said to the crewman.

"Sure is," said the man, throwing a dirty canvas bag onto his shoulder and walking away.

"It's about time. When can we board?"

Without turning around, the man said, "Dunno mister. Soon's the man says so."

The crewman disappeared around the corner. When Garner turned around he saw no other crewmen, just passengers. They looked confused too.

He pulled open one of the heavy double doors and walked into the station and up the stairs, heading for the office of the ticket agent. A small group of people had already assembled to watch the agent chalk something on the slate next to his window. When he stepped aside it read: "No. 213 to Knoxville departing approx. 7:30 a.m."

"Why's that, Garrett?" said a man whose suitcase was wrapped with thick twine.

"Train hit a truck down at Roanoke. Nothin's moving either way. Telegraph just come in."

"What happened?"

"Stalled on the tracks. Train hit it. Driver was still in there. He got killed."

"Whyn't the man jump out?" a lady said to no one in particular.

"Must a reckoned he had more time than he did."

The agent, Garrett, said, "Lots a folks do."

"Or he didn't want his car hit," said the same lady as before.

"Tell ya somethin', though, that ole boy never knew what hit 'im."

Surprisingly, no one laughed, even though the man said it like he was quipping.

"Anyways," said Garrett, "we can't get goin' till the track's cleared. Shouldn't be long. Half hour, forty minutes tops."

Garner stood picturing the driver trying to get his engine restarted, the man not wanting his truck, maybe his boss's truck, damaged by the oncoming train. He'd probably been confident at first he could do that, bold even, but then probably just turned hopeful as time got short. Garner turned away from the thought.

As long as they were still going to be a while, he might as well get something to eat. He walked over to the snack stand near the lunch counter. Two other people were ahead of him in line, and though he was hungry, he waited patiently, wondering if he could work the story of the truck driver not having as much time as he thought he would into his speech tonight. His turn came and he stepped forward, his eyes following the gray haired counter lady as she began wiping the pastry case with a little towel. Garner decided to be patient and not call her over. When she finished, though, she didn't wait on him. She turned her back instead and began wiping down the coffee urn.

He tapped a dime twice on the counter, just to make a noise that would say someone was there. She turned suddenly and looked at his hand, and then his face, her eyes narrowing, saying nothing, just cocking her chin at him. Garner wasn't sure how to respond—words didn't seem to be in vogue here—so he pointed to some sweet rolls and held up two fingers. She looked at him again before she dove for the rolls. Quite the goodwill ambassador, he thought.

She stood up, bagged the rolls, put them on the counter, and jutted her chin at him again. He held out several coins so she could take the correct amount, but she swiped them all and gave him the pastries quicker than he could follow. The man next in line stepped up.

Garner glanced at the pastry lady before stepping aside, but her eyes were ready for him, giving him that look zoo animals give people when they're alone in the building with them: "If these bars were removed, you'd not find me so amusing." Garner opened the bag and took one roll and put the bag with the other in his valise. He began eating the roll as he walked away.

Out on Kemper Street he debated taking a short walk while he stood eating the roll. He was trying not to think about what the truck driver's final minute may have been like. His eyes began following the erratic circle of a small, bug-picking bird on a tree trunk nearby. The name came to him: Black-and-white warbler, a sure sign of spring. That would be good, he thought: take a walk, look for birds, reclaim the good mood he'd awakened in.

From the covered walkway that straddled the railroad he saw a great blue heron slowly flap across the tracks, maybe a hundred yards away, and glide down behind the tree tops into what must be a marsh. He'd go look for it. He hurried down the steps to the platform.

An old couple sat at the end of the bench near the stairs. Garner went up to them and said, "Good morning, folks."

The man responded with the least possible nod.

Garner said, "Excuse me for interrupting you, but I wonder if you're going to be here for a little while?"

The couple's faces stayed stone still, but the man looked at Garner and said, "Prob'ly."

"Well, sir, I'd like to take a quick walk down to the other end of the station, but my bag would slow me down. Would you mind if I left it here?"

After a pause the man said, "We won't bother it none."

"Well, thank you, sir. I won't be long."

Garner put his bag next to the bench near them and walked away, a bit bothered by their flinty manner. As he walked he counted from habit the Knoxville train's cars: mail and baggage car, Pullmans (two), coaches (three), dining car, coach, and a last car that looked recently repainted a glossy forest green with bright yellow letters along the side that said, *Les Chasseurs*, the hunters.

Garner saw the brakeman sitting atop the rear platform steps reading a newspaper and said, "Good morning." The man looked up and nodded. Garner said, "Is that a private car."

"That's right. Goin' through to New Orleans," the man said, adding that it was an old car and had been ready for scrapping but was bought at auction by a sportsmen's club down there and sent up here to be refurbished.

Garner said he'd be curious to see it, but the man told him it was off limits, nobody was allowed in, it couldn't even have a fingerprint on it when it got delivered.

Then the trainman added, "Not too many people ridin' today, though, so you can move around in the other cars much as you want."

"Doesn't matter to me, I'm in a cabin."

"Good for you, but ... ah ... don't expect much service today."

"Why is that?"

"Why? Same's everything since the war. We're short handed. Not only that, somebody who was supposed to get the word to somebody else, didn't, so we got only two porters to Knoxville."

"Once we get going, could I go back and just look through the window of this car?"

"Can't, shades're drawn."

"Don't suppose they could be lifted, so a fellow could take a peek?"

"Nope, no sir, not you, not nobody. Even we don't go back there. Could cost a man his job."

"Just wondering," Garner said.

"That's okay," said the man as he returned to his newspaper, "Enjoy your ride."

As Garner approached the end of the platform, he began to hear the "kee-kor-ree" of Red-winged blackbirds calling, a sound that meant there was a marsh on the other side of the tall grass back here. If he hurried maybe he could see that heron.

He stopped before the pale of looming reeds, looking for a path. He saw none, so he parted the green stalks and pushed in, squishing through the mud toward the songs. It didn't take long before he made out a gap in the foliage ahead and guessed water was there. He moved toward it, keeping a steady pace, until only a single row of stalks separated him from the clearing. Taking his time, he leaned forward and parted the reeds.

And there, only a whisper away, was the Great blue heron, the sage of the swamp.

Today the heron stood on one ancient leg, looking into the dark water where tadpoles and crawfish lived oblivious to penetrating gazes and stabbing beaks. Above it, clusters of chinking blackbirds rode the sway of the reeds, like acolytes to the great bird. Garner took in all this and then looked, as far as he could, into the black center of the heron's awful yellow eye.

As he did, he felt the sun grow warmer on his cheek. After that, what was there to do but enjoy its warmth, smell this balmy air, hear these fervent songs, and let himself wish, with all his heart, to live forever? If not, so what—worse come to worse he'd be joining his dead son, Harry, drowned while boating only a year ago today.

The train whistle shrieked, and the blackbirds took flight. Only then did Garner notice that his feet felt wet. Black silt had come over the tops of his shoes—as though the marsh wanted to swallow him. The thought amused him. The earth seeking his return? Trying to reclaim him whence he came? He made a mental note to record that idea later, once he was settled on the train. It would make for an amusing anecdote in a lecture sometime.

He pulled free of the muck and turned around and hurried back, noticing along the way that most of the footprints he'd made coming in had nearly disappeared already. He grabbed a stick to scrape the mud from his shoes just as he regained the platform. Down at the station, people were lining up their baggage and grouping themselves near the steps of the passenger cars. He kept an eye on them as he knelt and scraped his shoes, then wiped them with his handkerchief.

Then he hurried down the platform to retrieve his bag, holding the dirty handkerchief by a corner, so it could dry a little. A surprise awaited him. The old couple who agreed to watch his bag were now sitting on the other side of the tracks. Where was the bag now? It held his lecture, his notebooks, some clothing, his shave kit, and his pistol. He jammed the damp handkerchief in his coat pocket and walked quickly, almost ran, back to the bench where they'd been sitting when he entrusted his bag to them.

The bag was still there, but a tall, lean man in overalls was sitting on one side of it and a blond haired boy, about twelve, sat crosslegged on the other side, looking in the bag. Garner approached till his shadow covered the man, who sat with his elbows on his knees, looking down as he ate peanuts from a wrinkled paper sack. The man didn't look up.

"Sir. Your son should know better than to touch another man's belongings. Tell him to stop at once."

The man looked up, placed a shelled peanut in his mouth, moved it to his side teeth, and started chewing as he said, "Tell im yerself mister, he don't lissen none t' me. Besides, he ain't my son."

"Well, he certainly seems to be your charge, sir, get him away from my bag."

"You got somethin t' say to him, mister, you best say it yerself. It's your bag."

The boy looked up at Garner with the shrewd glance of a camp monkey caught in a tent, the tip of the his tongue protruding at the side of his mouth. Garner stepped up and grabbed his bag and snapped it shut as he walked away.

When he'd gone far enough, Garner stopped and looked back. They were gone. He figured them for local thieves who worked the station. He rummaged through his carryall, but didn't notice anything missing.

Maybe they weren't thieves, he thought, maybe the boy was just simple-minded, beyond the man's control. Still the man should have apologized. Or corrected the boy, he thought, as he showed his ticket to the conductor, father or no father. The conductor pointed him to the first passenger car and he hurried past the other travelers to board the train for Knoxville.

Clara on the Train, Linder too

Not recovered yet, and wearing a snug plum-colored jacket and skirt she'd bought in Lynchburg to go home with, Clara Lydia Talbot, lately of Knoxville, Tennessee, thought she recognized Garner down on the platform talking to the ticket checker. She lifted the newspaper from her lap and looked at the picture and back again at him. It was him alright. Wearing a much nicer suit than you usually see. She watched him go out of sight, probably to board a private cabin in the car ahead.

She looked again at the news article. It said his name was Richard Lynch Garner. He was a scientist and explorer who hailed from Abingdon, Virginia. That's close to Bristol, she thought—when she was coming down here the train passed through Bristol, she'd seen a sign, "Abingdon -18 miles."

The article also said he studied apes and monkeys and gorillas in French Equatorial Africa. That can't be easy, she thought. It must be why he looked so serious. She read on. Professor Garner would visit Knoxville tonight to tell everyone about his recent discoveries leading the Collins-Garner Expedition for the Smithsonian Institution in Washington, D.C. Mostly, he would talk about social life among gorillas. Gorillas, and even chimpanzees, lived in families, but very few people knew that. Mister Garner would show projection pictures of the gorillas. Tomorrow he would return to Washington. Then he would pack to go to Cuba for some rest. After that, he would return to Africa.

Clara put the paper down while she pictured herself meeting Garner by bumping into him on the train. That probably happened to him all the time. He probably hated it too, strangers coming up and blabbing. But who knew, he might find her interesting. Wouldn't that be something? It could happen, she thought, she should keep an eye out for him.

With no warning, her blood dropped and she felt weak. She was sick again, and nervous, but told herself it was better to be here on the train and free than in that Crittenton maternity home another day. Torture chamber was more like it. Those girls were all too crazy back there, and the doctors and matrons were even worse. Not crazy, but too controlling. It was like a jail there. Not to mention needing to get away from anything that reminded her of babies. She rested the side of her head against the window.

Clara would also have recognized the man and boy Garner had run into earlier if she'd looked up just then, and it would not have been a happy recognition. The pair had just come out from behind the station to stand in the shadows under the eaves. The man waited a bit and then walked out on the platform and looked around like he was expecting someone. He put an unshelled peanut in his mouth and crunched it, as he walked to the station window, casually spitting out pieces of shell as he looked inside, the paper bag dangling beside his face as he shielded his eyes from the glare. He'd barely had time to look before he turned around and went back to look up and down the empty platform some more. He took his hat off and was about to run his hand through his hair when he happened to glance up at the train and saw Clara Talbot, who did not see him, already aboard, her head resting against the window, dozing.

His eyes went wide. "Damn," he said. He had to get on that train and get her off. He hurried back under the eaves and snatched his travel bag and made for the rear of her car, hoping he had enough time to grab and drag her from the train before it left. He hadn't said a word to the boy, who needed a moment to catch the drift before he, already twenty paces behind, went running after the man. The conductor stopped in mid-signal to let them board, then gestured 'all clear' to the front and stepped up behind the boy.

Linder entered the rear of the coach and saw her sitting up front, her back to him. It had taken him nearly three months back in Knoxville, of going to the library, reading about unwed mothers, asking questions, going to the social agency the library lady recommended and saying his sister had a problem back home, what should she do? till he finally narrowed it down to she must have gone to a Florence Crittenton home, but which one? Finally, the one that was both out of town, but not too far, was in Lynchburg. He'd come after her on an educated hunch, and been right.

But ain't like just like her? he thought. He'd only been here three days tryin' to stalk her and here she was, already heading home. Always one step ahead. There is absolutely no way of predicting the mind of a woman and goddam but this was frustrating as hell. The train wasn't movin' yet. He needed first of all to know if she had the baby with her. If she did, that gave him something to work on. If she didn't, he needed to get her the hell off this train before it chugged away. Leavin' his newborn to fend for himself in this nasty city!

He started up the aisle to see what the situation was—baby or no baby? He got halfway when a big man stood up to remove his jacket, blocking the aisle. Linder figured to give him a second to get it done, but the man stretched and adjusted his suspenders and trousers and bent his knees and then reached overheard to bring his jacket back down to search the pockets for something he'd forgotten. Linder wondered if he could knock this fellow down and get by him twice, the second time dragging Clara. Sitting at the window next to where the big man stood, an equally big man sat snoring Linder didn't think he could handle two of them and an angry Clara so he said, "Mind lettin' a fellow past?"

The man stepped inside his seat row without looking and Linder brushed by. The man leaned back into the aisle blocking Eddie, whom he hadn't noticed. Linder slipped into the empty seat behind Clara and stood to look over. No baby. She was slumped with a newspaper held in her lap, her head resting gently against the glass. He noticed the part of her neck scar that rose above her collar.

The shape of the back of her head, her hair, her lovely neck, once so familiar and now so distant from him, seemed to him as though seen across a graveyard through a mist and it all near took his breath away. His urge to raise hell diminished in the viewing. The months of following her, keeping far enough away to not be seen, had nurtured the growth of an awful resentment toward her, the kind he'd been born with, but now, this close, after all that time, he saw for a moment only the things that had made his heart ache back in Greenville, the same old admiration and longing.

Dragging her up the aisle past those two men seemed unrealistic. Maybe he could wake her and talk her into coming with him to talk things over. Maybe she'd be impressed that he'd come this far to see her and their child.

The train lurched slightly. He bent and looked out the window. It looked like the platform was moving away but it was them that was moving. Where was Eddie, anyway? He looked back just as Eddie tugged at the belt of his trousers. He put his fingers to his lips to tell Eddie "sssh" while he looked at her from above and behind for a second.

He'd hung around the station since daybreak. He'd done that every morning for the past couple of days, knowing there was only one morning train to Knoxville every day. He also came back for the sole afternoon train too, later in the day. She'd have to take one or the other and he wanted to intercept her and keep her in Lynchburg until she gave him what he wanted. Then, out of nowhere, as though he hadn't put a plan to his scheme at all, suddenly there she was and if he hadn't glanced up and seen her at the window, she'd have gone off without him

He wished things he could just tip his hat and say hello and ask her if they could talk for a minute. That was a joke though. After four months of thinking she'd scraped him off her shoe, she was going to get nasty if she saw him again, no doubt about it.

He looked again at the back of Clara's head and the same old trick happened: his first reaction was that little extra heartbeat a man gets when a woman's beauty catches him off guard, the little tick that precedes the jolt that opens the gates of sadness.

At that point the train jerked as it rounded a bend. Clara sat up straight and looked out the window. Linder could only grip the edge of the seat and be carried toward Knoxville, too late to get her off the train. He wasn't going to give up though. He just had to find out from her who had his baby and go back there and get custody.

He turned and led Eddie to another seat five rows back. Somewhere she'd not suspect their presence while he figured out what to do next.

Garner settles in

In the coach ahead, Garner had begun to enjoy having a personal cabin. He removed his coat, tie, and collar, and laid them on the seat across from him. He started to removed his sleeve garters, but decided against it because he didn't like his cuffs touching his wrists when he wrote. Feeling loose in his crossed suspenders, he sat by the window, and faced forward, so he could look for the rolling hills of his childhood in southwestern Virginia. Tonight's speech would be the last on this fund-raising tour and he wanted to make it a good one, give them something to remember him by. Next week a short rest in Cuba, then back to Africa.

The train rose from the cut near Lynchburg onto level ground for a while. Garner found the scenery unremarkable—a few stubbed hills in the near distance, the occasional back of a house, a horse cart bobbing lightly down a parallel road. But then the train entered a wooded area.

As various trees or bushes came into view, their branches close to the window, Garner amused himself by trying to name them: "Table mountain pine ... *Pinus pungens*," was the first—knotty, aggressive, among the first to regenerate fields. He looked for another. At the speed the train was going now, most of the foliage was an unpleasant green blur, too close to the window. The train diverged from the embankment, allowing him perspective: "American aspen ... *Populus tremuloides*." Fissured bark, flowers drooping like long, slender caterpillars. Another good one.

The naming went on for a while: poplar, cottonwood, beech, red mulberry. Then they entered a series of narrow valleys where the woods were thicker and grew closer to the window, so close, in fact, that a branch slapped the glass near Garner's face, making him blink. A scrape followed, then more, until the succession of slaps and scrapes was so quick and close that it was a challenge just to keep his face at the window. He held his place, blinking now and then, while the train bored through the riotous spring green. His eyes soon tired and couldn't focus and somehow the branches started seeming like living creatures desperately running alongside the train, trying to get through the glass and grab him. His nerves fraying, he was about to turn away when the train emerged into sunshine and meadows.

The assault left him breathless. That was awful, he thought. Like Mombassa, when some Africans had run beside his train as it left the station, clamoring and trying to reach through the windows to take his luggage until the train gathered enough steam to make them let go.

He turned from the window and looked at the seat beside him. A nap would be lovely, he thought. He started to clear the seat, but stopped. First things first, he thought. He'd better rework tonight's speech some before he lay down. Holding his writing case in his lap, he noticed that the pebbled leather had worn to a smooth black and brown in many places. Signs of age and service. He felt affection toward it and ran his fingers over it. His former wife had given him this case. It surprised him that something so intimate had not always been his. He removed his refillable pen from the case.

Without intending to—the day was becoming memory-ridden—Garner recalled that the pen had been a gift too, from the publisher McClure himself, soon after his first reports from Africa had boosted the Colonel's magazine circulation. Those were good days, he thought. The great circulation wars. Lectures at the Cosmos Club at Madison Square Garden, correspondence with Edison and Bell, nights of champagne, oysters, and great cigars. The University Club in Philadelphia, The Explorer's Club, the Smithsonian, the National Zoo. Terrific, terrific times, he thought. He set a clean sheet of paper in the writing pad, laid the stained blotter on the seat beside him and prepared to write.

Linder brooding as he sits behind Clara

Linder could not see the back of Clara's head when she slumped in her seat, so every now and then he had to stand and look to assure himself she didn't give him the slip again. So far so good. At least in the sense that she was still there.

Following her back to Knoxville was going to take at least eight hours. He didn't think he could convince her to get off at any of the whistle stops. So, there, it'd be at least eight hours. Then there'd be the convincing, demanding, or begging, whatever it took to get her to tell where the kid was. Then the train didn't go to Lynchburg but once a day and after that it would be another eight hours getting back. Let's just hope the kid wasn't adopted out already, then he'd have another set of opponents to deal with.

He hoped he could get her to listen to reason and be a little fair, accept that he had some rights here too. Maybe they'd go back together, tell them folks she changed her mind 'cause she and the baby's father were getting married. Gonna be a family.

Fat chance. He could kiss her ass from here to China and she wouldn't tell him a thing. He'd have to get one up on her somehow before she'd tell him anything . He sat up again to see what she was doing. This time, she wasn't there. He jumped to his feet and started up the aisle, his blood in a panic, but then he saw she was curled up across two seats, sleeping.

He looked back for Eddie. The boy had his head stuck out in the aisle, tracking Linder's every move. Linder motioned him forward and the boy came up and sat beside him, the aisle seat again.

Being this close started bothering Linder's nerves. He crouched over the seat to look at her, just to glimpse, but lingered when he saw she'd she was sleeping heavily. Same curly brown hair that looked red in the sunlight. She slept so soundly you'd think she didn't have a care in the world—a thought that made Linder want to thump her square in the middle of her back so she'd know otherwise, help her join the rest of the human race.

Garner writing

Garner had written:

"NEW DISCOVERIES AMONG THE WEST AFRICAN GORILLAS." and then sat looking out the window for a while. Now he was writing again, outlining what he'd say tonight. His little "Talks," as he called them, varied little from town to town, but a fresh review usually helped make his presentation livelier. Staying fresh for these speeches was getting harder to do, but he had no choice, people paid good money to attend. Except for the occasional wealthy patron, like the most recent expedition's Philadelphia sportsman, Alfred Morris Collins, there was only one other way to get funded: Go around the country waving a tin cup before wealthy men until enough of them "sponsored" an expedition in exchange for glory and a reputation for public service. Not to mention a percentage of his box-office.

——*Gorillas of two types: lowland and mountain*
——*I studied lowland.*
——*Hard to see, thick jungle, elusive creatures*
——*In capturing for zoo, or museum exhibition, sometimes necessary to shoot mother and capture baby who still clings to tree. Natives cut tree down and baby is captured.*

Gorillas were different from the other animals he shot, he thought. At first it had been easy enough to squeeze the trigger, but in recent years the consequences had become harder to witness. The gorillas acted like they were being murdered. They made a hideous fuss that added a frantic, judgment day desperation to what had seemed to the shooters to be the simple act of sacrificing a lower life form for science.

Fuss or no fuss, the gorillas died and their skins and bones were taken to America and reconstructed in a way that barely approximated what they'd looked like when they were alive.

Back in the United States, Garner had gone to visit the new gorilla diorama in the National Museum in Washington. He'd personally known and observed all four of the animals in the museum's display for weeks before he'd shot them, but they were unrecognizable now. Not that they didn't look like fine examples of gorillas, but he couldn't see any resemblance to the individuals he'd known.

When he began to remember the dying shrieks of those animals and the sight of Aschemeier, the taxidermy apprentice, pickling their skins, he capped his pen and looked out the window again.

Linder sitting behind Clara

Linder put his knees up against Clara's seat, pushing it forward slightly, just for comfort, not enough to wake her up. He wondered if something in her handbags would say who adopted his kid, or what orphanage he was in. If so and he got it from her, he could just get off at the next train stop and go back to Lynchburg. He leaned over and told Eddie what to do.

The boy got on the floor and squeezed under Clara's seat. Didn't take him more than two ticks to be back with a small needlepoint bag. Linder looked in it. There was what seemed to him a bunch of woman's junk in there, but no papers or certificates. But, wait, hold on, he told himself. His fingers found a knotted-up hanky with something hard inside. He palmed the hanky to keep Eddie from seeing it and told the boy to turn sideways and not look. Eddie turned, then starting wetting his finger and drawing little animals with his spit on the smooth dark seat leather.

Linder undid the handkerchief knots. He guessed a small watch was inside, but it was a gold locket, the kind that holds pictures, on a chain whose clasp was broken. What a thrill! He squeezed it tight, happy in the knowledge that he knew whose picture was inside. He turned to the window and opened one side. Tiny pieces of baby hair. He closed it and, scarcely breathing, opened the other. A baby's picture. "Oh, man," he said. He bit his lip and steadied himself to keep from trembling. The baby's eyes were closed in deep slumber.

Linder envied him that sleep. He himself couldn't remember ever dozing so peacefully, not in his whole life, he'd never been so trusting. He couldn't tell too much, the picture being so small and the baby's eyes closed like that, but Linder thought the baby looked more like him than Clara and that small similarity was enough to make a great determination rise in him: It was plainer than ever that this little boy needed rescuing and that Linder was obligated by blood to be his saver.

Eddie turned around and began watching him. "Everything's's okay," Linder said and he tousled Eddie's hair. Then he put the locket and hanky in his chest pocket and buttoned it. He turned to the window again. The space between his cheeks and nose had swelled with pain and he breathed slowly from the back of his throat, the way people must do when they'd too stunned for rage but not yet ready for tears. He looked out the window, picturing himself carrying the boy away from some orphanage, angry and sure of himself, the nurses and director standing in the doorway unable to stop him, staring at his back, and perhaps one of them, just one was all he asked, thinking he was within his rights, and brave to assert them.

After a while though, he was too agitated to sit still. Clara didn't deserve to sleep this long. He wanted to know where the baby was before they got to the next station—so he could get off and go back to Lynchburg. He wasn't sure how to awaken her though. If he hollered everyone else would get nosey and maybe butt in, but he couldn't bring himself, not just yet anyway, to touch her. Then he got the idea to rattle her seat. He put his feet against the seat and pushed forward to get her attention, but she didn't react, so he pulled his legs back quickly and let the seat slam. Again, no reaction. He stood and leaned over the back of her seat. She was still sleeping, but he felt she'd notice if he went hard enough, so he began rocking her seat with his feet. Eddie joined in, like it was a game.

Linder felt the resistance up front change and then saw Clara's face came over the back of the seat, wide eyed, like a raccoon coming out of its nest to see what was shaking the tree. Her eyes met Linder's and widened, shifted over to take in Eddie, and came back, full and hard, on Linder. Then she dropped beneath the horizon of the seat back, saying nothing.

Linder had been all set to fight back against a bigger reaction, her looking shocked maybe, or some shrieks or complaints or angry questions, so in a small way he felt insulted and belittled by her silent disappearance. Because he'd only thought about counterattacking, he had no entry into the argument he sought and everything he thought to say fortunately sounded stupid to him before he said it, especially with Eddie present, so he sat in dumb surprise for a moment telling himself she probably didn't know what to say either.

It came to him that he had to keep things moving if he wanted to keep the advantage, so he slumped down and started rocking her seat with his feet again. He knew she would say he was being childish, but he didn't care, this was serious business. Eddie joined in, pushing as rapidly as he could, his face lit up like it was father-son day on the rides at White City.

They kept at it for a bit, and then just as Linder was wondering how long she would tolerate being rocked, there was no resistance to their pushing. Linder stopped and waited for the argument to begin, but it didn't, and by the time it dawned on him why, he could only get to his feet in time to see her go through the front door toward the lead coach.

Eddie looked up at him and started rocking the seat again like he hoped Linder would join the fun again, but Linder just put his hand on the boy's knee and stepped over him to go after her. When he got to the door, he saw through the window that she was walking through the next coach with purpose. She went to a private cabin door and went in without knocking. A few seconds later, the mustached man who'd caught Eddie pilfering his bag stuck his head into the corridor, looked up and down, then withdrew, shutting the door.

To his surprise, Linder's feelings were hurt all over again by the sight of her going in there with that man, but at least now, he told himself, he knew the real reason she'd given up their baby.

Garner's intruder

Above the sounds of the train, Garner had heard bustling coming up the corridor in his direction. He stopped writing and cocked his head to listen and guessed someone was bumping luggage against the seats as they moved about. Perhaps a local stop was near. The noise surprised him by stopping outside his door. Then the handle turned, the door opened, and in stepped a pretty, young woman, who looked at the empty seat—but not at Garner—and then stepped inside without a word. Garner was taken at once by her fresh, good looks, which were accentuated by exceptionally long eyelashes and soft brown eyes. She was full figured and slightly plump.

Nonetheless, he had specifically booked a cabin for one and had paid the extra charge for such.

"Good morning, ma'am," he said.

"Good morning, sir."

She hadn't closed the door yet, being intent on getting her small suitcase and two large handbags inside.

Garner said, "Here, I'll get the door for you," and stepped over to the doorway. He wasn't sure who she was or where she'd come from, so he stuck his head into the corridor and looked around before closing the door. "I'll get my things out of your way," he said, grabbing his jacket and tie and collar.

"Oh, please, don't trouble yourself," she said, half a beat behind him.

"Quite all right. Wasn't expecting company." He didn't intend to be as blunt as he probably sounded, but he also didn't want company, pretty or not, and he was already regretting the sprawling nap he wouldn't be able to take if she stayed.

"I'm sorry. Am I intruding?"

"Not at all, glad to have company," he lied. Then he added, so he'd know how miserable to be, "Are you going all the way to Knoxville, ma'am?"

"Yes I am," she said.

They were both quiet for a moment. During this lull she began to adjust her hair and the act of lifting her arms also raised her blouse. Garner watched as afterwards she pinched her shirt at the waist, pulled it down, and then adjusted her collar by lifting her chin and twisting her neck slightly, drawing his notice to a scar on the side her neck. Thin, pink, and slightly raised, it began just below her chin and ran down to and under her low-collared shirt. Garner wondered if an interesting story lay behind it, though he doubted it could in one so young. Still, it was an unusual, and dangerous, place to have been cut.

She broke the silence. "Are you also going to Knoxville?"

"Yes ma'am. I am."

"Good, I'm pleased to know that." She punctuated her statement with another head-tilting smile. "However," she said, "before I intrude on your time another minute, I must confess that I have no ticket for this cabin and hope you will not mind my being here. I was quite comfortable back where I was, in the coach car behind this one, but some rude persons kept pushing the back of my seat. I tolerated them at first, thinking it was accidental, but it became so annoying I couldn't stand it any longer. When I stood up and turned around, I saw a man and boy with their feet up where they don't belong. I started to address the man but he just ignored me. Can you imagine a father making such a bad example for his boy?"

Garner knew at once she'd run into the bag-peepers he'd met earlier. Not a pair he'd want sitting behind him, but he didn't say that, though, hoping she would leave, or at the very least, stop talking. He merely nodded, keeping sympathy out of his eyes so she wouldn't be encouraged to go on.

He did not tell her he'd already met the pair and that the man was not the boy's father. He wasn't sure why he kept that to himself, other than his desire to keep the day unentangled. Besides, her occasional hesitance when she spoke made him think she was choosing her words more carefully than her breezy manner let on. Something was not quite right about her.

"And so, sir," she was saying, "when I realized that being near these people would only make my nerves worse, I picked up my bags and moved away from them. They frightened me, to tell the truth. Do you mind my coming in here like this?"

And there it was. The first of several decision points that would make Garner's day what it came to be. Handed to him plain, clear, and certain. The decision was his. He could erase this woman and reclaim his future merely by saying, "Yes, I mind ... I'm tired ... and thinking of my son who died ... and have work to do." She'd have to leave him alone then. He knew that if he spoke up, he should so at once and not let her expectations build. To delay would be cruel, so he should send her away. But instead, he looked away from her, out the window.

The train was approaching Roanoke now, slowing, and as they came around the bend into town he saw the crossing where the accident must have happened this morning. The gray truck that the train hit was off to the side, crushed and twisted, and a few people stood staring at it like it was to be memorized, while others smoked and talked a little.

An old man knelt on the bent hood, his head poked through the broken windshield, looking inside. Garner found it hard to imagine a man had been inside when the train hit it. He tried to picture what it must have been like, stuck on the tracks and seeing the engine light coming through the dawn to kill him.

He looked at the young woman in his cabin again and nodded as though she'd just said something, realizing he'd misjudged how much time had passed since she'd come in. It was his turn to speak, obviously, to decide. As though someone else called from a cave inside him, he said, "That's okay. Sit there as long as you like, ma'am. I'll see that you're not disturbed."

"Oh, thank you," she said.

"In the meantime, I have some writing to do which must get done before we get to Knoxville. I hope you'll excuse me; I'd best get started."

She had decided not to let on she knew who Garner was, so he wouldn't think she had picked him to protect her just because he'd been in the newspaper. "Thank you for letting me stay," she said. "I won't bother you, I really won't. But I must say I'm fascinated to hear you're a writer. I work in a bookshop myself, and I love to read," she said, leaning forward, "I'd just love to hear about your work, Mister ...."

"Garner, ma'am. Richard Lynch Garner, originally from Abingdon, Virginia, but for many more years, what you might call a citizen of the world. And I'm not a fiction writer, if that's what you were thinking. I'm a scientist and I write about my work."

Her face brightened and she clasped her hands together. "Oh, how fascinating, Mister Garner. I'm Clara Talbot, Clara Lydia Talbot, to be exact, originally from Greenville, Tennessee, but for the past year from Knoxville. And I must mention to my credit, so you don't think I'm too too provincial, that for the past three weeks I've lived in Lynchburg, Virginia."

Garner said nothing. She added, "The James River is really quite impressive, don't you think?"

Her manner when she talked was to turn her face full at him with her lovely brown eyes wide open and her eyebrows lifted, as though she'd just had a revelation she was sharing. Garner had smiled back the first few times she did that, but this time he withheld the smile, determined to cut this little drama short and get back to work. There was something strange, manipulative, about this girl. Everything she said now seemed unconnected to why she'd come in here.

"I'm sorry, Mister Garner, I'm keeping you from your work. I'll just sit here and be quiet and let you get on with it."

"Thank you, ma'am. I appreciate your understanding."

"Just one more little thing, Mr. Garner, if you would. Could you promise me something?"

"Ma'am?"

Sitting straight, as a seminary girl should, and holding her head as though it were unattached and needed balancing, she said, "Would you promise me—if you have the time, that is—to explain just why you called yourself 'a citizen of the world'? I'd really like to know more about what you meant by that. It's such a beautiful expression."

He nearly flinched. Her manner seemed straightforward, but how could anyone sound so naive? Perhaps she was ribbing him? He couldn't tell. He smiled and said, "Yes, ma'am, I'll try to find the time for that." They both sat back, almost simultaneously. Clara began looking through her handbags and Garner uncapped his fountain pen again. He held the blotter to his pen to see if the tip had dried. It hadn't. He put the blotter closer to his leg, bent over and began writing.

Clara watched Mister Garner begin writing, just out of curiosity, but found her eyes lingering long after that, amazed that someone could write with the boldness and decisiveness he exhibited in the simple act of scratching a pen across a piece of paper. This was a man who knew his own mind, not someone who chanted the same foolishness as everyone else back in the "Booboisie" of Greenville she's left behind. That was Mister Mencken's term for the average American, especially small town people with small minds. She'd been reading her uncle's passed along copies of The Smart Set mailed along faithfully each month from Baltimore ever since she was twelve. A wonderful world waited for her entrance, a world of books and theater and fine art and parties where men and women practiced free love, where even married people could live a life of anti-monagamy. She couldn't wait. She just needed to meet the right persons, or person, she thought, looking at the fine black hairs on the back of Mister Garner's hands.

From the side of his eye Garner had been noticing increasingly agitated movements in Miss Talbot's corner. He shifted his gaze to observe her. Her two handbags sat agape on the seat while she rummaged through the suitcase on her lap. Her actions were more frantic than systematic. Her neck was flushed. A small blue vein pulsed at her temple and a few wisps of hair stuck to her damp forehead. She was breathing loudly, punctuating her exhalations with low grumbles. Garner joked to himself that she looked ready to blow.

He tried to start writing again, but the gorilla sacrifices were still too vivid in his memory and Miss Talbot's movements were too distracting. He sat up and turned toward her so she'd know he was watching, was perhaps even willing to help if that would quiet the commotion.

She obviously hadn't found what she was looking for, because she suddenly stood up with her back to Garner and upended the contents of the suitcase onto the seat. Then she throttled each handbag and violently emptied its contents on top of the first heap. She began pawing through the pile of hankies, medicine bottles, clothing, undergarments, hatpins, keys, pieces of paper, unwrapped candies, hair combs, gloves, a bracelet, a map, railroad time tables and some make-up containers.

Garner tilted slightly so he could see around the energetic Miss Talbot, whose back blocked his view. At the edge of the litter, he saw a coin purse and a small rolled-up certificate.

Before he could notice any more, she suddenly turned and stared at him. The wispy strands of hair plastered to her sweating forehead now looked like she'd walked through a web. Garner kept his face still, in what he hoped was an calming expression, while he capped his pen and pulled the flap over his writing pad. Then he sat back, arms folded across his chest, legs crossed, and returned her stare.

She continued looking at him, but the storm seemed to have passed. She turned around and shoved her jumble into the corner of the seat. The veins on her neck and forehead subsided and her skin color nearly resumed its pink.

She softened her gaze towards him, smiled briefly, and took a fill-up breath before saying, "Mister Garner: The look of amusement on your face tells me you think you know something about women. If that is the case, then I do not need to tell you that I'm having a problem?"

She looked knowingly at the explosion of things she sat amidst, as though she were a detective who had come upon a crime scene and knew at once what had happened. Perhaps how also, and why ... even who.

"It does look that way." He resisted asking if he could do anything to help. She seemed like the type who'd accept your hanky for her tears and then blow her nose in it.

"And you look like a wise man, Mister Garner."

He stared, resisting a blink.

"And since you are wise, you might know what to do about my problem."

Here it comes, he thought. But he was wrong. She had more preambling to do. "Furthermore, I'll bet you'd not only know what to do, but be capable and forceful enough to do it, you being a citizen of the world and all that." She sat up straight, as though the appeal of her request might be enhanced by a better view of her figure, and looked at him again as he slumped, almost hiding in the opposite seat. He wondered how, despite his saying so few words she'd found a means to corner him with them.

Simultaneously, he did notice her waist was small, in contrast to her ample bosom and that her hands were delicate and white. The sight created a pleasant airiness in his throat and chest, a feeling that used to be the prelude to a long afternoon of pleasure. He sat up, blinked, and nodded for her to go on.

"I need something done for me. I might be able to do it for myself ... I'm sure I have the nerve, but being a woman, the persons involved will not heed me. These are not gallant people, sir. They lack even the most elementary forms of courtesy. They would only respond to a man. An authoritative man. A man of the world like you, Mister Garner." She broke the gaze to pick a pearl from a broken strand on the seat and put it in her palm.

Garner hurried to stop whatever was happening before it could start.

"Well, ma'am, I'm not one who gets involved in other people's personal business." She stared at him patiently as though she intended to give him his run before she opened the creel for him to jump in.

He went on, "These situations are usually more complicated than they seem at first glance. That's why I try to stay out of them." She still looked patient, holding a tiny grin, like a mother listening to a child exaggerate a tummy ache. "As far as you fixing the problem for yourself ... I'm sure a capable woman like you can devise a means. You needn't involve me just because I happen to be traveling in the same railroad car as you. I'm sure that if the need arises you can be quite clever, Miss Talbot."

She looked away, the edges of her jaw begin working as her body tensed. He thought: Good, let her digest that. She'd see he was making sense. He turned his head to look through the window.

"Clever ?" she said. The red had returned to her face. "Why would you say that, Mr. Garner. Call me 'clever'?" Garner remained silent, hoping this thunderhead would pass, waiting for a question he could answer without arousing her further.

She went on, this time with a mildly coy smile, but eyes still angry. "When you called me clever, Mister Garner: Were you referring to my somewhat unique method of finding lost objects?"

"Just what is your problem, Miss Talbot?" he asked.

Her eyes changed from belligerent to anxious, as though she realized she had underestimated him. She looked softer now. He guessed she was sizing him up for a different approach. "My, you are quite direct aren't you, Mister Garner? Since you asked, I'll tell you what my problem is. One of my handbags, this needlepoint one here, held an object of great value. Some of that value was monetary, but most of it was sentimental. Do you want to know what that item was?"

"I guess so, ma'am, if you care to tell me."

"I do care. The object was a locket my grandmother gave me before she died. My grandfather gave it to her before he went to fight the Yankees at Murfreesboro. He bought it especially for the occasion, to keep her safe from harm. It had his picture on one side and a lock of his hair on the other. Have you ever seen such a locket?"

"Yes, ma'am."

"Good, then you know how wonderful they are. And this one worked. It really did. My grandfather stayed safe all though that horrid war. When he returned, they raised their family. Eventually...they left the locket to me. I've worn it since I was a child. I'd be wearing it right now if the clasp hadn't broken when I was in Lynchburg and I didn't have time to get it fixed. I tied it in a handkerchief and put it in my handbag ..."

She turned away and went silent, her lip quivering slightly, forcing Garner after a few seconds to say, "And now the locket's missing?"

"Yes, stolen."

Garner thought her story sounded fake, created during the telling. His face expressionless, he said quietly, "Would this have been your grandfather on your mother's side or on your father's side, Miss Talbot?"

She started to answer his question, but stopped when she saw the tiny restrained curves at the corners of his mouth. She looked stunned, "You don't believe me."

Silence. Garner looked at his boots.

"Ordinarily," she said, "I'd get up and go sit where I'm not being disrespected, sir, but a strange curiosity makes me linger. I wonder whether you just don't believe me, Mister Garner, or whether it's your habit not to believe anybody. Do you think I'm just making up stories to make your train ride more entertaining?"

Silence. Garner was thinking that he'd raised enough hens to expect a certain amount of wing-flapping and running from one side of the yard to the other. But you couldn't take them too lightly, either. A quick peck could draw more blood than you'd expect.

"I'll tell you what I think, ma'am."

He took the marsh-soiled handkerchief from his pocket and began to rub his boots as he talked. "I believe you did lose something. You say it was taken from you. And you think it was taken by those two fellows that were pushing your seat, the father and son. You want me to find them and make them give me the locket so I can give it back to you. You also want me to give the big one a punch in the snoot." He wiped the back of his heel with the cloth, then folded it neatly and returned it to his jacket pocket.

"And to think that you called me clever, Mister Garner. I never spoke half of what you just said, and yet you discerned the truth. You are much more observant than you let on." Tilting her head slightly, she smiled and crinkled her nose. Garner didn't smile back, knew that pretty girls pretended such gestures were "gifts,' while they were actually like the flourishes used by card sharps to distract you while they manipulated the deck. He removed his watch from his vest pocket and started rewinding it. He hadn't meant to say so much but felt he should let her know he was on to her.

The rails changed notes. He looked out the window and saw they were running beside a stream. Cows had gathered in the shade near a willow whose branches hung to the ground. In one place the green curtain parted and settled again as though someone had just slipped through it and was hiding. Garner closed his eyes for a few seconds and gave his watch stem a final turn.

She was talking again, "I admire a man of few words, Mister Garner. I really do. But you are a man of so few words I'm beginning to think of you as a man with nothing to say. An unfeeling man. Maybe a smug man." Garner put his watch back in his vest pocket and patted it once. "And not just a smug man. A selfish man," she said.

Selfish? That one amused him. He'd heard it often enough back in Cincinnati when he was married. He wondered if he'd hear the other accusations that usually followed.

"Yes, selfish." She took a quick, almost giddy, breath to fortify herself for the daring words she was about to say, "Because you are a man who wears the guise of respectability, a man used to esteem, a man who plays the gallant when it suits him. You probably love to flutter women's hearts with tales of your worldly adventures. You look and act like a strong man, a protector, but it seems to me that there's no knight within the shining armor you affect to wear, just a self-centered man who doesn't care about anyone but himself."

The vigor and the eloquence of her attack surprised him. Her face had the triumphant look of someone who was dumping your dead pig from a wheelbarrow onto your lawn and saying, "I found this in my garden." Whether she was right or wrong, he felt she hadn't known him long enough to talk to him so familiarly.

"Whoa, ma'am. You'd better pull in the reins a little."

"Why? Is that a threat? Which of the many things I've said has bothered you? Or is it that I didn't curtsy when I addressed you?"

"There's no need to talk like that Miss Talbot," he said flatly. "I do believe I mentioned that I have a speech to write. And this little theater piece we're enacting is not going to get the job done." He reached for the writing pad. She paused for a two count, then said, "I take it that's your way of saying 'no'."

Silence. Just the gentle rocking of the train. Garner had his fountain pen out again and was unscrewing the cap. "I take it I'm on my own," she said. He said nothing. "Very well. Maybe a woman can accomplish the duty a man declines to do." She stood and neatened the spilled trifles on the seat, then put the two empty purses on top of them and laid the suitcase, unbalanced, over the pile.

"I wouldn't dare ask you to keep your eye on these things. Your speech needs writing. Pardon me for wasting your time. I may be a while before I return to claim them."

And then she was gone. Garner braced himself for a door-slamming exit and was surprised when she simply went out and gently clicked the door closed. Through the opaque panel in the door he saw her image waver, then disappear. He stared at the blank frosted glass and felt no urge to call her back.

As patient as a spider

During the time Clara had been frantically looking for her locket in Garner's room, Linder was enjoying the luxury of the private cabin at the rear of *Les Chasseurs.*   He'd kept the shades drawn and found the dim light soothing as he waited for Clara to notice the locket was missing and come looking for it. She'd search the train over and then decide he must be hiding back here.

The photograph of what he assumed was his son would be hard to give up, but he was willing to exchange it for information about where the child was. He could always have a new picture made, a better one, with the kid awake and smiling. He passed the time trying to predict what she'd do next, something he'd never managed in almost two years of knowing her.

Frustration and anger drove Clara away from the safety of Garner's cabin and down the aisle, intent on doing battle with Linder on her own, but with her energy drained almost as quickly as it had arisen. She sat on the last armrest before the door, feeling stunned and humiliated by Garner's indifference and his suggestion that she might have made up her story. A young woman traveler ought to be able to get help from a man without conditions imposed. It was not her fault that she had this problem, she'd tried to do right by everybody, but the parts beyond her control were now turning against her.

Where had Linder come from anyway? What was he doing in Lynchburg? It couldn't be any coincidence that he was on the train. He must have been following her, but for how long? She wasn't telling Garner any lie when she said Linder had her locket, he must have. Either he, or that boy—who must be the son, Eddie—must have gone into her

140

bags while she was sleeping. She moved from the armrest to the seat, wishing she had a quilt to burrow under.

She thought of Mister Garner's room behind her. Thirty feet that felt like thirty miles away. She wished she could go back in there and sit quietly across from him for the rest of the ride, safe from Linder and his ugly games. Garner would protect her if she stayed in there, he just refused to come out and get involved with Linder. She couldn't really blame him, he hardly knew her, but that left it up to her to deal with Linder and try to get her locket back. She straightened her skirt and went through the door into the next coach, the one where Linder had snuck up on her earlier. He didn't really want the locket, she thought, he just wanted to get a hold over her again.

As she walked into the car, not having bags to carry made her feel vulnerable and intensely aware that she was on her own. She braced herself to confront him, but Linder was gone. That's his style, she thought, he's waiting somewhere down the train, having set it up so she'd have to come to him. He loved turnarounds, he excelled at them. He had more patience—no, patience was a virtue—he had more 'waiting ability' than anyone on earth. Of the nasty kind. She wasn't sure she was willing to play that game with him. She slunk down into the same seat she was sitting in when they first snuck up on her.

Some girls talking loud behind her startled Clara. She sat up and turned around, thought staring would seem rude, and turned back again. But the spell of confusion concerning Linder passed with that small bit of activity. She decided she must look for him and retrieve what was hers. She took a quick breath and stood up.

Only those school girls and what must be their chaperone rode in this coach. She passed into the next car. In the middle of the car two big middle aged men with identical thick eyebrows snored against one another, their mouths wide open. Close by, a half-dozen novice nuns sitting behind an older nun, could barely suppress their giggles every time one of the sleeping brothers snorted.

The third car was nearly filled with noisy young and middle-aged men passing around paper sacks that obviously held liquor bottles. They drank like they were in a hurry, though it was still morning and the ride would be long. No sign of Linder and the boy, though, which didn't surprise her, Linder not being the type who would bother a woman in front of other men. She moved on. The next car was the dining car. Two porters and a ticket man sat at a table drinking coffee, the latter counting a thick stack of forms. It would be good to know they were there if she needed help. The fifth car held only three people, a family probably, all sleeping in the first rows of seats.

Linder's little game was getting aggravating. She was tempted to go back, and let him come to her, but knew that waiting would aggravate her more than taking action did. She thought she should have tended her bags more carefully, but how in the world could she have known he was going to come creeping up after all this time? How'd he even know she was on this train, anyway?

Then it occurred to her that she could wait here and drink some tea and maybe Linder would get impatient and come in here to the dining room. He couldn't do much to her here where they'd be on public display. If there was trouble she'd run in the next car where all those men were. He wouldn't dare try anything in there. Besides, she was thirsty, and hungry, and sipping some hot tea would make her feel better. She took a seat at a small table in the middle of the room. The waiter came and she ordered tea and biscuits.

Some time passed. She didn't even notice, but the waiter was back and her cup was empty. She declined his offer of more as she considered staying put versus going backward or forward. She noticed while she sat there that her foot was jiggling. That settled it. Waiting was not her way. She was sure he had the locket and he'd never offer it back. She left the table, continued through the dining car and on through the unexplored part of the train. The next car was unoccupied, which made for a sinister feeling. Why was no one sitting here?

She passed through, crossed the wildly swinging platform and came to the door of the last car, which was painted an odd grassy green.

The door had one small eye-level window covered by a bright yellow shade pulled most of the way down. She bent slightly to look through.

On the other side Linder's boy sat about ten-feet back in the darkness, staring right at her, looking smaller than she remembered. He sat up when their eyes met. Figuring she had the advantage of surprise, she turned the doorknob at once and went in. The boy dove under his seat in the dark.

Inside the car all the shades and curtains had been drawn, making the interior so dim she had to pause a minute and let her eyes adjust. The seats and furniture were arranged like several long parlors and were draped in white muslin, creating an odd landscape of soft shapes with sharp angles. The car smelled unpleasantly of fresh paint.

She guessed Linder was back there. She walked past where the where the boy had disappeared, needing to put her hand on the furniture now and then to steady herself.

Behind her back, the boy hurried to the door, which he opened just enough to slip the "Do Not Enter/Private Car" sign back over the door handle. He also pulled the door's window shade down. He then knelt on a seat and watched her walking unsteadily toward the rear where Linder waited.

Clara half-expected Linder to jump out from under one of the draped forms and try to scare her. When she'd gone most of the way and he hadn't, she figured he was waiting in the private cabin at the end of the car. That would be like him: trouble her to the maximum extent. When she got down to the cabin door, she paused and listened. An odd shaking sound came from within, like a muted rattling from a broken toy.

What a damned game-playing fool he is, she thought. She opened the door and stepped in and gave the nearest window shade a quick tug. It snapped up, lighting the room. She was sitting on the padded bench, shaking a paper bag while looking down as if he thought he was alone. "You big, dumb ass," she said.

He looked up as he took a peanut from the bag and made a show of looking it over before he shelled it and leaned forward and offered it to her with a big, proud, stupid smile on his face, saying, "Want a peanut?" She slapped it out of his hand and said, "I want my locket."

"You sure I can't offer you a peanut?"

"No, just the locket."

He started in at once: Long time no see. Are you upset? How you been feeling lately, anyway? Anything I could do for you? While she just stood there wishing she had a man's strength so she could beat him up and take back what was hers.

Eight months and he hadn't missed a beat. Eight months of thinking she was free of him, her life suspended till she was free of the baby he'd put in her. Eight months, and now he was back and would want either the baby or her, or both. The awful predictability of the coming conversation nauseated her. She stamped on the peanut he'd dropped and his smile fell with it.

He stood up right away to intimidate her, but she poked him in the chest and told him to return her locket immediately. "What locket?" he said, with a small, nervous laugh, before changing his tone and saying, "It belongs to me now."

"No it doesn't. You and that boy took it from my bag."

" 'That boy' has a name. It's 'Eddie.'"

"You two took my locket and I want it back."

"You shouldn't have gone to Lynchburg."

"What do you mean by that? I can go anywhere I want. What does Lynchburg have to do with anything?"

"Everything, that's what. You been followed, Clara. I know why you went there."

"You followed me?"

"Not right away, but yes, we found you."

"You actually followed me?"

"Wasn't hard."

"You had no right to follow me."

"Not how I see it, I got a claim here."

"You have no claims on me or anything of mine."

"Not true. That baby's half mine."

"I want my locket back."

"Well, you ain't gettin it back, not till we make a deal here."

"What do you want?"

"I'll put it t' you plain as I can: You tell me who you gave the baby to, I'll give ya back his picture. You ain't gettin' it otherwise. You don't want the kid, you want his picture. I don't want the picture, I want the kid."

"You're not fit to be a parent, neither am I, that's why I went to Lynchburg."

"Who're you to decide who's fit for what?"

She started to say something and he leaned forward in anticipation, but she stopped and looked away and bit her lip.

After a few seconds of silence he sat down again and leaned back and said, "Possession's nine-tenths a the law." He patted his top pocket. He can't be that dumb, she thought.

Just then Eddie came in, looking like he hoped he wouldn't be noticed if he hunched his shoulders a little and didn't look at anyone. He knelt facing the window and began humming as he wet his finger and drew on the glass. When Linder turned to say something to him, Clara grabbed for his pocket and got her fingers on the handkerchief and started to pull it out. Linder grabbed her wrist and bent her arm behind her back. At first she struggled so he pulled it harder until it hurt so much she stopped resisting and stood still.

Eddie pressed his forehead against the window and put his hands over his ears as he began singing nonsense words. The train had just then slowed to go through a small town crossing where some people stood watching the train pass. Still in Linder's painful grip, Clara brushed eyes with a boy on the street standing beside his bike, she and Linder and Eddie framed by the window into a family portrait: "Boy holding ears and crying while Man twists Woman's arm backward." That was just an instant, like all a single photograph could hold, then they were going through the countryside again.

Linder let go of her arm.

"You hurt my shoulder," she said.

"Stay outta my pockets."

"You should stay out of my bags."

He grinned and shook his head once, like he was amused by her impudence, but didn't want to be distracted. He turned to Eddie and told him to go back up front and keep his eye on things. She could tell the boy didn't want to leave. Every once in a while he sneaked a look at her.

"Keep an eye out for 'mustache man.' You see 'im, git down here 'n' tell me right away." The boy just stood there, looking down. "Go on now, we all got jobs to do. That's yours." No reaction. He put more force in his voice, "Git. When I say 'git,' I mean 'git'." The boy left, as sullen as if he'd been banished from Eden.

Linder shut the door, put his hand at the top of her chest and gently pushed her back against the door. He stood face to face and penned her head with his arms while he leaned against the door with his hands. She felt surrounded, her view blocked in every direction. He said in a soft voice, "I missed you, Clara."

Garner learns a few things

After Clara left his compartment, Garner stretched out on the seat for a short nap. Now he was awakening again, and he couldn't help looking over at the disarray she'd left on her seat and feeling disturbed. Why hadn't she returned yet? He took out his penknife and began to dig out the last traces of marsh dirt from under his fingernails. He'd never seen anything like it, the way she'd behaved.

As clumsy and conniving as her speech had been, she'd managed to strike a note of valor near the end which almost got to him: The Grand Finale. He grinned. A theatrical piece. Had to be. The whole performance sounded overblown. It wasn't the story, but the bravura that had tempted him to get involved. He curled his fingertips inward to inspect his nails. Good enough. He started on the other hand.

The fingertip on his fourth finger had been bitten off twenty years ago by a young chacma baboon at the Cincinnati Zoo while Garner was demonstrating his understanding of monkey speech. The bite created some picturesque blood, and hurt enough to make him want to swear, but he put a handkerchief over the wound and squeezed hard, telling the reporters, "Gentlemen, you've just witnessed how necessary are the powers of speech. If my assistant here had spoken to me instead of taking such rash action, I wouldn't have to terminate my demonstration at this time. Someone please tell Mister McKinley." The reporters laughed and his line was quoted in every story about Garner up until President McKinley was assassinated in '01.

He scraped and thought some more. If she'd been truthful, he thought, he had an obligation to help her. But she hadn't. In telling her story she'd hesitated at certain intervals, and her eyes had hinted of deception. He'd seen her type before. The stations and ports of the world were filled with people who preyed on travelers. What's more, he'd already met that tall fellow she said was bothering her and he looked like trouble. His eyes were empty and he looked worn clean through. The boy too. It was better to stay away from people like them. He wondered if the three of them were in cahoots. What if they'd been trying to set him up so they all could rob him?

He pictured her again, her smooth, fair skin and delicate neck and full bosom. Imagining her caused him to feel a vague tugging. A wave of regret at their age difference. Too bad, he thought, she'd be a lively companion. Never anything wrong with admiring female beauty though, even if from a distance. He picked up his writing pad, removed the cap from his pen and returned to his speech:

> GORILLAS.
> — Great difficulties capturing them for zoos (live in deep jungle forests, danger of fever, poisonous snakes, wild animals, shy animals that avoid contact).
> — To capture for captivity, must get young ones. Shock of sudden change to Civilized life too stressful for adult constitution.
> — Orphans?

Garner looked up, trying to remember which of his glass slides depicted the 'orphan' idea. He couldn't remember but could decide later, during set-up at the lecture hall. 'Orphan' was one of those terms the press loved to criticize, saying he was describing gorilla life in human terms, but they didn't bother him. The audiences loved it, and they paid the bills, not the freeloading press. Human terms like 'orphan,' or 'uncle' made the pictures more understandable.

After two pages, his hand cramped. He capped the pen and put it away, hungry enough now to open his carryall and reach in for the paper bag with the remaining sweet roll.

He groped in the bag, but he didn't feel it. Removing his shirts, holstered revolver, and shaving kit, he put them neatly on the seat beside him and then pulled out his socks, slippers, bathrobe, and two collars. No sweet roll. Not a crumb. Taking the bag by the lip and bottom, he started to dump it, like Clara Talbot had, but suddenly understood what had happened and sat down, holding the bag tilted on his knee. He felt ridiculous.

That boy on the platform had taken his roll. That's why he looked so sly when he got caught. Garner looked at his things again. Nothing else seemed to be missing. He looked at the revolver lying atop his shirts and considered himself lucky to have lost only a pastry. As he slumped into the corner with his arms and legs crossed, he wondered if Miss Talbot had been truthful about those two stealing a locket from her. He still didn't quite believe the story about her grandfather and the Battle of Murfreesboro but maybe she added that part just to give weight to a trifle. The locket perhaps marked a birthday or a young romance. He could forgive that. He might owe her an apology when she returned.

For a while after that he just sat with his cheek resting against the cool window glass, trying to think of nothing in particular, but continually returned to thoughts of Miss Talbot. He wondered if he should go look for her, just in case she was telling the truth.

Just then the train rocked into a curve and Miss Talbot's empty suitcase fell to the floor. He started to put it back, but knew it would just fall over again if he laid it on the pile as she had, so he stood it upright against her seat. He glanced for a moment at the jumbled pile of stuff she'd left. It was too disorganized to appeal to his curiosity, but for the moment he couldn't resist sitting on the bench and looking at it. This rubble made little sense to him, not the way a man's would. In a workshop, or campsite, he could look at a man's tools and know his intentions, his ambitions, and even his character to an extent.

In that respect, some of Miss Talbot's obvious traces—jewelry, face powder, scented stationery, ribbons, barrettes, trivialized her from Garner's point of view. Certainly the contents of her bag marked its owner as a female, but only another woman could know what was particular, or individualistic, about Clara Talbot from these things.

Yet, trivial or not, there he sat, on the outside looking in, wishing there was some riddle here he could master as proof against the indelible loneliness he felt. He reached over and touched the small stack of clothing on the bench. Hankies on top, then bloomers and brassieres, a lightweight sweater, two blouses, more, all folded neatly. As a formerly married man, a pile of laundry spoke to him of easy comfort with another human being. It said they were ready to go on with life again, everybody's clothes washed and dried and folded. He missed that kind of intimacy.

Today would have been his son Harry's birthday. He wished he had someone else in his life who knew that when he mounted the podium tonight to address a thousand people. Or someone who knew that tonight's celebrated speaker had grown up the son of boot maker and never been formally schooled, and had gone to Africa on his own. Or how much loneliness and fortitude it took to be the solitary white man, the only English-language speaker around for months at a time, as he lay in the bush waiting to see the gorillas in families, always in families.

More than anything just then, he yearned to gently touch one of these garments and feel a personal connection with the woman who'd worn it. When he pictured himself doing that though, he felt stupid. He and Clara Talbot had no history, and what's worse, his access to her personal things had been unearned, gained only by nosiness. He felt ungentlemanly and somewhat ashamed.

A door opened and closed in the corridor. He went rigid, ready to jump back to his seat, but there was no further sound. He looked at the pile again: A hair brush, some hat pins, a handkerchief, a broken strand of fake pearls, a brooch, a rolled scroll with her name written on it, but no address, some receipts ....

Someone was humming in the corridor, just loud enough to give notice of his approach. Garner crossed over to his seat in time to pick up his pen and writing pad before someone rapped twice on the door.

Before Garner could answer, the door opened and a porter leaned in, still holding the knob. He was a light-skinned Negro, middle aged, with a freckled face that had little bumps on it and hardly any eyebrows. A deep squint made it hard to read his eyes.

"Good aftahnoon, suh. Sorry to disturb you. Just wanted to make sure everything was okay."

"More or less," said Garner, "We making up any of the time we lost this morning."

"Oh yeah, we tryin' to. Ah hate to tell ya this, but we gonna have t' take water when we hit Strawberry Plains. That'll be about a half-hour stop. But we'll be in Knoxville by 4:30, I garantee ya."

"I see. Well, thank you," reading the porter's name tag, "William."

"You're welcome, suh."

"Oh, wait, William, just one more thing."

"Yes, suh."

"There was a lady sharing this compartment with me for a while. A young lady wearing a plum colored skirt and coat." Still leaning in from the doorway, William's gaze flicked quickly at the jumble on the seat and then back to Garner. He didn't say anything.

"She left here over an hour ago to take care of a little problem and she hasn't returned."

"Yes, suh."

"I wonder if you've seen the lady somewhere on the train?"

"No, suh, I have not."

"You haven't?"

"No, suh."

"No, huh? How about a tall man with blue jean overalls, traveling with a boy about twelve years old."

"No suh, didn't see nobody looked like that either."

"Well, if you do, the lady's name is Clara Talbot. If you see her before she detrains, she needs to be reminded that she left some of her possessions back here." William didn't look at the pile again. His eyes flicked over to the floor beneath the window and then returned to Garner's face without changing expression.

"Yes, suh. I see the lady, I'll tell her to come back 'n' get her stuff 'fore she leaves. Good mornin', suh. I'll go look 'n' see if the lady's out there."

Garner let him have the last word, merely nodded as the porter pulled his head back and closed the door behind him. He leaned forward and looked under his seat to see what William's eyes had gone to. The scrolled certificate that had fallen out of Miss Talbot's emptied bag. He picked it up and unrolled it. The thick paper had fancy engraved borders and a center vignette that depicted an upward-gazing angel that brandished a sword in one hand, a banner in the other, the banner reading *Virtue*. A gold seal adorned the bottom-right corner. The document attested that Clara Lydia Talbot had stayed at the Florence Crittenton Home, 18th and Taylor Streets, Lynchburg, Virginia from April 28 to May 13, 1920. She had successfully completed "The Crittenton Course in Domestic Science." Her advisor was the Reverend Merrill Chase.

She didn't seem like the type, Garner thought, putting the certificate back in the envelope. She was too feisty, too educated, really, to work as a servant. Didn't she say she worked in a bookstore? Why would she work to attain a Domestic Science certificate? Perhaps, he thought, she wants to be a governess to some rich people and needs credentials. Still and all, he never took her for the type. He put the certificate with the pile of things she'd left on her seat.

He couldn't resist looking at a small group of receipts she'd left. Five were for commonplace things—shampoo, hair pins, stockings, face powder, a white blouse. The sixth was from Garvey's Watch and Jewelry Store, 411 E. Main Street, for a 14-carat gold, double-sided locket and chain. That must be the locket she said was stolen ... but ... the receipt said it was purchased new on May 11, two days ago.

So much for family heirlooms, Garner thought. She'd told him that locket was her grandmother's. And compounded the lie with what amounted to heresy here in Virginia, invoking a false civil war history to trick him into helping her reclaim that a thing had been purchased only two days ago. The Battle of Murfreesboro, indeed.

She must have thought she had to goose him to get involved. She probably hoped he might be the Southern Gentleman sort who'd fight for family honor—the source of a very common Southern dread: pursuing an ideal only to discover on one's deathbed that it had been a false cause. He pictured the truck driver who got killed by the train this morning, either by being too brave, or simply too slow a judge of how quickly bad things can happen. He remembered his footprints being sucked away by the rising muck in the swamp this morning.

He changed the subject. Tomorrow he'd leave Knoxville and start getting ready for his return to Africa. "French Equatorial Africa"— words that still had a magical ring, even after four trips. There was nothing wrong with his life, he thought, that keeping busy wouldn't cure. Food always helped too. He decided to go to the dining car. As he stood and put on his jacket, he looked once more at Clara Talbot's rubble. He was sorry he'd looked at her things. If she was in trouble, she'd got in it herself and would get out of it herself. After all, he laughed to himself, she's got a certificate in Domestic Science.

The joke failed to remove the disappointment he felt, however. He did not know that the Florence Crittenton Homes were for Unwed Mothers. Perhaps such knowledge may have sent him bounding after to help her. But it was hunger alone, just simple appetite, that moved him to leave the cabin and walk down through the train toward the dining car.

He had no idea if he'd say anything to her if he saw her along the way. She was probably sitting somewhere telling her locket story to another stranger. He'd nod as he went by, if it seemed appropriate, and keep walking. Maybe he wouldn't. He'd have to assess the situation.

He went out of his cabin and past the two snoring brothers and the young nuns. He didn't see Miss Talbot, or the man and boy. The third coach was crowded with burly men in shirtsleeves, probably lumber workers. Bottles were being passed around and rough laughter overrode their loud conversation. In the dining car the porters stood and ate lunch behind the counter next to the busy cook. He thought it strange they'd both be eating at the same time when the train was shorthanded. Not a good allocation of employees when they were understaffed.

And then it occurred to him that if they were shorthanded and nearly all of the employees were here in the dining car, he might be able to sneak a look at the sportsmen's car at the rear of the train without anyone stopping him.

Garner explores *Les Chasseurs*

Eddie saw Garner coming through the empty car up ahead and ran back to tell Linder, who still had Clara trapped behind the door.

"That man's comin'."

"Open the back door," Linder said.

Clara's heart lifted: Mister Garner believed her. He was coming to help her. Linder reached overhead and pulled down strips of muslin he'd torn earlier. Before she realized what was happening, he'd tied her hands.

"What are you doing?" she said. From behind her, he whipped another piece around her mouth and dragged her roughly out of the cabin, through the rear car door, and onto the railed platform. The noisy, shaking platform and the sight of the rapidly sliding scenery made her want to scream. Eddie shut the door. Linder laid her on her side against the rear wall of the car, so she couldn't be seen by anyone at the window inside. When she dared to look up, squinting to see where they were, the earth tilted toward her at tremendous speed. Her stomach churned. She feared choking if she vomited with the gag across her mouth.

"Please, Mister Garner," she thought. The only direction she could look that didn't make her sick was straight down the track, far down, where the rails merged. Even then she could only open her eyes briefly because the air was alive with flying grit.

"Gimme the knife," Linder said to the boy. The boy gave it over. Linder opened the long blade and stuck it the skeleton key hole, wiggling and pushing it as far as it would go, less than an inch, while he jiggled the door handle. The handle had a little play but the door wouldn't open.

He motioned Eddie to sit on the other top step of the platform while he crawled to Clara's side and got down between her and the edge. Every now and then he would look aside at Clara and then lean forward enough to look at the door handle. He had a disgusted look on his face.

Garner saw the "Do Not Enter" sign, but tried the door anyway and it opened easily, a surprise, given the fuss the brakeman made this morning. He entered. In the dim light, the draped furniture reminded Garner of an unlit theater stage—the parlor set.

He opened one of the shades and lifted the muslin from several chairs and tables. Very nice, he thought. Those duck hunters down in Louisiana are going to have a good time with this coach.

He decided to look around some more. There was a bar in the middle of the car, unstocked as yet. The hunters would probably have no problem supplying their own Volstead Cocktails. At the end of the car were two rear compartments he assumed were sleeping cabins.

He opened the door on the right and saw that it had bunk beds, no mattress or linens yet, and a small night table. He closed the door and stepped across to the cabin on the left. Just as he touched the doorknob he noticed under the acrid odor of paint and new upholstery the smell of peanuts. He sniffed again, gently. His skin tightened as he recognized the smell. He wished he'd brought his revolver. He considered hurrying back to get it, but worried that they might still be here, and, in fact knew he was here. He decided to confront them all.

He pushed the cabin door open quickly while remaining in the doorway, ready for anything. But all he saw was a nearly empty peanut bag on the floor, its edges rolled down. A scattering of broken peanut shells also.

He went out to the rear door window and lifted the shade. He couldn't see much of the deck through the small window, other than the outer railing and beyond it the ever-lengthening recession of tracks.

The door's handle had some play to it, but was locked. He wondered why this door was locked but the first door was not. He could think of no likely reason other than the employee negligence.

That fellow with the peanuts and his overly-curious boy had been here. What was their game? And had they really been bothering Miss Talbot? Perhaps he should have believed her. Even if the locket was new, didn't he have an obligation to help her get it back? Surely, if its theft was a lie and part of a swindle she ran, why would she bother to buy it new? And, if a swindle, why had no mention been made of money? She hadn't asked him for any.

That's when he wondered: If they're all together, why had he not seen them together on the platform when his bag was molested? Perhaps she'd been honest when she said she did not know them.

If he saw her again, he'd be more sympathetic and try to be more helpful. It was surprising, though, that he'd walked the length of the train and not seen her. He'd look for her again on his way back to his own cabin. But first, he'd stop and get a bite to eat in the dining car.

Out on the rear platform, amidst the roar and confusion, Linder turned to Clara with a grin and shouted, "Looks like your boyfriend done run out on ya."

On impulse she said, "He'll be back."

"Oh yeah," he laughed, "Ya think so?"

But he looked worried when he said that.

Garner meets Bobby Williams

Garner took a seat in the dining car and looked up from up the menu just in time to see the porter, William, walk into the kitchen. William must have seen him. Surely he'd have said something if he'd seen the lady, man or boy. Garner stared at the kitchen door, prepared, if William reappeared, to call him over to be sure. He'd tell him the mysterious trio seemed to be missing. Maybe together they should search the train and ask people if they'd seen them. William's employee uniform would legitimize an inquiry that might otherwise seem foolish.

A hoarse, thin voice from behind him said, "Excuse me, sir?" Garner turned. The backlit figure that spoke to him seemed like a small, thin, old man whose clothes draped him with room to spare. Bending away from the sunlight in his face, Garner saw what looked like a young actor made up to portray an old man. The boy, or man, was possibly frail, or ill. Garner nodded reassuringly and said, "Yes?"

"I hate to bother you, sir ...."

In Garner's experience those words always preceded a request he probably didn't want to oblige, but this young-old person with basset hound eyes seemed lost. He nodded for the boy to go on.

"Sir, I ain't eaten for a while and I'm broke. Could you spot me a meal?"

The boy's oddity touched him. He said, "I guess you look like you could use a meal. You're welcome to join me."

"Thank you sir," the boy said.

"Good to have company," Garner said, "I'm hungry too." The boy sat down. "What's your name? I'm Richard Garner."

"I'm Bobby Williams."

"The waiter should be here in a second. Where you from, Bobby Williams?"

"Williamsburg, sir. First time for me, going through Tennessee."

"Is that right? Well, it's nice country but it tends to repeat itself after a while. Knoxville where you're headed"?

"Yes, sir. For a while."

"It's a nice enough place."

"That's what I hear."

"You in school?"

"No sir, just travelin'."

"Just traveling, eh? Been anywhere ?"

"Lots of places ... Maryland ... West Virginia ... Ohio. North Carolina, too."

"Sounds like you've been around. What kind of traveling you do?"

"Beg yer pardon?"

"You a drummer?"

"Drummer?"

"A traveling salesman, something like that?"

"Not hardly, sir, just a travelin' traveler. I go places just to see what's there." Garner liked that expression, "a traveling traveler."

At this point, Garner realized table service must have ended for today. He told Bobby to come to the counter with him. Bobby asked for fried chicken, sweet potatoes and lemonade. Garner ordered a pork sandwich and lemonade. They brought their food to the table and began to talk again.

"So, you don't have an objective in mind, with all this traveling, Bobby?"

"Nothin' particular, sir. I just want to see as much as I can before I wind up in just one place."

"I think it's good for a young man to see the world. Get some idea what folks are like outside his home town. You on your own?"

"I got a sister in Alexandria, but she's married, and has a lot of kids to take care of, so yeah, I'm on my own."

"How you support yourself, if you don't mind my asking you"?

"No, that's okay. I do a little this, little that. I help out in general stores, do deliveries, wash dishes, sweep floors, write letters for people that can't read or write, that sort of thing. Jack of all trades."

"And then what"?

"After a while, I push off 'n' go somewhere's else. I like movin'. I've eaten ice-cream in six different states so far and mean to in a few more."

"More than a few left. Let's see: forty-eight states, minus six sampled, that would leave you with forty-two to go."

The boy laughed a little.

Garner excused himself and went back to the counter. He returned with lemonade refills and another plate of fried chicken and sweet potatoes for Bobby.

"Go, ahead," said Garner.

"Thank you, sir."

"Think nothing of it. I was saying that eating ice cream in all forty-eight states could make for a meaningful life's work."

"Would, indeed, sir, 'cept I probably ain't ever gonna get that far." He turned a bit to face Garner more fully, allowing himself to be seen better. "How old you think I am, Mr. Garner"?

Garner looked. The boy was short in stature—with his back against the seat, his legs wouldn't quite reach the floor. His arms and legs were thin. His eyes were large in his head, like a child's, giving him a puppy look, but they were tired-looking and baggy, and his skin was almost translucent as though with age. He looked like a very sad puppy. And in the midst of this patchwork face sat a somewhat pinched, beak-like nose. The train entered a stretch of bright sunlight and in that moment's glance Garner could see that the boy's thin and patchy hair had turned partially gray. Then the bright backlight went behind some trees and in the gloomier light he ventured his guess.

"Well, I'd say you were sixteen. How's that for a guess?"

"Pretty good, Mr. Garner. Just one over." With a tinge of pride, he said, "It ain't easy to guess my age. Most folks have no idea."

"Well, Bobby, maybe I cheated just a little. I do believe I've heard of 'progeria' before, but I've only seen pictures of people who had it."

"Oh, you were pretty close Mr. Garner. It ain't progeria."

"No?"

"No, it's something else they call Werner's syndrome." He sounded proud, in a resigned way. "Progeria starts when you're real young and the kids stay real little. Then most of them die of old age before they're teenagers." Garner nodded for him to go on. "What I got usually don't hit people till they're in their thirties. But every once in a while it hits a teenage kid. Then he's done with by thirty. I been warned the last ten years are rough."

"And that's what you have?"

"Yep. One of the few." Garner asked him how he knew this. "When I was twelve I stopped growing and my hair got gray so my folks took me to the doctor. First time I was ever in a doctor's office. He didn't know what it was, so he sent us to another doc. He didn't know neither, so he sent us all to another doctor, and so on until I got to Richmond and a doctor there knew what it was. He said a guy named Werner, a German doctor, first noticed it."

"Is there a cure for it"?

"Sure, Mr. Garner. It's real simple. I just keep going till I get balder, weaker and sicker. Then, when I'm about thirty I crawl in a pine box and wait for the cure."

The boy's manner of speaking invited no response. Such private joking couldn't be joined. Condolences would sound hollow. Garner wondered what it would be like to young and faced with such a future.

Bobby said, "You travel much too, Mr. Garner?"

"Yes. All over. I'm going to give a talk tonight in Knoxville about my scientific research. I study wild gorillas and chimpanzees, mostly in Africa, sometimes in zoos."

"You really do that? You're not just teasin" me?"

"Not at all. In fact, tomorrow, I'm leaving from Knoxville to go pack my fourth expedition."

"Your fourth! That's something. Where you goin'?"

"West Africa. Gorillas mostly this time."

"What do you study about them, Mister Garner?"

"Just about everything, but especially how they talk to each other. I always wanted to know what animals were saying to each other. So, I decided to figure out their language. And if I could do that I'd know what was on their minds, how they think about things." He fiddled with his hat while he spoke, as though the hat was a problem that needed solving.

"They think like people?"

Garner was scanning a group of people walking into the dining car and didn't hear Bobby's question.

Bobby said again, "Do they think like us, Mr. Garner?"

"Do they think like us? Yes. Yes, they do, in many ways. They seem to know they have families: fathers and mothers and brothers and sisters and aunts and uncles and all that sort of thing."

"Enemies, too"?

"Enemies? Yes. They have enemies, mostly rivalries between males. But there are also females who like to push other females around. Much of it's just showing off, trying to intimidate, but some of it's real enough. They often injure one another, sometimes even kill one another."

"Just like people, huh"?

"Yes, but not as bad." He paused, then added, "They have the same major enemy humans have."

"What's that?'

"Humans. Biggest enemy of gorillas, chimps, giraffes, squirrels, all the animals on earth, and especially their fellow humans. You can quote me."

"Yeah, I know. Mr. Garner." Bobby went quiet, as though remembering.

"Yes. Anyway, if you'll forgive me for making a personal remark. I was wondering a minute ago if you were making the best use of your time and talents by just being a drifter who's looking for new places to eat ice-cream."

"Watta ya mean, Mr. Garner"?

"I mean you seem to be a bright fellow. You should be able to do just about anything that requires a good mind and a steady hand. Settle down a bit, learn a trade."

"Well, thank you, Mister Garner, but there's too many places and things I won't get to see if I settle down."

"Okay, I withdraw the question. Sounds like you've done some serious thinking about it."

"Maybe. I don't have too much choice Mr. Garner. Don't have time to double back if I go up a blind alley."

Garner stopped fiddling with his hat while he thought about that. It seemed strange to a man who'd always chosen his destination. Then he said, "I guess when it comes to having time to make mistakes, even ten times a hundred years isn't enough time to make all the mistakes you'd need to make. Not if you wanted to find out what you were best suited for in this world."

"Have you found out"?

"No, don't believe I have, or ever will," he said. He took his elbows off the table and sat back, his hands on the armrests.

Clara confesses

As soon as Garner was gone Linder sat Clara up and untied her. He threw the muslin strips he'd tied her with off the back platform. Clara opened her eyes just then and watched her bonds fly away, wishing she were free too. The bindings hung and fluttered in the train's airstream for a while till they lay down and turned to specks in the distance.

After a silence, Linder said, "Well, your lover boy ain't come back for you yet."

Partly to torture him back, partly because maybe she wished it was true—she turned to him and said, "He will. He cares about me."

Linder said, "If he cares so much, why didn't he come down here when you did, try to help?" He laughed again, but she could tell he was trying to read the truth of what she said.

She said, "I didn't tell him you took my locket. I just told him I needed to walk around a bit." Linder turned to look at her, so she added, "And that I'd bring him back some coffee. That man just drinks coffee by the gallon." Sighing.

That detail stopped Linder like his plow hit a buried rock. After a brief silence, looking crafty, he asked, "Why didn't ya tell him 'bout your necklace?"

"Because he has a violent temper. His war experiences made him that way, I think." She paused, and then said, matter-of-factly, "I didn't want him to shoot you. He carries a pistol."

Linder laughed, then changed the subject. "Where'd ya meet him?"

She stayed quiet and let the story come to her. Up till now she'd made up a few things just to put a little fear, or if not fear, caution, into

Linder by encouraging him to think she had a protector. But now that she'd started, she chose details that would give her the satisfaction of hurting him.

"Come on, where'd ya meet him?"

"Through the bookstore," sounded right.

"How's that?"

What followed was how she imagined her life in the bookstore should have been: "He came in one day to buy some books, very philosophical books ... of the highest taste ... and we talked. His name is Richard Lynch Garner."

"Go on."

"You're thinking he's a Northerner, but he's not, he's from southwestern Virginia, but he doesn't talk like it. He's very refined. His diction is near perfect." She knew that would hurt him. "Mister Garner bought lots of books and we shipped them to his Washington address."

"He got more than one address?"

"Of course. He divides his time between Washington and New York. Which, really, nowadays is what a writer has to do if he's to stay current. Not that he's a fiction writer, mind you, he's a ... "

"I don't give a hoot what he writes, why's he goin' to Knoxville?"

"Oh, he's just giving a speech tonight at eight o'clock at Mechanics' Hall for a thousand people, that's all." Linder had no answer for that, so she went on. "Well, we sent the books to his *pied a terre* in Washington and when he sent payment for the books, he sent me a charming little personal note along with it." She'd always wanted to get a 'charming personal note' from a male admirer.

"And you wrote back to him."

"Of course. It wouldn't be good business not to."

"And he wrote back to you again?"

"Oh yes, more charming letters." Might as well imagine the best.

"Charming," he repeated, as though holding the tail of a dead skunk he'd pulled from his bedroll.

"Yes, in a graceful, but masculine hand."

"What were you two doin' in Lynchburg?"

"We simply agreed to meet there."

"What, after ya finished yer business there?"

"Yes, we only re-met this morning as a matter of fact. He never knew of or saw me in my condition."

"In yer 'condition'?" He practically snorted that line, bothering her enormously. She went quiet, staring at the receding rails.

"Why weren't you two sittin' together on the train?"

She didn't have a ready answer so she waited for him to provide one. But he didn't, and instead said, with a threatening tone, "I asked ya a question."

"Richard had work to do for his big speech tonight and he needed privacy. So I respected his wishes and sat out there." Nice touch, "Richard."

"Big speech? What's he, some kind a politician?"

"No, he's a scientist. He studies gorillas."

He laughed when she said 'gorillas.' He got his big, stupid, superiority grin on his face and then said, "Where's he do that, New York City?"

"No, in Africa. West Africa."

"Oh yeah?" Then he leaned forward and stage whispered, "He ain't no colored man under that suit, is he?" He laughed loud. She went silent again. It took nearly a minute for his mirth to subside. When he calmed down, he asked in an indifferent, obviously fake, tone, "So, where'd ya say this speech was tonight?"

"At Mechanics' Hall on Gay Street, at 8 p.m."

"You gonna be there?"

"Of course, I wouldn't miss it for the world. It's a shame you're not invited, you might learn something." His face looked like a landscape a dark cloud was crossing. He said, "What happens after his speech tonight?" She tried to remember what she'd read in the newspaper this morning. "Mister Garner will return to Washington and pack before going to Cuba for a brief vacation. Then he's off to Africa for his next expedition."

"You're going with him, aren't you?" Linder said.

She opened her eyes to the dizzying sight of the rails rushing away from under the platform. What should she say? If she said 'no,' he'd follow and torment her forever, and if she said 'yes,' he'd try to stop her from going, maybe even go after Garner.

Maybe if she told him about the baby, he'd leave her alone after that, but she knew he'd keep the locket just to torment her and the locket was all she had left. Her face flushed and she turned her head away from him and watched the ground whizz by, wishing she could fall off the train and start over where nobody knew her. She couldn't speak.

Linder was squeezing her arm. "You're going with him, ain't you?" He'd dramatically combined discovery and declaration in the same breath. She was unable to think through the possible consequences of whatever she might say. Linder drew his own conclusion. "You got rid of my kid so you and him could be together, didn't you? So you two could leave the country together."

She knew she should say something to change the direction she'd started Linder, and hence herself, in, but she froze. He moved in front of her so he could grab both her arms. He tried to force her to look at him, but she turned her head and closed her eyes. He shook her, saying, "You'll never get away with it. I'll stop you both. Give me what I want or somebody's gone to die. I'm warning you."

"Give me back my locket," she said, crying at last. "Give it to me, or Richard will take it from you."

Linder laughed and said, "I hope he tries."

Garner and Bobby

Garner and Bobby both leaned to the dining car window when the train abruptly began to slow down. Several people in the dining room made public guesses as to why this was happening, but no one said anything convincing. Garner figured it was the water stop the porter had mentioned earlier, they must be near Strawberry Plains, just about sixteen miles from Knoxville. He watched as the train slowed and then stopped.

The porter William came in at that moment and Garner hailed him and asked if this was that water stop. Yes, it was, he said, any minute now they'd start backing up onto the sidetrack. He added, "Shouldn't be too long. Don' worry, we'll get y'all to Knoxville in time."

"Thank you," Garner said. He wanted to ask about the young lady in the plum skirt and jacket who was missing, but the porter was already gone.

"Mister Garner," Bobby said, "do you think I could do the kind of work you've been doing in Africa"?

"Maybe. Some of it, but I don't know for sure. Some of the work is hard and physical. Other parts, you'd need to know some mathematics and chemistry, know something about animals, know how to get around in a foreign port, how to get your specimens preserved and shipped back to the United States. And so on. That's just some of it."

"I guessed as much, Mister Garner, but I'm a quick learner."

Garner looked at him. He hadn't figured the boy might want to get a job. He nodded at him as though thinking it over and looked out the window.

The train had stopped near a high embankment built through a swamp. Garner saw no birds but didn't expect to, this early in the afternoon.

He turned back to Bobby and answered carefully: "I don't think it could be done. There are some little jobs that need doing and I might say 'sign on' if times weren't tough, but this time the money isn't there. The sponsors have been tight this time around. I've even fewer people than I need and I don't know how I'm going to feed them. I'm sorry young fellow. The money isn't there to hire an extra hand."

"Oh," Bobby said.

Garner knew that one sick person doubled the healthy's work and this project had to finish, down to the last detail, on time. His career had never been more tenuous. Attacks in the press about the accuracy of his research findings, snickers about his penchant for native women, about his drinking and irascibility in the bush, had preceded him everywhere on this fundraising campaign. The boy made fine company on a train ride but how would he handle a situation that called for nerve, or will, or action? He looked again at Bobby who was looking out the window. Big ears like an old man, skinny, droopy, sad eyes. Such a shame.

Then he thought of something: "There is one thing, Bobby." The boy said, "What's that"? Garner turned from the window and said, "I could use help at the lecture hall tonight." When Bobby asked him what kind of help, he said, "Well, this is a fund-raising talk to the general public. I usually show glass slides to illustrate such talks. You could run the slide projector for me."

"Is it hard to do"?

"Not at all. You'll be an old hand in no time."

"Okay, sounds great, Mister Garner. Thanks." Bobby returned to looking out the window, his elbow on the ledge, his hand covering his eyes like a salute. He was wondering what the pay would be and whether Garner would be offended if he asked for it up front rather than risk the possibility of Garner skipping town without paying him.

Clara tumbles

Linder got doubly nervous when the train stopped. For a minute he wondered if it was because someone had seen them out here on the platform. Or maybe Garner had got the engineer to stop it so they could come back here and nab him. But when no one showed up he relaxed a little, though not enough to make him feel they should stay out here. He stood up and grabbed Clara's arm and pulled her over next to the door.

He started trying to pull the knife blade from the keyhole. It was stuck, so he had to grab it with two hands and try to wiggle it out. No go. He tried up and down and side to side, pulling and muttering. Then he went too far and snapped the blade off. Curiously, the blade fell out of the keyhole when it broke. "Dang," he yelled. He picked it up and tried to set it back in but the pin that held it was gone.

He turned and looked at Eddie. "Sorry, boy. I'll getcha a new one, promise." He handed both parts to Eddie who sat back down and started trying to reattach the blade to the case. Linder, in the meantime, pulled furiously at the door. The handle wouldn't turn.

"Oh man. They got it so it locks from outside."

Clara wanted to laugh that the fox had outwitted himself, but kept quiet.

He stared at the handle for a little bit, then pulled her to her feet and over toward the edge, with his back to Eddie so the boy wouldn't hear.

Whatever was coming next Clara wanted to avoid. She looked down. If she jumped it was about four feet to the ground and then she'd probably fall down the slope into the marsh below. That's what she'd have to do. It might hurt, but it would be better than enduring the scene she knew was coming.

He'd stop her, though. He was too close. Maybe some crewman, right this minute, might be coming up the tracks to throw a switch or something and he'd see them out here and she'd be saved.

Linder put his face close to hers and said, "Let's get straight about the baby." She turned her head away. He pulled her chin toward him. "You heard me."

She said "It's over. Let it rest."

"Not for me it ain't."

"I don't want to hear anymore Linder. Let me go."

"You ain't goin' nowhere till you answer me."

"What do you want to know?"

"Where's the baby?"

Clara wondered if she could shove him hard enough to break free and jump. He had one arm beside her head and the other poised to grab her if she moved. She wanted to ask him if he wanted to recruit the baby for his pickpocket gang, but held her tongue. She dropped her eyes.

"You two put that baby up for adoption, didn't ya?" She wondered if kicking his shin might break her free.

"He made ya do it, didn't he? Garner."

"You're talking like an idiot."

When she said that, some blocky unbalanced thing inside his head must have toppled. A wild, trapped, look entered in his eyes and his face turned mean, a look she'd never seen before. He turned his head away but held onto her arm so she wouldn't run off. He looked down the tracks, looked up to the sky, looked everywhere but at her, obviously trying to overcome some strong, destructive urge.

Clara looked over at Eddie sitting on the top step, turned away from them, his shoulders and back hunched, his neck drawn in.

Then, the train jolted and began moving again, slowly, this time, but backwards along the sidetrack. The train's speed picked up a little. Any faster, and Clara feared she wouldn't have the nerve to jump off. She wanted to scream, had wanted to since she first turned around and saw Linder sitting behind her this morning.

And then Eddie was beside Linder, pulling at his sleeve, his eyes wide and confused. Linder turned and yelled, "Watta ya want?"

Eddie said, "The train's goin' backwards," in a frightened way, like he needed to be sure someone else knew things weren't going the way they should.

Linder's hold relaxed when he turned to looked at the boy. Clara shoved him, breaking his grip, and jumped from the backward-moving train.

Dead Tree Angels

"Look, a lady!" Bobby said.

Garner leaned to the window in time to see Clara tumbling down the steep embankment. His first thought was, "So, she didn't get off at Bristol." The train passed the point where he'd seen her bounce down the slope. He said to Bobby, "I'll be right back," and hurried out to the next car. He walked half bent, trying to see her through the windows, but the train kept moving farther from the spot where he'd seen her. What he did see was the bag peepers, bounding down the embankment, flapping their arms in a desperate struggle to keep from falling. They were going opposite the direction where Miss Talbot had fallen. Garner straightened up and ran through the car yelling, "Stop the train! Stop the train!"

He ran into the lumbermen's coach, saying, "A woman fell off the train." Some of them shouted they'd also seen her roll down the embankment. A half-dozen men followed Garner to the next car, Garner shouting, "She must've been pushed; two fellows pushed her and jumped off. They're getting away." The two big brothers with the thick eyebrows joined the posse going through their car, everyone heading for the engine and shouting for the brakeman to stop the train. As they barreled through the last passenger car, the brakeman and two coal tenders appeared ahead of them, blocking the aisle, their arms folded.

The brakeman shouted, "What are you men doing? What do you want?" Garner stopped three feet away and said, "A woman got thrown off the train by two men who jumped off after her. She's probably hurt pretty bad. Get this train stopped so we can help her."

The man looked like he was going to stand there and think about it. Garner said, "Stop it now! We mean business. Stop it or we'll go up there and do it ourselves."

"Hold your horses, mister, don't try to tell us our business. I'll go tell the engineer," the man said, and then hurried forward. Within a hundred yards the train began braking and a hundred yards later it stopped. Garner and the others moved to the exit. The brakeman and signalman blocked their way, the brakeman saying, "This is railroad business. Go on back to yer seats. We'll take care of it."

Garner and the other men held their place. With a last look of warning, the two railroad men went out the door, removed the safety bar in front of the coach steps and went down. As soon as the second man stepped down, Garner whipped around the aisle and went down the steps, the crowd right behind him.

The signalman stepped up to block Garner's way, but Garner pushed his hand away and went right by him, saying, "Don't touch me, and don't get in my way. I know that lady and I'm going to find her." The men following Garner also brushed past the two trainmen on the narrow ledge beside the track. A few stooped for a second to pick up railroad stones, just in case, as they walked nearly single-file along the narrow walk, hurrying after Garner.

After about forty yards, Garner spun around without breaking stride and, walking backwards, faced the others and said, "She was wearing a plum-colored jacket and skirt and a white blouse. Stay alert." Then he turned face front again without losing his rhythm or breaking stride. It was a deft move, a bit fancy, but worth seeing, and memorable enough, given the circumstances, that one of the beetle-browed brothers would drunkenly imitate the move in a speakeasy later on tonight.

Despite Garner's injunction to stay put, Bobby Williams also left the train and was trailing the men. He'd begun about fifty steps behind and after five minutes of huffing and puffing as fast as he could, he was a hundred steps behind, and out of breath. He stopped and sat down on the rail to recover, removing his cap as he did so, and fanning his face while he looked around. From where he sat he was at eye level with the tops of the trees rooted in the marsh below.

Most of the trees were nearly plush with May foliage, but the one just across from Bobby stood out for the smooth-limbed simplicity that death and years of exposure had brought to it. The tree's bark had peeled away, and the trunk and limbs had been bleached by sun and wind to the kind of soft, light gray that invites touch. Bobby's gaze moved along the limbs until it was stopped by the sight of two shirtless, thin, white-haired, white-skinned boys sitting on a branch near the top. Still as birds before they flush, they looked back at him at eye level.

Bobby stopped fanning his face and looked from one boy to the other several times. They looked identical. No one said anything—and in fact all three of them seemed so accepting of the other' presence, the situation seemed empty of wonder. Bobby imagined this was the way angels looked at one another. A shout from up ahead, where the men were, reminded Bobby of why he'd come out here. He looked at the boy nearest him and just using his eyes asked, "Where's the lady that fell down the hill?"

A moment of primitive silence followed while a drop of sweat formed at Bobby's temple and then ran down across the side of his cheek, brushing his earlobe along the way. Then the tree boy slowly moved onto his stomach and used both hands to pull himself farther out on the thick branch until he stopped and stared unwaveringly at a spot on the edge of the marsh. Bobby took the cue and followed the direction of the boy's gaze with his own eyes until he saw, unmistakably, a small patch of plum behind some thick bushes the men had passed. He hoped Mister Garner would be pleased with him.

He stood up and took a final look back toward the boys in the tree. One was gone already, the other descending with gracile confidence. Bobby looked down the tracks. Garner and the men were well past the site where the lady lay and were getting farther away. He looked at the tree again. Both boys were gone; a small flock of crows sat in their place.

Bobby walked, jogged and limped towards Garner and the men, who had slowed down. When he'd nearly caught up, one of the searchers noticed his hurry and yelled, "Hey Mister Garner, this little feller's trying to catch up to ya. Maybe he seen somethin."

Garner turned, and started back towards him, possibly to scold him for not staying on the train. When they met, Bobby was too winded to speak, so he grabbed Garner's sleeve and started down the embankment on a long diagonal. Garner followed, nearly stumbling several times. They marched to a small grove of sumacs. Bobby pointed. Garner stepped forward, bent to look through the stems into the thicket and then stood up. He turned toward the other men, cupped his mouth with his hands and yelled, "Down here boys." Garner looked at Bobby and patted his shoulder before he started flattening the bushes so they could get to the nearly unconscious Clara Talbot.

In the swamp with Linder & Eddie

If Bobby had looked up in the dead tree a second time and asked the white-haired boys, "Where's the fellas that pushed the lady off the train?," they might've pointed to a man and boy hiding halfway across the marsh.

Linder was watching the rescuers try to pull Clara from the thicket she'd tumbled into. He figured it would take a while to get her back on the train, something the engineer must've thought too, because the train started moving backwards again and soon was out of sight. From where he lay the bunches of men looked to Linder like a squad of nervously busy ants who'd just found a juicy bug. No, not a bug, a bee. A big fertile bee, maybe a queen. That would be her. He forgot if queen bees had stingers. No matter, did or didn't, she sure did.

The spectacle of the tripping, sliding ants on the embankment amused Linder at first, but soon grew tiresome. The marsh breeze had died and swarming gnats had started to include his face in their swirl. He rolled onto his back, pulled up his collar, and turned down his sleeves. High overhead the wind had torn a white cloud from the mass and was blowing it toward him, like an accusation. Linder drew in his neck and rolled back onto his stomach. He turned slightly to look at the boy beside him.

Eddie was on his knees, his butt on his muddy heels. He was in no mood to talk to Linder after what he'd seen on the train, so he was watching a water strider and wondering how it kept from falling through and drowning. It reminded him of swimming once near O'Keefe's rock. A chunky boy had said, "Watch me everybody. I'm gonna do the Dead Man's Float. Watch." The boys stopped splashing and watched him lie back with his arms and legs akimbo. He floated until the current tried to pull him to midstream and swallow him. At that, the boy broke pose and waded back to the shallows. A boy visiting from Virginia said, "That ain't nuthin. Here's how we do it back home. This here's the Real Dead Man's Float." He lay on his stomach, his face submerged, arms and legs laid out, and floated. Everybody watched as the creek rotated him slowly out of the eddy. He didn't break like the local boy, just let the water carry him. The other boys moved up onto the bank to see. Hoping. He went away silent as a deadman, disappearing around the bend while they stood rooted to the mud.

The beauty of the boy's passage seemed to Eddie as perfect as the arc of an arrow before it disappeared over the tree tops and he stood breathless on the bank until his awe was struck away by the sight of the dead boy walking back through the waist-deep water, his lips tight and blue, his bony, shivering arms wrapped across his chest, trying to hug himself back to life.

Eddie's recollection of the boy stopped when he sensed Linder was about to speak, a criticism probably, so he threw a palm-sized stone near the water strider. The stone missed, but made the water say "Clung."

Linder whispered harshly, "Watcha do that for, Eddie?"

Eddie just sat, still on his knees, watching the spot the water-word came from.

"Ah'm talkin' t' you. Don't do that again. You're gonna get us caught, ya hear?"

Linder's words were blending to a senseless froth in Eddie's ears as he watched the ripples from the stone rushing toward him. Maybe they were trying to climb out, get ashore, to thank him for the life he'd given them.

"Eddie, you hear me"?

Eddie finally spoke, "Linder, why'd you tell that man I weren't your son?"

"What man?"

"The man at the railroad station."

Across the pond, the two railway men, who'd passively watched the other men struggle until now, had fetched a stretcher and were handing it down. To Linder it looked as though the ants had finally figured out how to get themselves coordinated. Linder knew Eddie was staring at him. Without turning his head, he began explaining.

"I shouldn't a said that. I should a just said I ain't your father."

"Same thing, Linder." Eddie said. He was slapping a flat round stone he held in his palm like a mud patty. "If I'm yer son, you're my father."

"It ain't the same. You're only my son 'cause you were born to yer ma and me.

"So?"

"So, after that I ain't done enough to claim I'm yer father."

At the railroad embankment, some of the ants had hoisted the queen bee's stretcher shoulder high and were struggling to keep her level as they handed her uphill. The slope was overlaid with a scree of jagged cinders that gave way when walked on. Some of the men slipped and got cut, mostly on their knees or palms, but one of them got a pea-sized cinder in his chin that set a slow dribble of blood running over his jaw and down his neck.

"You're confusin' me, Linder."

"It's like this, Eddie. Yer ma chased me from the house and made me live back in the woods. That leaves just you 'n' her back home. You call her 'ma,' she calls you 'son,' and I ain't there."

"Why'd she chase you?"

"Danged if I know and I doubt I could explain it if I did."

Eddie was silent, staring at something beneath the surface of the pond.

"Like I said, you call her 'ma,' but you don't call me 'pa,' or 'daddy,' or 'father.' You just call me 'Linder,' and I call you 'Eddie.' Been fine all along so why you complainin' all a sudden?"

Linder turned to see if he'd been understood, but Eddie wasn't looking at him. He was leaning forward, one hand on the bank, the other poised above the pond until his free hand suddenly darted into the water like a heron's beak and pulled out a small gray crawfish which he held aloft by the tail.

"Ma says it's 'cause you're cheap, too cheap to act like my father."

"She's got money on the mind."

Eddie put the crawfish on its back, its tail curling up and down, the swimmerets fanning, like it was trying to crawl away by walking upside down across the sky.

"Leave that thing alone Eddie."

"I'm just lookin' at 'im."

Linder didn't answer because he remembered something, "Your mamma mention the money I just give her?"

"That was two Christmas's ago, Linder."

"And how about the new dress I come back from town with last July? The one from Wanamaker's up north."

"Wrong size, she said. And you left the customer's name in the box."

Linder looked back at Eddie who had pulled off all but two of the crawfish's swimmers. The boy's focused stare showed he hadn't used up all his curiosity yet. "Cut it out, Eddie," Linder said, grabbing for the crawfish.

Eddie was too quick. He pulled the little marshman away, turning his back to Linder in the same motion so he couldn't reach around. Before he could be stopped, he pulled the last two legs off.

"Aah, that's mean, Eddie, just mean. That's about the meanest thing. That ain't no way to treat a critter that never done nothin' to you."

Eddie concealed the crawfish's body in the grass and began arranging the thin legs to make a circle on the mudbank. When he finished, he sat back to look and then leaned forward again and pushed his first finger into the middle of the circle, making a post hole. He bent over and put his lips to the hole and drooled bubbly saliva until he filled it.

It was too crazy for Linder. He looked across the way. The men carrying Clara had neared the top of the embankment. A wave of melancholy went through Linder. He turned back to look at Eddie again. What he saw disturbed him. Hoping for the effect desperate words sometimes have, he said, "I gotta tell you something, Eddie."

Eddie had made another finger hole beside the first one and filled it too with spittle. He was listening but not seeming to, because he was focused on inserting the crawfish's claws into the holes he'd gouged.

"There's two ways a lookin' at these things," Linder said, "There's the boy's way. He's just for hisself. Gimme, gimme."

Eddie said nothing.

"And there's the father's way. He don't mind the boy sayin' 'gimme' but he wants somethin' in return: The boy should make him proud to say 'That boy's my son.'"

Silence.

Linder continued, "Well, Eddie, that me me, business don't work. Not with me it don't. It's what they call a one-way street."

Nothing from Eddie.

Clara had arrived at the summit. Four men carried her stretcher waist level as they walked the tracks. The train had returned and waited fifty yards away, right before the embankment.

Linder tried again, "We gotta have a two-way street here. I mean if I give somethin' t' you, you also gotta give me somethin.'"

The crawfish wouldn't balance, even though Eddie had forced the claws deeper into the holes. Its belly kept curling over, bringing the crawfish down with it. Eddie looked around, found a twig and snapped it to the right size. He pushed it into the dirt between the first two holes and used it prop the crawdaddy upright, its claws staying in the holes.

"Look, Linder, he's doing a handstand."

Linder ignored him.

"Don't ya get it? This's a circus, Linder, and this fella's doin' a handstand for people."

"It ain't no circus, Eddie, and that ain't no handstand. It's a goddam execution, you ask me. A goddam upside-down crawfish execution."

Eddie laughed.

"It ain't funny, Eddie."

"He's a' acrabat, Linder."

"Never mind that. I'm tryin' to tell you about one-and-two-way streets. Things gotta be two ways for us from now on. You gotta act right and stop all the nonsense."

Eddie looked at Linder like he'd never seen him before.

"Don't look at me like that. I'm tellin' you what ya gotta do."

Eddie said nothing, just lay chin down facing the circus he built in the mud. Linder looked over at the railroad bank. The procession was nearly out of sight, the stragglers now passing the dead tree whose branch pointed into the swamp. On that same gray limb from which the two white-haired boys had seen everything, a single crow now sat and stared at Linder like he was trying to remember his name.

"And one last thing, Eddie. You gotta stop bein' mean. That was plain mean what you done to Mister Crawfish there. He didn't ask to join no circus."

Lying on his stomach Eddie now had his arms at his sides pretending he had drowned and come face-to-face with the undersea circus kingdom. Eddie thought: What is, what really is, is down here, far, far away from where they said it would be.

"So, Eddie, you do what he says and ol' Linder here'll feel like he's yer pa. He'll say, 'Eddie there, he's my son.'"

Eddie cocked his head sideways to look at the crawfish's black stalk-mounted eyes. The deep hum of Linder's words, of having his attention, made pleasant vibrations inside Eddie. And the warm sun on his cheek was like having his mother there too. They were all three together now, floating.

But Linder started to say something else and the mood went. Quick as a snapping turtle, Eddie swung his arm and slapped the crawfish into the pond. Almost in the same movement, he scattered the circus ring like the dead embers of a campfire.

Linder sat up, not surprised really, just regretting he'd put so much into trying to reach the boy. The backs of Linder's eyes hardened and swelled, ready to scald his face with tears. He kept them back but it took a few minutes. Then he said, "Well, Junior, I see where all that talkin' got me."

Eddie said nothing.

"It's okay, boy. Some other time."

Probably from seeing Clara again, he thought. Made me want company. He pictured Clara, lovely, lying unconscious in a train cabin, attended by people he didn't know. She was on her way back to town with her new boyfriend and here he was in a swamp with Eddie.

Eddie was seeing the crawfish in the shallow water near the mud bank. Its tail flicked occasionally, raising a small cloud of milky glitter that settled slowly over its back. On the bank a few feet away, flies and ants contested for its feathery legs.

Across the marsh the train made a loud, shuddering noise and began moving again, gathering steam quickly and chugging past them right to left. Linder's eyes followed the engine and the passenger cars as they curved away. In a little while all he could see was the rear deck of the green car, where he'd sat with Clara, getting smaller and finally passing from sight. Even then he stared at the empty rails until he heard no more clacking.

The silence made him feel left behind, sad again.

Then he remembered. He turned to Eddie and surprised him by starting to spiel like a country auctioneer while unbuttoning his top overall pocket, "Well, now, Eddie, let's change yer tune, change yer tune," he chanted as he pulled out a small lavender handkerchief. Holding it in his palm, "I say lookee here folks, lookee here."

Linder peeled the hankie to reveal a gold chain and locket. He picked up the chain and dangled it so the locket sparkled as it slowly revolved.

"This here's for your mama. Nice, huh?"

"You gonna give it to her?"

"I got it for her."

"You took it from that lady's bag. The lady you called Clara."

"Ain't you the smarty pants!"

"I saw you."

"Okay, perfesser, I'll tell ya somethin' you don't know: Takin' ain't always stealin'." Linder stood up, then Eddie, both brushing dirt and grass from their clothes.

"Sometimes takin' is just gettin' back what belongs to you."

"That belong to you, Linder?"

"Heck yeah, it does. Especially what's inside."

"What's in there?"

"Nothin' that'd interest a kid. Let's leave it at that."

Eddie said nothing, just put his head down and looked around.

Linder rewrapped the locket and chain and stuffed them back in his pocket, but didn't button them in because he had to stop Eddie from throwing another big stone into the pond.

"Cut it out, Eddie! You done enough of that."

"Just throwin' a stone, Linder."

"There's been enough stone throwin' for one day, let's get goin."

They edged around the marsh, then climbed up onto the railroad tracks and began walking in the direction the train had gone. The stones between the rails were not flush with the ties, so they had to walk at first with their heads down, watching where they put their feet as they moved along. After a while, their feet got a feel for how the ties were spaced and they picked up the pace a little, but it was obvious that it would be slow going this way.

Linder wasn't even sure how far away Knoxville was, but he was determined to get to the "showdown," as he'd decided it would be, where he'd catch Clara and Garner together. She'd bragged away too much information for her own good. Mechanics' Hall tonight at eight.

Linder didn't know if a road was nearby, a river, or what, so there was nothing to do but keep plodding, follow the train, and trust fate to make the way obvious after a while. Eddie tugged his sleeve, but he didn't turn around. Nursing his bitterness, he didn't want to be distracted. Eddie tugged harder. Linder turned and looked, ready to be sarcastic, but Eddie was pointing down the track behind them.

In the distance, emerging from infinity, a speck coming toward them grew slightly bigger every time Linder blinked. It was so indistinct at first, it might have been anything coming their way, but the gleam of the rails and smell of the coated ties predicted an oncoming train. Linder was reluctant to let go of the spectacle and move away, so he stood there trusting the place in himself where warnings were stored to get him off the track in plenty of time.

He and Eddie stood there staring and then, though the train still seemed far away, everything—the rails, the ties, the stone and spikes and plates—started to hum, as though they'd come alive. The rails tensed, as though bracing, and Linder prepared himself to witness some wonderful thing that was about to happen. And then he had a vision of himself on the train, standing beside the engineer and looking out the window, seeing himself and Eddie facing the oncoming train like a pair of thieves caught by doomsday.

He pulled Eddie's shoulder and together they jumped from the tracks and ran away from the train. Just ahead a trestle crossed a narrow creek. They ran toward it and scuttled down its side embankment, tucking themselves under the arch of the stone arcade. The rumbling built towards them, the loudness ascending, until finally, when it still seemed a few seconds away, the black iron mass was roaring overhead—deafening, urgent, and crude.

Linder sat with his arms around his bent legs, his forehead on his knees, like a stone in a flood. Eddie, though, was like a curious creature called from his burrow by a rumbling herd. He moved up as close as he could to look through the quaking ties at the great beast's underbelly. As each new set of wheels clacked the joint near his head, Eddie flinched, but being so close was thrilling. He held his position, unable to get his fill of it, until a cinder fell in his eye.

It hurt. He blinked rapidly. He rubbed his eye. He held his hand over his eye. The pain was sharp. He pulled out his shirt tail and tried to rub it away but that made it worse. Tears flowed rapidly from his burning eye. The train did not let up because of his pain, it just kept roaring and dropping more cinders on the back of his neck. Eddie scooted down the bank and sat like Linder, braced with his head down while the fallout continued. Then the train was over the trestle and gone, taking the noise and shaking with it, though a fine shower of dust and grit kept falling through the ties from above for a while. But it was quiet at least. Until Eddie started howling.

He scrambled down to the edge of the stream and sat there yelling, "Linder, help me. My eye hurts. It really hurts. Ouch. Ouch. Linder."

"What happened Eddie? What is it ?"

"Somethin' from the train got in my eye. It hurts. I can't get it out."

"You were lookin' up weren't ya? Come here, let me see. I bet you was lookin' up."

"Ouch. Get it outta my eye, Linder."

"Hold still. How can I git it, ya don't sit still?"

"It hurts."

"Course it hurts. It's your eye. Hold on, I see somethin'."

"Hurry."

"There now, hold on, I think I got it." Keeping his gaze on the corner of Eddie's eye, he pulled the handkerchief out of his shirt pocket, and started using it to work the cinder from under Eddie's eyelid.

Eventually: "There ya go. Good as new."

"Still hurts."

"But you don't feel that thing in there no more, do ya?"

"No."

"It's sore from rubbin' it. Just wait a bit." He put the handkerchief back in his pocket, looking satisfied with his mastery of the problem, then stood up and stretched. As if noticing the creek for the first time, he said "Let's go see where this crick leads." He walked down the embankment on a diagonal in the direction the water flowed.

Eddie's eye hurt. He wasn't sure he wanted to walk anymore. He looked down at the stream. Right where Linder had sat was the locket. Linder's back was turned. Eddie grabbed the locket and chain and quickly stuffed them in his own shirt pocket, not saying a word. Linder yelled back, "Let's follow this a ways, it might be quicker."

Eddie said, "My eye hurts. I wanna wait here."

"Suit yerself," Linder said, disappearing downstream.

Eddie scurried up the sloped bank under the trestle and went out the side opposite where Linder had gone. He looked back. No Linder.

Then he left the tunnel and climbed halfway up the bank to hide in the dappled shade. Bracing his feet against the slope, he sat down, feeling he had to hurry. He pulled out the locket and held it by the chain, letting it twirl as Linder had done back in the marsh. It didn't sparkle the same way. Here in the shade it looked cool, dull, almost gray.

He was tempted to give it back to Linder, but brushed that thought aside in favor of compulsion. Ownership could be figured out later. He rested the locket in his palm and let the chain collapse onto it. He wondered why Linder said he owned what was inside and why he'd said it wouldn't interest a kid. He looked for a way to see the sides. One end had two little buttons that sprung back up if you pushed them down. He did that a couple of times while he watched a spotted water thrush walk along the creek bank into the tunnel.

Then one of the locket sides opened a little. Eddie held it so it would open fully. Inside was a little nest of tiny pieces of hair. Eddie took a pinch between his thumb and finger and rubbed the tiny hairs hair between them. The hairs were thin, really fine, and the lightest shade of brown. He looked some more but all that was in there was hair. Eddie couldn't figure why hair was inside a piece of jewelry. He looked at the hair some more and began to find it offensive. He twitched his fingers together and let a little tuft fall like a dandelion puff towards the black sooty earth.

As Eddie watched it float down, his gut twisted a notch. He had to tighten his lips to counterbalance the feeling the hair gave him. He looked at the locket again and pushed the other button down to open the other side. A photograph of a dead baby was inside. He knew it was dead because the baby's eyes were closed and it wasn't curled up like it was sleeping. His aunt had a picture like that in her parlor that his cousin had showed him. They took the baby's picture when it died so they'd remember it. But why would Linder want to own a picture of a dead baby? It didn't make sense. He probably just wanted the lady's jewelry. Eddie decided to throw the picture away.

But just then, the water thrush flew back out of the tunnel, in a panic.

The real Deadman's Float

The thrush fleeing the tunnel meant Linder was back, probably sneaking up on him. Eddie snatched up the baby hairs he'd thrown away and put them in the locket and shut it. Some tiny hairs still sticking out looked like roots coming out of cracks in a flower pot. He shoved the locket into his pants pocket just as Linder stuck his head out of the tunnel and yelled up, "Gotcha." Linder's boots were tied together and drooped around his neck.

"What're ya doin' up there? We gotta go."

"You hurt my eye."

"I didn't hurt yer eye. Why you sayin' that?"

"You rubbed it too hard."

"Don't talk like a baby, Eddie."

"You didn't have to rub that hard."

"Forget it, and come along, we got the answer to our problem."

Eddie got up and walked crossways down the embankment, guessing Linder didn't know he'd lost his locket. They walked through the tunnel, and followed the brook.

"Atta boy, Eddie," Linder said, "We're movin' again."

There was no path beside the stream. Linder told Eddie to take off his boots like him and follow him. They waded through the shallow stream in their bare feet, using rocks as stepping stones where they could, and in a little while came out to where the stream met a creek that they followed to a bend. There Linder stopped and told Eddie, "There's a surprise jest around this here bend," back behind the bushes.

When Eddie came around he saw Linder standing proudly beside a faded powder-blue skiff whose rear end floated in the shallows, its bow tied to a cottonwood tree. And just beyond Linder and the boat, Eddie could see that this creek entered a river.

"Why walk when you can ride?" Linder said, smiling, "That river right yonder is prob'ly the Holston, which gets us back to Knoxville." He walked to the cottonwood and untied the boat. Then he went to the bow and dropped in his boots and socks, noticing a bunch of small animal traps in the bottom and a pile of fist-sized stones near them, probably weights for the traps. He'd threw the traps and most of the stones out, thinking it wouldn't be right to take more than you need from someone. He waded out to the stern and pulled the boat into the water till most of it was afloat. "Go on, get in," he said. Eddie climbed in. Linder walked to the bow and got ready to push off.

But just then: Thunk. Somebody punched him in the meat of his back just below the shoulder blade. It was intensely painful. He went "aarrgh" and arced backward as he reached one arm up behind him to touch where he'd been struck and in the same motion spun around to see who hit him.

Twenty feet away, a tall, bearded man, with a big stomach that bulged his braces, stepped out of the treeline. His small dark eyes looking out the slits of his fat cheeks looked cold and mean. One hand was cocked behind his shoulder holding an apple-sized stone ready to throw, the other held a handful of resupply. He took a half-step forward. "That ain't yours, sonny," the man said in a deep, flat voice.

Eddie flinched, thinking the man meant him and the locket.

Linder said, "What's wrong with you man? You crazy or sumpun?"

"Get 'way from mah boat," the man said making a small circle with his stone hand. Linder yelled, "Whoa, easy with the rocks, man, you made yer point." The man's arm stayed cocked. Linder rubbed his back and said, "We weren't taking your boat friend. I was just showin' it ta the kid here, what it's like. The boy's never seen ..."

"Get it back on shore."

"Okay, boss, I'm on it right now." Eddie stayed in his seat, his outstretched arms holding the sides and rocking the boat in a gentle, almost imperceptible rhythm while he hummed under his breath. Linder pulled the nose of the boat back up onto the muddy shore. Over his shoulder he said to the man, "That yer only way of saying' what's on yer mind, throwin' stones at people? I think you broke somethin' in my back."

The man raised his arm again, "Hurry it up."

"Take it easy, boss. I'm doin' what ya said."

"Tie that boat up and git outta here."

Linder felt the man sensed he was delaying, not ready to give up the boat. Which was true. He had to get to Knoxville and walking wasn't going to get him there in time to break up Clara and her Richard man.

He headed for the tree, the tie line in his hand, but stopped halfway and said, "Look, I hope there ain't no misunderstandin' here. This boy here never seen a boat like this. I was tellin' him I used to run muskrat lines with a boat like this. He didn't even know what that meant, so I set 'im in the boat, let 'im get the feel for it. That's all. We was on our way after that."

He noted that the man had three stones in his supply hand and none of throwing size near his feet. He could maybe handle that. The man spit to the side without taking his eyes off Linder or lowering his rock. He said, "Okay, you said yer piece, now scram."

Linder remembered the rocks in the boat. "Okay captain, we're on our way. But I gotta get my boots outta the boat so don't get too itchy with yer trigger finger there."

"Just hurry it up, you bullshit artist."

Linder put his head down, like he got the message and was being humble now as he walked back to the boat, supposedly to get his shoes, but he was hot now. To his mind, it was one thing for the boatman to defend his boat, even throw stones, but it wasn't right for him to try to unman him with words in front of his kid like that. Linder's ears were hot and his jaw gritted as he bent into the boat. Real quick, he put one of the rocks into a sock and grabbed a second rock for his other hand.

It was over quick. Linder whirled and faked throwing at the man as he ran at him, closing half the distance between them in the time it took the man to flinch and duck, one arm up across his face. As the man unflinched to throw his own rock, Linder made him flinch again and by then had swung the loaded sock onto the center of the man's bald head. "Uuhhh," the man said, falling to his knees and clutching at Linder's belt to keep himself up. Linder grabbed the stone through the sock and smacked it down on the man's head again, then hit him with the other hand's stone and then hit the man right-left, right-left a few times until the bleeding man let go and fell down and Linder could stop swinging.

His thumb hurt. He'd hit his right thumb on the first knuckle and it was scraped and bleeding. But the fight was over. The man lay on his side, sprawled over the slab he'd fought from, one whole leg twitching, his head bleeding. Linder stood over him, panting, ready to give him more if he moved. He was in a wild mood and didn't know what to do next.

He noticed Eddie looking at him and said, too filled with savage pride to stop himself, ever the teacher, "See, Eddie, that's how ya win a stone fight." Then he looked down at the man again, as if looking for agreement. His whole body, was flushed with so much left-over energy he wanted someone else to step up and do the fight all over again with him. It had happened too fast. One minute his heart was beating hard with the plan and the next it was pounding in victory.

Then he noticed how quiet it was here. Just the sound of the creek and the call of a peewee back in the woods. Linder sat down on a rock next to the man. Then he got up and looked at the scene from 20 feet away. It seemed to him that what happened here was important, or should be important, but there was no one here to verify that. All it was to Linder, and the man, was a dispute, and they'd settled it privately.

Some advice would help. He had no idea what should happen next. He noticed he still had a blood-stained rock in his left hand and he threw it in the water, knowing it should get washed.

He looked at Eddie staring at him from the skiff and then looked again at the man. Of the two, he felt more comfortable with the boatman, so he sat beside him again. The man had stopped moaning, and Linder wished he would wake up. They could talk about the fight. The man could sit up and maybe apologize. Or even congratulate Linder and tell him he won fair and square. Linder would tell him 'no hard feelings.'

Flies were already drinking from the pool of blood collected in a shallow rock fissure near the man's head. Linder brushed them away with the back of his hand but they settled again the moment his hand was still. Things were looking serious in a way he hadn't imagined. He shifted his thoughts. The boatman started the whole thing with the first rock and then said that 'bullshit artist' insult. Linder idly picked up a flat stone and put it against the man's back, wanting to hit him there and ask, "How you like it, heh?" Too late, the man was dead. He leaned back feeling the sun like a balm on his neck and hands and scuffed-up bare feet, and let his mind, which had been prepared for a thousand decisions, calm down until it could focus on just one or two.

Clara put him here. She should've just told him where the kid was and he might have let it go at that. But she had to spite him and cut him off from their kid. And then put so much time pressure on him, leaving tomorrow, he'd had to kill a man, this damn fat man beside him who'd rather die than share his boat.

He had to get moving, he had no more time to waste, he had to get to her and make her talk. It didn't seem right though, to just leave the man lying there alone. He reached over and patted the man on the back like men will do after a fight.

Eddie was still in the boat, holding the broken knife blade Linder between his fingers and thumb like a pencil, and was scratching wavy lines on the faded blue paint. The lines were meant to ask the question: Is there was a way to know what's inside something, or someone, before you looked?

Linder was announcing everything he found in the man's pockets. "Plug a tobacco ... seventy-eight cents ... a empty shotgun shell ... wire cutters ... a lock key." He tossed all but the coins into the creek. Just before he tossed the tobacco plug he held it up and said, "Dirty habit, Eddie, don't ever get into it."

Eddie was too busy carving questions into the boat to look up.

Linder pulled the fat man down to the water and stopped to get his breath. Then he stepped in and tugged him free of shore and let go. The water rolled the man over facedown and took his legs downstream while his upper body stayed put. He was partly floating, partly beached, parallel to the shore. Linder pulled the man's boots off and threw them into the middle of the stream and then grabbed his suspenders and walked him in deeper until he was floating a little. With a shove from Linder the man got caught by the current and started downstream, toward the Holston, more submerged than not, disappearing and reappearing like an bad thought.

Eddie watched, thinking the man didn't look as convincing, as the Virginia boy had that day when they were all practicing the Deadman's Float.

Linder pushed the boat out till it let go of the bottom, then climbed in and stood up, using an oar to push off some more. When they got out to the deeper part he sat down and started rowing.

When they entered the Holston a short time later, Linder looked over and saw the boatman snagged by a branch of a tree that had fallen into the water. The swift current dipped the boatman under the water, then eased up to spring the man back up, like a primitive ducking stool. As they drifted past, Linder said, "See, that's what comes of poking yer nose in someone else's business." But it didn't sound right, even to him, so he said no more and just kept rowing, trusting that if he kept to the middle of the river they'd stay clear of obstacles. Without much more effort they got into the quiet middle of the river and Linder's mind was free to wonder what he was doing in a stolen rowboat, racing a deadman down the river.

About a half hour later, he wasn't watching when the boat scraped bottom, spun around, and stuck on some submerged rocks near a small island. Three goats on the island lifted their heads to look as Linder tried pushing off with an oar. Eddie and a big albino billy goat whose eyes were like keyholes stared at one another. Though he tried looking from several angles, all Eddie could see inside the goat was what looked like an unlit cave. Linder bumped into him as he put the oar against the upstream edge of the rock and pushed them off.

Five minutes later, a film of water covered the floor, and in another five minutes the quiet pool was two-inches deep. Linder knew he should head for shore, but they weren't far enough away from the boatman yet. If anybody found that guy, he was the likely suspect. He rowed faster and got Eddie bailing with a lard can, wanting to go as far as he could before they had to go ashore.

Before long the boat became too sluggish for him to control. The river was wide and slow along this stretch and the boat was low in the water, almost filled. He wanted to see ahead, perhaps spot a good place to get ashore, so he stood up on the seat and looked around. His stance wasn't balanced right though, and he tipped the starboard side under water and the unsecured oar floated out. A small dock up ahead seemed like a good spot to row toward and he began inventing a story he could tell if anyone was around. When he sat down again though, the missing oar was floating to the side of them, well out of reach. He wasn't a swimmer and he didn't trust the current with Eddie and he couldn't chase it down in a logged boat with just one oar.

They were still in the center of the river, being carried along by the current. He wanted to get ashore and get the boat fixed. He used the oar every way he could think of to paddle or steer the boat toward shore. Nothing made a difference, a situation that struck him as both comical and dangerous, and thus a continuation of the life he'd lived since he was born. There was no use fighting it, the boat would go where it wanted to go and that was that.

Then he corrected himself: the boat wouldn't go where it wanted to go, it would go where the river wanted it to go. He looked at Eddie bailing, humming, oblivious. That kid's in his own little world, he thought. Turning back, trailing his hand in the water, he thought: Yeah, the river goes where it wants to go and it takes along whatever's on it, which today is us.

But then, he got another thought: Even a river doesn't go where it wants to, a river goes where the earth makes it go. A river's just water running downhill, trapped inside the banks, helpless as coal falling down a chute, just along for the ride. Linder didn't know what shaped the earth so his thoughts stopped there. But he was relaxed for the first time that day.

Hanging around the station waiting for Clara hadn't been easy on his nerves. And things sure turned ugly quick when he tried to talk to her. And then she went and jumped off the train. That was crazy, though he had to give her credit, not too many gals had that kind of nerve. The problem was that she forced his hand. He had to jump after her, and it would have been okay if he could've got her alone out there, but then her boyfriend brought his posse out and spoiled that possibility.

What he couldn't figure was what difference would it make to Clara or her Richard man if Linder wanted to raise his own kid. And why wouldn't she tell him she had a kid and gave it up? Now here he was, in a leaking rowboat that wouldn't steer, floating downhill to Knoxville. And, if anyone needed some more laughs, they could think about this: If that boatman got found by somebody that knew him, he and Eddie were out for a Sunday row in the evidence.

He pictured telling the cops, "We found it in some weeds." That was true, it was in the weeds when he found it.

He looked at his shirt sleeves carefully and saw he'd missed some blood spots behind one elbow so he tried washing them off by wetting his fingers and rubbing the spots. He saw Eddie's feet on the seat beside him and turned around to see what he was doing. Eddie had stopped bailing. The boat was like a floating tub and Eddie was lying back with his face up, submerged to his ears, holding the sides of the boat, letting the river water lift him. His own little world, Linder thought. We might drown and he thinks it's Saturday night bath time. He said, "This is what comes from killin' that crawfish, Eddie. You can't kill a critter like it was a toy in some game."

Eddie lifted his head, "It wasn't a game, it was a circus."

"Some circus," Linder snorted, "Where's your bailin' can? Get bailin.'"

Eddie sat up, dipped the can into the boat water and dumped it overboard. Linder put the remaining oar in the water and used it to keep the boat from turning broadside as they continued riding the river. The river was quiet. They fell into an easy rhythm, one that encouraged musing, remembering even, but the boat had veered into an Eddie near the south bank. When Linder saw how close they were to shore, he grabbed the oar and jammed it into the water. It touched bottom half way down, so he started poling them ashore. It worked. In a matter of minutes they emerged from the boat and scrambled to the trees. Linder tied the bowline to one of them. The logged boat bumped the bank a few times, then gradually caught the current again, doing a lazy half-spin before it stuck and lay there, half submerged.

"Sit here a minute, Eddie," Linder said, "I gotta think."

It was shady where they sat on the hillside and their damp clothes quickly turned cold. Eddie started shivering right away, but Linder didn't notice. Like every shipwrecked sailor since time began, his thoughts turned to the woman who's set him adrift. He took a narrow match-safe from his shirt pocket, screwed off the lid, and withdrew a rolled-up paper—the note Clara had sent him with the peach pie that day. It was the only letter that Clara, anyone really, had ever sent him. He read along to the remembered sound of Clara's voice.

> *"Dear Linder Charles:*
>
> *As promised, here is the peach pie I made for you. I hope you enjoy it. I'm very sorry that the funeral of an old and dear cousin kept me from giving it to you personally. It would have been a pleasure to have gone on that picnic you invited me to. If you ever feel inclined to issue another invitation, I might try to make myself available to accept.*
>
> *Sincerely yours,*
> *Clara L. Talbot*

The first time Linder read that note, he regretted all the negative things he'd said and done that day, especially cursing the cousin of

Clara's for dying. Why, if that cousin hadn't died, Clara wouldn't have needed to write this note, the most well-spoken words ever said to him. This note had been special to him ever since the day he picked it out of the pie. Almost worth the trouble he'd been through.

And worse, lately he'd taken to scrutinizing Clara's letter as though he was reading the fine print of a contract he'd made with Hell itself. A violated contract. He'd read it over and again looking for some tell-tale sign of deception he'd missed the first time. He'd believed what she said was like a contract to deliver certain goods which had not really been delivered. He'd paid full price for what turned out to be promises only half-delivered. He searched relentlessly for a word, a phrase, an inflection, comma, tone, even extra pressure of the pen in some place, that might have revealed back then what she'd really meant if he'd only been alert enough to notice.

Wet and disgusted, he sat on the river bank, knowing he'd be accused of assault because Clara jumped from the train, and murder because the boatman was out there in the river and nobody would believe it was a case of self-defense. It was funny to think that he was on the run from the trouble he was heading towards.

He noticed Eddie was shivering and felt bad for making him sit there in his wet clothes in the shade that long. He rolled up the note and put it back in the tube and screwed on the top. Down below he saw again the half-sunken boat. Time was being wasted. They were going to have to get out of these woods, up into the sunshine, and look for help. "Come on," he said, "maybe somebody'll help us get this boat fixed."

In Garner's cabin

Clara lay in Garner's cabin, wanting to seem unconscious. Once they pulled her from the bushes she knew she needed a story and she hadn't figured one out yet. She felt the men, with great fuss and effort, carry her up the embankment and back to the train. She let her eyes open briefly now and again to see where they were taking her, but then closed them and tried to think. She hurt everywhere. Last night she'd slept at the Crittenton home. Today she was on a train, going home. She pictured her apartment. That was home now. She worked in a bookstore. Those were comfortable images. She started feeling nauseated and tried breathing softly, but she might have to sit up. She'd have to open her eyes, but was afraid of what she might see. She dared to peek.

Mister Garner. Right where she'd first met him. Obviously looking after her, but which Mr. Garner was he? The one who rejected her, or the one she told Linder was her beau? She breathed slowly until her stomach settled down. She remembered pulling away from Linder and jumping. Her head hurt. Her hands felt scratched. As she slipped back under, she wondered if Linder might still be on the train. For now she was too sleepy to care.

Bobby Williams was in the car too, but Clara hadn't turned his way to know that. He'd noticed her sneaking looks at Mr. Garner and wondered why she didn't say hello or thank him. He knew enough about appearances to hold his tongue.

Garner was waiting for her to feel well enough to sit up again. If he'd had a dozen questions about her before, he had a hundred now. Looking at her shoulders he felt tender and protective. But still a bit wary too.

Clara looked again. He was at the window, seemingly lost in thought. He had a large masculine nose and full mustache. What probably had been a commanding jaw when he was younger was softened now with extra flesh. He had bushy eyebrows. He struck her as a man whose ordinary face had gained good looks with age and the habit of command.

Her anger returned. He'd refused to help her, even though there was enough truth in her story that he should have. Where was Linder, anyhow? It wasn't like him to give up so easily.

Garner sat at the window, his elbow on the sill, bracing his chin with his hand. The sound of her breathing changed in a way that said she was awake, but he didn't look over or say anything. She'd let him know if she needed anything or was ready to talk. Though he worried how much of anything she'd say would be true.

Clara continued to study him, trying to work up enough contempt to deflect the questions he might ask. She noticed her bags, repacked, beside him and thought that was considerate on his part, but before gratitude could dilute her resentment she dismissed the thought and closed her eyes again. She needed to think.

Her scalp felt raw. So did her knees and elbows and the insides of her wrists, but she couldn't sit up to examine herself for fear that Garner would talk to her or that he'd see her pain and be sympathetic, another thing that might weaken her right to be annoyed. Nursing anger was hard enough without being subjected to these insignificant little decencies. She told herself the pain would go away. She didn't need his sympathy.

That line of thought left her off guard for what happened next. Without warning, quick as a lantern slide, an image of the baby projected in her mind's eye. A warm smile reflexively creased her face just before she saw the child dead again. Her insides collapsed. Her throat squeezed. Recognition and pain jumped the threshold together and overwhelmed her. She moaned like a struck deer and immediately

Garner was at her side, touching her brow, his soft words like rites from a foreign tongue. The low timbre of his soothing voice brought her eyes wide open.

His face looked calm, neither sympathizing nor prying. She started sobbing again. She tried to stop a few seconds later, but couldn't. She covered her face and turned away, still sobbing.

Garner wasn't sure what to do. He hardly knew this woman, had only met her this morning in fact—under less than pleasant circumstances. He felt sorry for her, but wondered why she had lied to him. And tried to manipulate him in a way that exposed him to danger. There was nothing simple about this woman. Her troubles seemed deeper than what a stranger should have to know.

He stayed beside her though, his hand on her shoulder, believing that was all he could do just then. When his son Harry died, Garner's friends had tried to soften his grief by patting him and offering words intended as solace, but treating him as if his emotional equilibrium had to be restored as soon as possible. People seemed to feel, he thought, that sadness was a deviation from life's natural course. A person's tears, about anything, make his friends feel helpless.

He remembered a small death he'd seen once. He'd been studying baboons in Kenya's Rift Valley, keeping his distance but following them. After a long day's march the troop descended a steep cliff and ran across the plains below towards another cliff where they'd probably spend the night.

Left atop the cliff, wheeling and staggering was a small young male baboon. He sat and watched the others disappear into the golden twilight. Garner wanted to hurry along and watch the main troop settle in—that was his study. But the sight of the lone young baboon touched him, so he eased closer until he sat some ten feet away and together they watched evening descend.

Later the half-moon came up. The stars were bright and clear and close. He heard a violent wheeze and turned to see the little monkey now lying on his side, his ribs going quickly up and down. Garner looked up at the moon for a while. When he looked over at Flynn again, he was still. There, he thought, Every living creature deserves a witness. Ever since, he'd felt that was the most we can do for one another.

Clara, lying on her side, faced away from him, had quieted. Garner looked at her and felt grateful he was given this moment of usefulness. He'd seen her through terrible stress. Surely, some peace would come of this. And then he looked at Bobby Williams, sitting with his skinny legs crossed, lost in thought, desperate, disintegrating child that he was.

He was glad for their company. He'd begun the day alone and burdened by the anniversary of Harry's death and now he had souls other than his own to worry about. People who needed him. His heart opened to Clara and Bobby and in a very real way he hoped they'd all know one another a long time.

Clara sees the Man in the Moon

Clara had to turn around sometime. For one thing her hip hurt. She'd talk to Mr. Garner as soon as she knew what her own questions were.

First and foremost: Was Linder still on the train? If he was, she knew he'd be coming for her. He thought the baby was still in Lynchburg, waiting for adoption. Maybe he even believed that she and Garner had arranged that together. Anything was possible with Linder. And she couldn't avoid him, either. She needed to get her locket back somehow. Maybe if she told Mr. Garner the truth he'd help her.

She shifted slightly because her elbow and hip hurt. Garner, still beside her, asked if she wanted some water. She nodded and he helped her lift her head enough to sip from an enameled cup. When he put his hand over hers to steady the cup, she was surprised by how pleasant it felt to be touched gently. She shook her head and lay back and closed her eyes again.

Linder was sure to come back, soon as he could, she knew that. She considered what might happen if she told him the baby died. Maybe he'd leave her alone. But she didn't trust him to return her baby's relics. He'd spite her. He'd taunt her with them, or burn them up right in front of her. She didn't think she could take that.

The men who'd carried her up the hill probably thought she'd been crying because she was a woman and was easily unnerved. Being taken lightly bothered her, but it would be useless to tell those big "he-men" that being unmarried, and unassisted, and uncomforted, and all alone, through pregnancy and delivery, and losing a baby she chose to protect from its father, wasn't easy.

Her returning anger made her feel stronger. She needed a plan for getting the locket from Linder, but she didn't want the police involved if she could avoid it. She knew the look they'd give her when they opened the locket: Loose woman. Mean woman. Linder was sure to get the cops' sympathy when he started speechifying about father-hood and all the trouble he'd been through. A country man that loves his kids is what they'd see. Someone who got taken by a flapper.

Garner was out too. He'd had his chance to help. Now if he found out she'd been pregnant he'd put two and two together and be as disgusted as she was that "four" was Linder. Once he knew she was tainted, he'd want nothing to do with her.

Anyway, it was none of his business. No, what she'd better do is tell as little as she could. When Linder came after her, probably to her apartment, she'd make a bargain with him, an exchange: the locket for the name of the folks to contact at the Crittenton Home in Lynchburg. Let them tell him the baby died. If he came back after her, she'd even have the picture hidden where he couldn't find it. She hoped he knew she was only kidding about Garner being her boyfriend.

She sat up a little. Garner asked her if there was anything more he could do for her, but she mumbled a weak "No, thank you." He nod-ded and then bent to put the cup away and the space he had occupied in her line of vision filled with the sight of another person, a little boy. Maybe not a little boy. She concentrated. Maybe he was a little man. Bobby sat against the backrest with his feet up on the bench, his hands on his knees, his chin on his hands, his head tilted so he could see Clara.

The train rounded a bend. The sunlight in the cabin swung about and illuminated Bobby's face, the strangest little face she'd ever seen. He looked like a wax boy left in the sun. He seemed to be smiling at her, though his teeth were not showing. Altogether he seemed to embody the sad, drooping aspect of someone who's never had a good day. Clara wondered if he might expect her to alleviate his misery or reciprocate some affection he was about to offer, like a sad, vigilant dog who might interpret your slightest movement as an invitation to come tail-wagging over and lick your face.

Garner finished fiddling with his carryall and sat up again, blocking her view of the boy. He turned sideways to them, reached over to pat Bobby on the head and said to Clara, "Miss Talbot, this is Bobby Williams my fellow traveler. He's the one who found you. He's also my technical assistant, so he'll be operating the magic lantern when I give my talk tonight in town."

Bobby grinned. Clara loosened a slight smile.

"And Bobby, this lady is Clara Talbot, our fellow traveler and the recent victim of a pair of out-and-out skunks I hope we get to skin. Bobby grinned again. Clara made another weak smile. Garner crinkled his eyes as though delighted, but the rest of his face was still.

After the introductions, Clara eased back down, facing away from Garner and Bobby. All three sat in silence. Clara was worrying that Linder might be coming after Garner, and Garner was looking at Clara's shoulders, trying to gauge if he should question her about Linder. Bobby was feeling more miserable than either of them, regretting deeply that he'd let Mister Garner get the impression of him as some innocent kid when he'd really approached him with money in mind back in the dining car. He was still shook up from robbing a drunk back in Lynchburg last night, the first time he'd ever done that.

He felt he'd had to though, he was broke and hungry and leaving town required money. Every time he'd tried to earn some money, people looked at his face and acted like he was carrying the plague. He couldn't earn, or even beg, a cent.

He'd had to wait until dark, on an empty stomach, before he began staking out a speakeasy called The Roost. The object was to wait for the drunkest of the drunk to stagger out, some fellow so far gone he could hardly stand. Bobby waited in the shadow of a doorway across the street from the entrance. The air outside was cool and dry. The streets were deserted. A faint yellow moonlight lit the sidewalks. A newspaper, made conical by a quick breeze, tumbled to the middle of the street and sprawled open again.

Near midnight, three men left. Two went up the street together talking loud for this time of night. The third, a red-headed man, went the other way after staggering into the street. Bobby felt sorry for the man, 'cause he was about to get robbed and didn't know it.

Bobby gave him a head start, then followed from the other side. The man swung his legs and arms aggressively wide, trying to stay balanced. He kept sidling off though, and had to stop to put a hand on a post to steady himself, before setting off again, but stutter-stepping about every six strides.

The man turned a corner. Bobby waited a short count, then crossed and looked around the corner. The man staggered on, probably heading for a boarding house. A few steps later, he tripped and fell face down. He lay there a moment. By the time he'd worked his way to all fours, Bobby was beside him.

"You all right mister?" he said, as he pulled the man's arm up with one hand and reached into his jacket pocket with the other. He felt a pocket comb and a deck of cards with a rubber band around them, but no money. He got the man sitting and sat next him so he could get at the other pockets, all the while talking to distract the man, asking him questions, like where'd he have to get to, while he reached into the man's coat pockets. In one he found a pocket watch.

The man lifted his chin and turned to look at Bobby. His eyes and brows narrowed in suspicion and he jerked his head back for a better look. "What're you?" Bobby said, "Just trying to help, mister."

"I mean, what are you?" the man said.

Bobby didn't say anything, just put his hands on the man's shoulders and tilted him so he'd lie on his back. "Easy does it," as though it was his mammy tucking him in for the night.

"What's the goddam story here?" the man said. Bobby kept going through his pockets.

Looking at Bobby's face again, he said, "You from the moon?"

"Just trying to help you, mister."

The man tried to rise, but Bobby pushed him back down and the man acted like it was a relief to stay down. He looked like a knocked-out boxer coming to, trying to figure why people were pulling at him, lifting him, rolling him around, thinking "I had an accident, they're taking care of me."

As Bobby loomed over him, the cold blue light of the street lamp lit half of Bobby's face, casting his odd face with mixed shadows of youth and age. The man stared at Bobby's face, as though trying to understand it, like he'd seen him somewhere, until a look of dim recognition animated his face. "I know you. I jus' remembered. You're the goddammed man in the moon, right?" Bobby went away with more shame than money.

The train, meanwhile, was moving fast, trying to make up for lost time. At the speed they were going, Garner felt anxious he might not get to talk with Clara before they arrived in Knoxville. To his relief, she braced herself and sat up again. Bobby looked at Garner, who nodded slightly, then quietly slipped out of the room.

"Easy, now, ma'am, you might get dizzy if you sit up too fast."

"I'll manage, Mr. Garner. I just want to sit up a little. I was having trouble breathing lying there like that."

Garner said, "That was a nasty tumble you had back there."

"I guess it was."

"You guess it was?

"Yes, I guess. I don't remember it. But I hurt so much everywhere I guess it must have been a nasty tumble."

"Don't you remember any of it?"

"I remember being on the platform of the last car and then I remember being here."

"Were you pushed off the train?"

"I don't remember, Mister Garner."

Garner looked at her for a minute as he measured his next words, worried that if he didn't ask in just the right way Miss Talbot might not answer. Then he said, "We don't have much time until we get to Knoxville, Miss Talbot, so I'd like to be direct with you."

"Go ahead, Mister Garner, be direct."

"I'd like to know what happened after you left here this morning. You said you believed a man and boy had been bothering you by pushing your seat. And that they had taken an heirloom locket of yours. You were going to confront them to get it back."

"That's right. Because you refused to help me."

Back where we started, Garner thought. He pushed on anyway. "If I was wrong, I'll apologize sincerely to you and do everything in my power to make it up to you, Miss Talbot. In the meantime, if you'd like to see justice done all around, please tell me what happened."

"Mister Garner, why are you making it your business?"

"I'm not sure. Perhaps I feel somewhat responsible for what happened to you."

"That's good to hear, I feel the same way. Only I'd leave out the 'somewhat.'"

"Yes ... well, as I was saying, when I saw you falling down the hill it aroused a terrible fear in me that you might have been killed. And then, when Bobby and I found you, I was relieved to see you were hurt, but would survive.

"And then?"

"And then, Miss Talbot, I felt a deep anger towards the two of them, especially the man. It felt like a personal affront because it felt as though he had attacked someone I knew, a guest of mine almost."

"Mister Garner, you don't know a thing about me."

"I know more than you think I do, Miss Talbot."

Clara's eyes went involuntarily to the handbags sitting tidily on the seat beside Garner. Garner noticed that and was not surprised when she lifted her eyes to meet his and said softly, "What was it you wanted to know, Mister Garner?"

"What happened after you left here?"

"This probably won't satisfy your abundant curiosity, but I left here and went looking everywhere for that man until I found myself in that private car. He was in there, hiding out I suppose, when I disrupted him. Before I could get him to return my locket, the boy came in and say "Mustache Man"—that's you, Mister Garner —was coming, and they dragged me out to the platform."

"Mustache Man?"

"Yes, they acted like they knew you. Do you have a previous relationship with them, Mister Garner, something I should know about?"

"Why, of course not. Other than that they'd tried to rob my valise this morning while I was waiting for the train."

"Why didn't you tell me that when I came in here this morning?"

"It didn't seem important."

"But it was, wasn't it?"

"I suppose so. Anyway, what else do you remember?"

"That's all, Mister Garner. Somehow I got off the train and now I am back here."

"I'd like to ask if you'd ever seen those two fellows before."

"What do you think?"

"I don't think a simple pickpocket would welcome the amount of attention this fellow's drawn to himself—or do the kind of damage he's done—if there wasn't something personal about all this. So, yes, I do think you knew these men."

Clara felt she had little to lose if revealed some of the truth. They'd all be parting their ways in another hour or so. She ventured, "They're father and son, actually."

Garner stopped and narrowed his eyes, but didn't say more than, "When I had my own run-in with them the man said the boy wasn't his son."

"That sounds like something Linder would say."

" 'Linder' is his name?" His voice trying to control his growing curiosity.

"Yes, Linder Charles, and the boy's name is Eddie."

"And you knew them before?"

"Yes, but until today I had only heard of the boy, not met him. As for Linder, the last time I saw him was almost a year ago. Well, eight months to be exact. I had assumed, and hoped, I'd never see him again. Yet, out of nowhere, there he was on the train this morning, bothering me again." Her voice had taken on the indignant tone of a woman who's seen a dog walk in the parlor and lift his leg against the sofa.

Garner—intrigued, it seemed to her—leaned forward, as if to say "go on."

She shifted topics. "I must say, Mr. Garner, that I was more than a little disappointed when a man of substance like yourself found himself unable to believe me or help me reclaim my locket. In my mind you became one more lofty-but-dubious "man of action" in a long string of such who have not helped me when I needed the help their demeanor suggested they'd be able to offer."

Garner blinked, but said nothing. He thought her speech sounded rehearsed, as though memorized from a novel and held near the tip of her tongue for just this moment.

He said, "What happened next?"

But she had more questions. "Did you really come looking for me? What made you change your mind?"

Garner was genuinely caught up in her story, but still wanted her to tell the truth. He considered knocking her down a peg by saying he'd given up on her after he'd rummaged through her personal belongings and learned she'd bought the locket only a few days ago. And had obviously lied to him. And that he had only gone back to the dining car because he was hungry, and from there to the sportsmen's car when he realized he could do so out of curiosity and not get caught. His wanderings had not been motivated by her.

Not then anyway. But sitting amidst her personal belongings had affected him. The sight of her washed and folded garments had made her seem human, and vulnerable. They provoked tenderness in him. And a desire to protect her. He'd had to overrule that sympathy when he thought she'd been lying to him. But, having seen her fall and knowing something of her troubles, his reservations now seemed petty to him.

And he was happy to have her here, she and Bobby, both of whom might need him for a while. He was reluctant to give up that feeling after having felt alone and selfish for too long. And in a way, despite the strangeness of how they'd all come together, he remembered what it was like to have a family.

He still had questions though. "When you didn't return after a while I became worried about you."

Clara wondered if he had become more sympathetic to her situation, or if he was simply making a statement.

She said, "Thank you, Mister Garner. Too little, too late to save me from a heap of trouble, but you did have the strength of character to reconsider your rigid position, so I'll forgive you."

Garner wished she would drop her condescending manner, but he smiled and said,

"I did come back in the car where that fellow, Linder, held you. I even found a peanut bag on the floor so I knew he'd been here. You must have been right outside on the platform. I even tried that door. It was locked."

"Linder stuck his penknife in the lock, Mister Garner. That's why you couldn't open it."

"Why, that's ... frustrating ... a frustrating thing to know, Miss Talbot. To think that I was so close to being able to help you."

"I don't know, Mister Garner. Perhaps it's better you didn't come through that door. Linder was angry and he had another knife."

"Well, I'm angry now too, and I'm plenty comfortable around knives. He wouldn't be the first fool to pull one on me."

"I hope you two don't ever meet again, Mister Garner. He really seems to have it in for you."

"For me? Why? He doesn't even know me, other than his son trying to steal from my bag at the station before we boarded the train."

"He may not know you, but he thinks he does and that's just as bad, maybe even worse."

"What's that supposed to mean?"

Clara hesitated a moment while she thought of how to give Garner fair warning about Linder. Then she said, "For some silly reason, Mister Garner, Linder thinks you're my beau. He's jealous."

"Your beau? Why on earth would he think that?"

"Oh, he's the jealous type and when he saw me go to your compartment to get away from him, he thought he'd put two and two together. And then when you came looking for me, that about proved it to his eyes."

'What did you say to him?"

"I told him to mind his own business."

"Why didn't you tell him we just met?"

"He wouldn't have believed me. Besides I was tired of his bullying, so I didn't feel like answering."

"Miss Talbot, there's something important we haven't addressed here."

"Which is?"

"Why is this man Linder so concerned about who you keep company with?"

"Oh, he's the jealous type, I told you that already, Mister Garner."

"Yes, you did. What I'm asking is who is he to you? Or you to him, that he's behaving in this way?"

"He's somebody who would like to be my beau, Mister Garner. But I won't give him the time of day. He repulses me."

"Where do you know him from?"

"From back home. He hangs around the stables in Greeneville and makes sassy remarks to the women that come in town to do their shopping. If you make the mistake of talking to him, he's like a tick you can't pull off."

"You his gal?"

"Mister Garner!"

"Sorry. Have you ever spoken with him? Before today?"

"It's a small town, Greeneville, Mister Garner. Everybody talks to everybody sooner or later."

Garner said nothing.

Clara said, "In answer to the spirit of your question: Linder is someone who wants to have a relationship with me. I have no interest in a relationship with him. I thought he had been dissuaded from trying and I hadn't seen him for many months ..."

"Eight months, you said."

"Oh did I? Well, yes, that sounds about right."

"This would be in Greeneville?"

"No, Mister Garner, in Knoxville. I haven't been back to Greeneville since I left there a year ago. He came to the bookstore where I work in Knoxville. I have no idea how he knew I worked there, but one day he just showed up. I told him to go away and leave me alone and he did."

"Until today."

"Until today."

"When he sat behind you on the train."

"That's right. And a shock it was, too."

"What was he doing in Lynchburg, do you suppose?"

"Following me."

"Excuse me?"

"He thought I had a boyfriend in Lynchburg and was following me there. Why, I don't know. I don't know what he expected to happen. I had no idea he was there until he told me later on the train."

"Were you in Lynchburg visiting friends?" Garner wanted to see how much truth she'd offer him.

"My purpose in visiting Lynchburg is none of your business, Mister Garner. You're being a bit forward for my taste."

"I'm sorry. I'm letting my anger at his mistreatment of you cloud my sense of propriety. Please excuse me."

"Thank you, Mister Garner."

Garner searched his mind for another subject to discuss.

Clara said, "Mister Garner, I just remembered something Linder said that I feel I should tell you."

"Yes?"

"He said he was coming after you. He said he was going to follow you and catch the two of us together."

"That's preposterous."

"Why, Mister Garner? The idea that you'd be interested in a nobody? A young woman who works in a book shop and has no particular attainments?"

"No, no. You seem to have many ... attainment. I'm just surprised that he'd be jealous of an old man, one who's just met you."

"You're not that old, Mr. Garner," she said. "And besides, as I told you, Linder's mind draws conclusions quickly. He refused to consider any other reason for my being in a private compartment with you."

"But he's the one who practically chased you there."

"Linder always forgets what it was *he* that did that made someone else do what *they* did."

Garner thought, "Oh my goodness, what have I gotten myself into?" He didn't need a lovesick, vengeful hillbilly coming after him for an affair he'd never had the pleasure of experiencing.

He said, "What did you tell him about me, Miss Talbot?"

"I don't remember too much, but I think he asked me what you were doing back there and why you didn't come out with me to help me get the locket back. I told him you were a world famous explorer and scientist and writer, that you were from Abingdon, Virginia, and so on and that you were giving a public slide lecture at Mechanics' Hall in Knoxville tonight at 8 p.m. to raise funds for your latest expedition to Africa."

"Excuse me, Miss Talbot, but how did you know all that about me? I didn't tell you all that, did I?"

"You told me some Mr. Garner. The rest I learned from reading the Gazette this morning at the Lynchburg station. I thought it was quite interesting and I thought you might be an interesting person to meet, 'a man of the world,' so to speak. Maybe you'd come into the bookshop some day and I'd help you find a book. And it was all so sudden. I mean, I read about you and saw your picture in the paper and the very next moment there you were, getting on the same train I was taking. I recognized you right away. I wondered what it would be like to chat together about your scientific work and the life you've led, but I saw you go into your private compartment and knew I should leave you alone. I wondered if perhaps after your lecture tonight, when people came down to talk to you, you'd notice me—if I came, that is. That might be a sign of something, I guess."

"Are you saying," said Garner, "that it was no accident that you came into my compartment? That you knew who I was?"

"Partly an accident, partly not. When Linder and Eddie were pushing on my seat and bothering me and they stole my handbag, where was I to go? I knew Linder would follow me unless I had a protector. And after reading about you, I felt like I knew you, and that you were capable of protecting me, so I took a chance. It was all just a matter of your getting to know me a bit more. And, well, you know the rest of the story."

Staggering, simply staggering, Garner thought. She read a newspaper column issued as a publicity story by the lecture promoter and thought she knew me. Like I was an uncle who'd stepped out his portrait on the wall.

Clara said, "Well, to finish the thought I was talking about first, Linder kept insisting you and I had a relationship and that the compartment where you were working was our 'love nest' and he vowed he was going to keep me out there with him on the platform of the empty car all the way to Knoxville and then follow me everywhere once we got to the city, even go to your talk tonight in order to confront you. His behavior, the things he was saying, well, Linder's strange, but I've never known him to be that strange. He just sounded ... different."

When she finished saying that, Clara felt she'd perhaps revealed too much and should shut up and think for a while. She could think of no other way of ending the conversation than by saying, "Excuse me, I feel weak," and lying down on the seat again and closing her eyes.

Garner was a little perturbed by her abruptness, but accepted it without complaint because he also needed some time to think about the things she'd told him. He said she should rest up. She mumbled her assent, yawning, and cushioning her head on the inner side of her bent arm, set to slumber. In the next few minutes she shifted her body and settled into what Garner guessed was sleep.

His eyes wandered over her sleeping form. Her body was a purple landscape of ample curves that swelled and subsided with each breath.

Despite the troubles she'd brought him already and those undoubtedly yet to come, he remained drawn to her.

Did Clara see anything in himself? He wasn't in his prime, not physically at any rate, though mentally not so bad. He'd been many places in the world, published books, talked before distinguished groups of literary and scientific men. He could teach her things, introduce her to important people, show her the world. As flattering as it would be for him to have the companionship of a beautiful, intelligent young woman, it must be equally flattering for a woman to win the company of an accomplished man.

But why was he wasting his mental energy even thinking about all this? Tonight he'd make his final public speech, tomorrow he'd leave town en route to Cuba, and in three weeks he'd leave for Africa. He'd be away for at least a year. There was not time to get acquainted with this young woman. And further, it would be boorish to suggest it. She'd been injured today and probably wouldn't be able to walk without assistance for a while. From what he knew, that alone would be enough to set her against men for a while. No, he'd better turn his thoughts elsewhere. He was sorry he'd opened himself to such ideas.

Making a decision to quash the desire for her merely because of common sense was a futile exercise, because the threat of extinction only made desire stronger. Lovely, amateurish, Miss Talbot had pulled open a long-closed drawer that wouldn't go back in. The framework had swelled and the space was too narrow now for the drawer to return. For no good reason, he started humming

> Not since my lad left to live in the tide,
> Live in the tide, live in the tide,
> Not since my son left to live in the tide
> Have I felt the warmth of the sun.

Young he was and always would be. How could it be else, gone to live in the tide at eighteen? Twelve years passing could not make the boy thirty. Death gave him immunity from aging. Many things also stopped when Harry did. Garner never wrote that tide ditty on paper, just sang it sometimes when he was near water, when he needed to feign a light heart so he could bear some thoughts of the boy, the drowned boy. Funny it should come humming to his ear just now, he thought.

He turned from the window, away from the memory. What good were such thoughts? Who sought them? Why were they being revived with such vigor? He looked at his hands, resting loosely in his lap. Veiny they were, the skin rippling like a sand bar when he bent his wrists back. He pinched the back of one hand and let go. The ridge of skin settled slowly. Perhaps from some reluctance to resume old shapes.

He put his hands side-by-side, the fingers spread, and examined them. The two henchmen, he thought. They'd done his bidding time and again. There were regrets, of course: letters, touches, gestures, fists, women he should not have touched ... but the heart, not the hands, bore the blame. They looked tired and worn today. He felt an affection for them, old friends grown old with him like graying hounds.

He was thinking foolishly again, letting his road-weariness carry him away.

Right now, what he should be thinking about was whether to change his departure schedule enough to give him more time with Miss Talbot. If he had a week, perhaps he'd learn enough to know if he wanted to pursue matters further. If she were willing.

A week would also give her a chance to see if she had an interest in him too. If so, they could meet again in Europe. He could pay her way and meet her, take a respite from his work. And they could correspond. It would be a charming way to court her further.

That settled it, then. When she awakened, before they left the train, he would tell her of his plans to stay on a week and ask for the pleasure of her company. It wasn't the best time to propose such a thing, given her physical condition and all she'd been through, but it was the only time he had, so he'd do it.

Nearly the end of the line

As Garner reached his decision, Clara lay across from him, eyes closed, but half-awake. Too many things had happened today, starting with turning around this morning and seeing Linder sitting behind her on the train, the last person she'd want to see. She should have known he wouldn't give up so easily. Nothing had ever been that tidy with Linder. She should have seen it coming.

Mister Garner: It was nice, the way he'd been looking after her now. Truth be told, she liked him. He was slow to warm up, but when he did, he was nice. And not just about her getting hurt, but also about what she was thinking. He asked good questions and he listened to her answers. She didn't know men could do that. And he was handsome, too— though in a way that most girls her age couldn't appreciate. She wondered how she'd feel if he ever tried to kiss her.

Then she wondered how he'd feel if he knew what she'd done with Linder, or what she wanted to be like if she'd ever been accepted in Knoxville. She wondered how Mister Garner would feel if he knew she had recently had a baby—out of wedlock—or that if it hadn't died she intended to place it in an orphanage and walk away—her own flesh and blood. He probably wouldn't think she was a very worthy person.

She couldn't imagine enduring a conversation with him where she placed herself at his mercy, opened up and told him about what had happened to her and what she had done. And especially with whom. Even if he'd accept her anyway, she could not stand the idea of diminishing herself in his eyes. She'd only done what many others have done, but she got pregnant and all this trouble followed.

What was the use of wondering anyway? He was leaving tomorrow. Maybe she could go to the hall tonight though, that would be nice, see him give his talk, think "I know that man." Right now, though, her body hurt so much she didn't even know if could stand, let alone walk. Besides, the Linder situation made any such plans impossible. He'd said he'd come tonight and make things hot for Garner and if he could he probably would. The least she could do after bothering Mister Garner all day was stay away from there tonight so Linder wouldn't have an excuse to act stupid.

Those Who Trespass Against Us

The slope Linder and Eddie were climbing up from the river was steep at first. A thin layer of turf and scrub barely covered a rock-filled field. Then the hill leveled out as they emerged from the shade into a flat meadow filled with intense sunshine. Their clothes began drying at once. Catching his breath, Linder looked up the next hill which was covered by acres of yellow wildflowers attended by lazy black butterflies.

They began walking uphill again until Linder made out the roof of a shed and changed his angle to go toward it, across the field on a diagonal. This upper part of the hill was all flowering clover and occupied by thousands of noisy bees. Linder walked through them. Eventually the farm buildings seemed to rise up out of the earth like ships coming over the horizon.

Linder's first thought was that if the farmer that lived up here didn't help them, he was going to get what he'd given the boatman. He didn't have time to waste anymore.

When they got close enough to see the main farm house, Linder noticed a dirt road and motioned to Eddie to follow him out of the clover onto the road. Half way there he told Eddie that the clover meant the man kept beehives and you never knew when someone was gonna get touchy about your walking on his meal ticket.

By now they'd been in the sun long enough that their shirts smelled like they were being ironed. Except for his shoes, Linder was pretty well dried out and feeling ready for whatever came next. The rear of this house had a wide wraparound porch with three rocking chairs on it. Twenty steps later, Linder saw a mean-looking dog, kind of a collie-shepherd mix up on the porch watching him. He was expecting that. Most farmers kept a dog or two around to bite strangers, and a place this close to the river probably got more than its share of intruders.

What did surprise him was the weather-beaten farmer sitting in a faded green rocker with a baseball bat laid sideways across his lap. The pair of them reminded Linder of alligators he'd seen sunning in the Florida Panhandle—motionless, half-closed eyelids —too still to be trusted. Linder stopped fifty feet away and bent down to untie and retie his and the boy's shoelaces.

"Looks like baseball season 'round here, Eddie," he whispered. "That boatman thought he was a pitcher and this ole grump looks ready to play 'batter up.' Wait here a minute." Linder went towards the house, then stopped short of provocation distance and said, "Howdy, sir. This your place?"

The man didn't answer, wasn't even looking at him now, was looking to Linder's right, so Linder turned and saw the puzzle answered as Eddie walked past him and went up to the porch. Both men watched as the boy stopped in front of the sleepy-looking dog and reached his hand out for the dog to sniff. The dog seemed uninterested, but lifted his head off his paws slightly to sniff Eddie's hand anyway, more out of habit, or courtesy, than curiosity, and put his head back down. Everybody relaxed.

Then the dog bit Eddie's hand when Eddie went to pet its head.

"Ow," Eddie yelled, bending over, holding the bit hand with the other.

He backed away from the dog, then howled and ran toward Linder, holding his hand up, with his fingers splayed. Blood flowed down his wrist, going under the frayed cuff of his dirty blue shirt. Linder turned and glared at the farmer." You had no call to do that."

"Pilgrim there don't like his head touched," said the farmer, a trace of pride in his voice as though his jack-in-the-box had popped up on cue.

"Don't suppose ya might a said somethin' ahead a time?"

"Nobody asked," said the farmer.

Oh boy, Linder thought, this is gonna take some doin', talkin' to this guy. He'd had enough of that for one day. He put a lid on his anger for the time being and began stanching Eddie's wound with the first thing he felt when he reached in his pocket - Clara's hanky. As he had under the trestle when his eye hurt, Eddie was raising such a racket and ruining Linder's nerves so much he didn't notice the hanky was empty. Eddie knew though, and kept howling. The bite was at the base of Eddie's thumb, not an easy place to bandage, but eventually Linder figured a way to tie the handkerchief around it hard enough that Eddie was soon more bothered by the bandage than the bite. He shut up. "You shouldn't a touched his head," Linder said to Eddie.

Then he noticed the locket was missing. He pulled the hanky from Eddie's thumb and unrolled it. Then he looked in the grass all around where they stood. He checked every one of his pockets. Eddie knew enough to not meet Linder's eyes and kept staring at his bleeding thumb.

Linder pulled Eddie out of the farmer's hearing range and said: "I lost that jewel I got your momma. You seen it?" Eddie said he didn't.

"You sure?" Eddie sucked at his wound and shook his head.

"Well, dagnabit, it's gotta be somewhere."

He was going to ask Eddie to empty his pockets, but that thought came just as he remembered he'd last had the handkerchief out when he took the cinder from Eddie's eye. "Dang. I know where it is. It's under that bridge where you got ash in your eye." Eddie kept his eyes on his dog bite and said nothing.

There was no time for pondering fine points. He calculated that he did not have time to go back to the bridge and then get to Knoxville. Besides he didn't want to go anywhere near where he had the fight with the boatman, not during the daytime anyway, because somebody was bound to link him up to the body.

First he had to get to Knoxville and find out where the little fella was from Clara. Depending on how he felt when he saw her and her professor together, some head cracking might be necessary, but that shouldn't take too long. Then he'd probably go right to Lynchburg and get the kid and then go back one night and find the locket. But he had to get started right away and he didn't have a boat that worked.

He stood up and turned to the farmer, his legs apart and his arms folded across his chest, and smiled, despite the stony face the man offered in return. Linder nodded his head toward the baseball bat and said, "What team you play for, old timer?"

"Ain't nobody here playin'," said the man.

"Well, I seen that baseball bat there."

"It's there to be seen."

"It is, huh?"

"I reckon you know why."

"Yes sir, I take it you don't take kindly to strangers."

"Trespassers."

"'Scuse me?"

"Not strangers, trespassers. River people. Use the river all you want, mister, just steer clear of my place. You come up here, you're not a stranger anymore, you're a trespasser."

"Heck, brother, I always heard you river folks'd help your fella man if he comes to you in trouble."

"You heard wrong—brother."

There had to be an opening here somewhere, Linder thought. "Well," he said, sitting down with one knee up, his arms around it, "I guess that shows ya can't believe everything ya hear."

"Amen, there, stranger."

Least he didn't call me 'trespasser' Linder thought. Then he said, "Say, though, jest for the sake of arguin', don't you think it was kind a mean t'set yer dog 'gainst the boy like that?"

"I seen it the other way around," said the farmer.

"How's that?"

"I figured you set the boy 'gainst the dog, to take the dog out the picture."

"What picture would that be, sir?"

"The picture of that dog helpin' me if trouble started." He hefted the bat.

"Oh boy," said Linder, "hospitality sure is different 'round here."

"Be sure you tell that to the folks back home."

Linder smiled. The situation was still tense, but more relaxed than five minutes ago. He enjoyed this kind of back-against-the-wall bantering and would have strung it out longer if he had more time. He had to figure this old buzzard out and get him to help with fixing the boat.

He said, "That a real Louisville Slugger you got there?"

"It is," said the farmer in a voice that barely concealed his pride.

"I never seen one before. Looks good."

"It is good."

"What's it, a Honus Wagner?"

"Honus Wagner my foot, this a Ty Cobb."

"Oh yeah? He any good, Cobb? I might a heard a him."

"Don't tell me you never heard of Ty Cobb."

Linder chuckled softly, "Yeah, I heard a him, but I don't follow Detroit much. I'm a National League man myself."

"Don't matter to me who you follow."

Linder gave it another try, "So, that mean you don't follow baseball yerself?" Wondering if he could get close enough to the man to ask to feel the bat for himself. Then he could kill the dog and threaten the old timer into helping them.

"Naw, don't like baseball. This here's a gift from my son in Cincinnati. Only time I swing it's when river rats sneak up off the water."

"That often?"

"Often enough."

"I reckon that can be a problem."

"Not 'can be,' 'tis. Just like it says in The Lord's Prayer."

They were drifting away from baseball, but Linder thought that if he changed the subject the old man would get suspicious. He kept up the banter, looking for another opening. He said, "The Lord's Prayer?"

"They trespass against us," the farmer said.

"Holy smokes, pardner," said Linder, "I ain't much on prayin', but I think you left out 'bout half of it."

"What half would that be?"

"Why, the part that goes 'As we forgive those who trespass against us.'"

"Hah! I'll tell you somethin', riverman: I ain't big on prayin' neither, so I find it a whole lot easier to stop people before they do somethin' I gotta forgive 'em for."

Linder smiled. "Gotta admit, sir, that's prob'ly a smart policy."

The four of them sat in silence for a minute.

Linder was trying to figure out the man's weakness. Whether it was greed, or lust, or anger, or vanity, or just needing a friend—everyone had a soft spot.

This old farmer was mean and dangerous and enjoyed giving his words a hard edge. Most men try a little diplomacy with strangers, but this old crank seemed proud of being hard-hearted. This wasn't the first time he'd said, "Pilgrim don't like his head touched," after his dog bit someone. He'd probably been lying in wait the, whole time with no expression on his face, hoping even, that the boy'd touch his dog.

Linder figured the man's weak point was his pride, and that it covered his loneliness. He sounded rehearsed, like he thought ahead of time what he'd say if someone bothered him. He was the kind of man that wouldn't come in out of the rain till he was ready, because he loved feeling rained on. He'd put all his attention into details—kids too loud, window not shut, dinner not ready. Gives old men something to hang on to, something to drive other people away with, justify their cold lives.

Linder kept talking, looking for a chance to soften him up, so he could toss in a question about getting help with the boat. The man kept coming back to what seemed to be his favorite subject—"the damned human race," an expression he said was from a man named Mark Twain. The old man's words snapped out, clever and nasty, with a funny edge. They sounded like each time he came up with a new saying he'd go out and wait on the porch, hoping for trespassers, armed with his sayings, his Slugger and his dog.

Linder got impatient. He stood up and looked about for a club, brushing the dust from his overalls as he covered for his wandering eyes by saying, "Well, sir, if you don't mind my sayin' it, you seem prickly as a briar patch and none too invitin', so I guess we gotta move on. I guess you got yer reasons. Must get annoyin,' people comin' up from the river like this."

The old man kept quiet.

"This'll sound funny, but even though you been no help to us, it was good for me to meet ya. You got some powerful way with words. Wish I could express myself as good as you."

"Read a book once in a while," the farmer said sharply.

"Read a book. Well, thank you for your advice, sir. 'Read a book.' I truly appreciate it."

Silence.

"Any particular book I should read, sir?"

"*Pilgrim's Progress.*"

"*Pilgrim's Progress*, eh? Well, that sounds like a good place to start … so, that's a good one, you think so?"

"I know so."

"That what you named your dog after?"

"Now you're one ahead of the game already, Riverman."

Linder gave up on finding a weapon and decided to go back to the river and walk the banks until they found another boat. He gathered himself together to take the first departing step but then stopped as though a great and curious question had arisen within him and must be asked, "Say, Mister Farmer, those sayin's of yours, they from that book, *Pilgrim's Progress?*"

The man stiffened and sat upright immediately.

Bang. Right there, Linder thought, right between the eyes.

"I sure as hell did not get my sayings from any book, especially that book. They're my own words. I don't need sayings from a book to deal with what comes up here: 'River talk for river trash,' I say."

"There, ya done it again, mister. You just said another one worth repeating."

"Hell, man, I been sayin' that one for years."

"You have, huh?"

"Sure," said the man.

"Well, mister farmer, if I could talk like you I'd have three wives, two automobiles, and a hill of gold."

"You just make that up ?"

"Huh? Oh, yeah...guess I did, "Linder said.

"Well, you ain't so bad yourself," said the man.

They began talking, exchanging proverbs and bits of wisdom they'd accumulated along the way. It was obvious the old man didn't want to be alone again so soon. They bantered about book learning versus life experience and agreed that life experience was more important but that Linder's character would never truly improve until he got a few books under his belt. That would be the only way to have 'lofty thoughts' as the farmer called them.

After five minutes, Linder had to change the subject, "Well, listen," he said, "it's been a pleasure, but we gotta get movin'. But ya know, it would be foolish of me to spend so much time here and not take a chance on asking what I came up here to ask." Whereupon Linder explained how Eddie's mother was sick in the hospital and they had to get there soon because she wasn't expected to last much longer. And a friend of theirs had lent them a boat but it wasn't any too sturdy and started leaking after it brushed some rocks. And they'd lost an oar too.

The farmer must have enjoyed his talk with Linder, because he agreed to help them. He went in the house and came back out with a half loaf of bread, a small cheese and a jar of pickled beans for them. Then he led them over to the tool shed and gave them an extra oar they could borrow and leave for him with the river police in town. Then he found some materials for patching the boat and the three of them walked down through the clover and the yellow flowers and the trees to where the boat was tied up. The old man did most of the work of repairing the boat.

For a moment while the farmer bent over the boat finishing the last patch, Linder considered picking up the baseball bat and knocking the old man's head clean off his shoulders. He figured that would even the score for the humble pie the man made him eat. He didn't do it, though, because the dog was between him and the man, and looking bigger down here than he did on the porch. If he didn't get one of them on the first swing, he wouldn't have time to whack the other when it came at him. Then he'd be fighting two of them and the odds were against him. He didn't want Eddie jumping in and having blood on his hands.

As for Eddie's own blood—on their way back down here Eddie had pulled Clara's hanky off his hand and dropped it among the yellow flowers. He didn't want Linder to see the hanky on his hand and start wondering where the locket and chain were. Almost as soon as he dropped the hanky, the dog came over and began licking the dried blood at the base of his thumb. Eddie let him. They went like that all the way down the hill to where the boat was.

Now, next to the water, Eddie stood enjoying the dog's attention, thinking about how some blood that used to be in himself was now inside a dog. He wanted to make a drawing about that. Linder pulled Eddie's hand away from the dog, then looked at him and shook his head No.

Then they were in the boat and the farmer was shoving them off. Just to be funny the old man pointed and told them what direction the river was flowing. The farmer and Linder waved goodbye once as the faded blue skiff floated off, Linder struggling with the oars to keep the boat away from the middle of the river where the current was strong. As he did this, he told Eddie to open the paper sack the farmer had given them and divide the food so they could eat.

When he turned and looked at Eddie he saw the boy had rolled up his sleeve and was searching his arm for any fleck of blood the dog missed. When he found one he licked it, wondering if his other blood had turned into dog yet. "I hate to interrupt your tasty little meal, Eddie," Linder said, "but you shouldn't lick where a dog's licked. You never know where a dog's tongue has been."

The farmer watched them float around the first bend and out of sight. Then he grabbed his bat and went hurrying up the hillside, the dog loping ahead of him, and went back into the house. If Linder had given the farm buildings a pretty good looking over when he first came up the driveway he would have noticed an odd detail—an insulated black wire that went from the farmhouse to a wooden pole fifty feet away. From that pole, the wire ran to another pole, and another, and another, down the dirt road to the access road and then from pole to pole all the way to Knoxville itself.

The folks who knew him, Earl Pettigrew was his name, never wondered why a man who lived out in the country got a telephone installed—at great expense. For years he'd bragged about how many books he had and how he'd given himself more education than a school teacher. When modern inventions became available, he'd already read about them and knew how they worked and whether he wanted one. His was the first farmhouse in those parts to get electricity and among the first to get indoor plumbing.

His latest device, the telephone, had become one of his favorites. With it, he'd made himself the self-appointed patrolman for this stretch of the river. Folks said hardly a bug floated down that river without Earl knowing about it. Now he had a good one to call in. He cranked the phone and waited for the trunk operator to come on.

"Hello, Earl," the operator finally said.

"Look here, Nancy, I gotta talk to Bill Ward right away."

"What's happened?"

"Never you mind, just get him right away."

"Okay."

The phone rang seven times at the Riverside Police Station before it was picked up. Then there was a thirty-second wait before Earl heard a voice.

"Captain Ward here."

"Wardie, this is Earl."

"What's up?"

"We got a problem, a big problem. Two river rats just left here in a boat and they're coming your way. A tall man and a boy about twelve, both wearing overalls."

"Yeah?"

"They came up to my place asking help for their boat, which was leaking bad. I went down to help them, see."

"Yeah, go on."

"The boat they had was Buddy Parker's boat."

"Buddy Parker's boat?"

"Yeah, that's what I said."

"Buddy don't loan his boat to nobody."

"That's right, especially to strangers."

"You think they stole it?"

"'Course I do. Not only that, the man had blood around the bottom of his trouser legs, splattered blood. Up around the collar, too. And when he rolled down his sleeves there were bloodstains there too."

"That Pilgrim's work ?"

"No sir, Pilgrim just bit the boy a little, got his thumb, but that don't put blood on the man's collar or his rolled-up shirt."

"You're reckoning they jumped Buddy and took his boat?"

"Prob'ly more than that, Bill, gettin' beat up wouldn't keep Buddy from holdin' on to his boat."

"That's true enough. How long ago they left?"

"No more than ten minutes."

"And they're heading this way?"

"Gotta be. No way them two could go upstream. That man looked like he never pulled an oar in his life before."

"Buddy's boat's blue, right?"

"Used t' be. If you look real hard, you'll still see some blue. Buddy wasn't too big on keepin-up."

"Anything else?"

"Yeah, one more thing. I lent them two black oars. I want 'em back when you catch them."

"We'll get them and get your oars back to ya, don't worry. Ya know, I sure hope that ain't Buddy's blood on that fella's sleeve, Earl."

"I know what you mean, Wardie, Buddy owes me money, too."

Downriver, Linder was stroking faster than ever toward Knoxville, hoping to be off the river before the sun set.

A most unusual Day

Garner sat across from the reclining Clara as the train neared Knoxville. Bobby had returned and sat quietly. Now that Garner had made a decision to 'court' Clara, he was afraid that the combination of her drowsiness and the confusion that comes when people detrain, might prevent him from making his intentions clear.

He wished she would sit up, fully alert, so he could say his piece. And, at the same time, he was uneasy, not just that she might say "No," but that she might say "yes" and not be who he thought she was. He looked out the window, seeking a distraction.

The train was crossing a low trestle, and in the brook down below Garner saw a boy, switch in hand, tending three cows. Cows and boy stood strangely still, staring in wide-eyed horror into the tunnel the train was crossing over. Garner had a sudden vision of himself emerging from the tunnel with his arms spread wide, coming to tell them not to worry, the direction had changed, there was plenty of time to get out.

That's enough! he thought. He squeezed his eyes shut and rubbed them hard, trying to get the image of the stalled truck from his mind. When he opened them, Bobby was looking at him. "You okay, Mister Garner?"

"Oh yes," he said, "my eyes are tired, playing tricks on me.".

Soon the train slowed almost to a halt, outside the yards near Knoxville station. Garner put his and Clara's bags outside the compartment and asked Bobby to take the bags through the car to the exit and wait there. Clara sat up, but said she felt dizzy, and didn't know if she could stand. He told her he'd help her, that he was sure she'd be just fine, but first, before they left, he had something to say. She looked at him.

He said, "This has been a most unusual day, hasn't it?"

"Yes, most unusual."

He hesitated.

She said, "In fact, it's not a day I'd ever care to repeat—except for the pleasure of meeting you, of course."

"That's exactly what I wanted to say. I know this is rather sudden of me, but I wanted you to know that I've decided not to leave tomorrow. I'm going to stay on for a while, at least a week, in order to spend more time in your company."

The train had stopped and the porter cried through the open door, "Everybody off for Knoxville. Train's leaving in five minutes for New Orleans."

Clara stood up. She had to tell Garner it was impossible, that Linder was coming, that it was too soon after losing a baby, which Garner didn't even know she'd had, to be considering romantic overtures.

She said, "Can we continue this outside?" He nodded and helped her down the aisle to the exit. She stood at the top step for a second to get her bearings while Garner stepped down to assist her. Then, holding the handrail tightly, she stepped down and it was like stepping into a swarm. The noise and confusion from so many individuals moving at once, in so many directions, and at so many speeds, was overwhelming.

In her earlier imagining of this scene, she'd pictured herself shaking Garner's hand, thanking him, and walking away. In her present concussed and confused state, however, she could not assemble any thoughts to speak and could only smile at Garner, and nod, hoping he'd know this was goodbye from the look on her face.

Garner was also confused and, when he saw how distracted she looked, afraid that the surging crowd was going to carry her away before she could answer his request to meet her again. He looked for encouragement to bring up the subject again, but Clara looked like a sleepwalker. He reminded her, "I would like to spend some time together in the next few days. I've revised my calendar and will not leave for another week." She looked at him in confusion. He added, "In order to see more of you." She gestured toward the nearby bench and said softly, "I need to sit."

"Of course." he said, "Over here. There's a bench." They had taken just two steps toward the bench when Clara fainted. Her collapse was so sudden and total that she was lying on the platform floor before Garner could hold her up. Fortunately, he'd kept his grip on her arm so her head didn't hit the concrete. He crouched behind her and lifted her into a sitting posture.

Most of the crowd barely parted to go around them, but one man stepped over and helped Garner get Clara over to a bench. The man looked at Clara's face briefly, then left before Garner could thank him. Garner fanned her face until her eyes fluttered back to consciousness. Then he said to Bobby, "Go find a cab driver and tell him to pull up next to that exit over there. Get someone who looks strong." Bobby ran off. Garner said, "Are you all right?" She moaned slightly. "Listen, Clara, you fainted. You're in no condition to be alone. I'm having you taken to my hotel and arranging for a doctor to come see you right away. We'll see what happens after that."

Among the swollen, logy images jamming her mind at the moment, only Garner's face was clear. She couldn't remember his name though. She smiled apologetically

"Did you understand what I said, Clara?"

She was breathing better, stronger now, her color had returned, but she still couldn't say anything intelligible. Bobby was back, with a balding cabby whose thick arms filled his rolled-up sleeves. The taxi driver bent over and lifted Clara as though she were weightless and carried her to his cab. Garner told him to take her to the Fairfax Hotel and paid the fare in advance and gave the driver a note for Mister Helms, the manager, asking him to arrange a room and a visit from Doctor Woodruff for Miss Talbot.

Garner and Bobby watched the cab leave and then went to the station's baggage room. Garner changed the original orders for his trunk, and had it sent to his hotel room, preferring to assume he would be here for a week, even though Clara had not yet assented to his plans. He also had a porter take his heavy wooden box of glass slides and load them into a taxi. He and Bobby got in then and he told the driver to take them to Mechanics' Hall. Garner needed to set up the slide boxes for his talk and make sure all the lighting and microphones were set properly. He also needed to train Bobby to operate the projector and give him cues for changing slides during the talk. If all went well, they'd be back to the hotel before dinner. Garner wanted to visit Clara and talk some more if she felt well enough to do so.

As they rode in the taxi, Bobby looked out the window, his face expressionless though he thought it was fun to be in such a big, vibrant city. They stopped for a traffic light where the road intersected with the bridge road. Bobby looked at three boys fishing from the river bank on the other side. The strong current had pulled their lines under the bridge. Bobby wondered what river it was and what they hoped to catch. The light changed and the cab moved on toward the lecture hall.

Still coming along the river

Back under the bridge, the Tennessee river surged onward. Up-river, not far from where the Holston ran into it, Linder and Eddie were rowing this way. And just ahead of them, freed of the need for boats and schedules, the dead man, released from his ducking stool, floated in his own sweet time, now winning the race.

At the Riverfront Police Station, Captain Bill Ward and four deputies, had armed themselves with powerful flashlights and enough firearms and lead to turn Linder and Eddie into sinkers. They had just launched their motor boat and headed up the Holston to join the deputies looking two river rats stroking Buddy Parker's skiff.

At the hotel in Knoxville

Garner and Bobby were entering the Fairfax Hotel. Bobby looked spiffy in the new shirt, necktie, long pants, shoes, and socks Garner had insisted on buying him so he'd look good at the lecture tonight.

Up in Garner's room, a cot had been set up for Bobby in the corner near the bathroom. Bobby removed his new shoes and lay down, trying not to wrinkle the covers or make an impression. He lay there, light as he could, as long as he could, not wanting to ruin the mattress with his indentation, but finally got tired and let himself sink into the cot. It felt good, clean and fresh, but the comfort was hard on his mind. Even in these new clothes, he felt the clean sheets weren't intended for the likes of him and that no matter how clean or new his clothes were, he was soiling them further every moment he lay there. In this palace of luxury and cleanliness, his was the muddy footprint on the marbled floor, the smudge in the mirror, the stain on the linens.

The courteousness in this hotel bothered him also. Having been treated like a freak for so long he expected loathing as his due. When kindness opened to him, his first reaction was seldom gratitude. Suspicion came more readily—understandable, given the twisted motives some people have for being kind. To the givers, unfortunately, such suspicion smells like ingratitude.

As Bobby lay on the cot he could hear Garner humming in the bathroom and knew he was mooning over Clara Talbot. Not a good choice for Mister Garner, he thought. When they were taking her out of the marsh she seemed pitiful enough, roughed up as she was, but later when she sat up and talked, Bobby thought she had things to hide. She couldn't meet his eyes and her smile lay flat. At first, Bobby thought she was hiding her curiosity about his looks. But now, he suspected she was aware that he thought she was a fellow grifter.

Garner stepped out of the bathroom, just long enough to tell Bobby to put the blanket over himself and relax. A simple enough command, but one that reminded Bobby, as he looked at Garner's back, of when he'd first gone on the road. He'd gotten used to sleeping uncovered in cold barns and thought nothing of it until some thoughtless Samaritan laid a blanket over him one night. When he woke up, the discovery didn't make Bobby happy. Instead, he became angry and shed tears for all the times it had never happened before. Sometimes, good things happen just to taunt you, show you what you aren't ever really gonna have.

And another thing: You never knew how long anything was going to last, and most things never lasted long enough to bother getting used to them. Start liking a bed like this and then go back to sleeping in a barn? Not a good idea, far as he was concerned. 'Good enough' is bad after you've seen better.

What's more, Bobby felt he didn't deserve Garner's trust and generosity. Garner thought Bobby was a nice kid who'd had a couple of bad breaks. The bad breaks part was right, but you don't survive life on the road by being a nice kid.

Garner started humming a different tune, one that sounded more like opera than music hall. Bobby closed his eyes. Mister Garner only saw that woman's pretty face and was blind to her faults. There was at least one piece of justice in this business: Time was working on her as the Great Equalizer at this very moment and she'd be old someday too, and then she'd know what it was like to feel like a child trapped behind the wrinkled eyes of an old person.

He could not remember what it was like not be a freak. Normal life ended for him when he could no longer avoid seeing what looked like two tortoise eyes looking back at him in the mirror. Sometimes his face looked so stiff and pale it looked like the eyes were staring at him through a breathing hole in a box. After that he didn't need mirrors, the surprised faces of other folks told him all he needed to know.

Bobby hoped he'd do well tonight, be on cue showing the slides as Garner talked. It seemed straightforward enough. Maybe Garner would be impressed, employ him again sometime, maybe on one of his travels. Being his assistant would be good. Better than last night in Lynchburg when that drunk he robbed called him the Man in the Moon.

Garner emerged from the bathroom wearing a dark blue bathrobe. He saw Bobby lying uncovered on the cot and walked quietly over to put a quilt over him. Bobby was awake but kept his eyes closed, so Mister Garner wouldn't know his kindness was wasted. Garner returned to the bathroom to shave.

A minute later, Bobby's pale face appeared in the bottom right corner of Garner's shaving mirror. Garner said, "Need to borrow a razor?"

"Oh heck no. I mean, no thank you. I don't need one of those just yet." He hesitated and then said. "This sure is a swell place."

Garner had spent more time in hotels than houses during his adult life, but enjoyed seeing this one through the boy's eyes. He said, "Glad you like it. Everybody deserves a nice place once in a while and I guess it's our turn. What do you say to that?"

"I'd say that's a good way to think about things, sir."

Garner finished shaving, cleaned and dried his blade and returned it to its case. He looked in the mirror from several angles, rubbed his cheek, tilted his chin, then turned it so he could see how it looked from the side. Looking at Bobby in the corner of his mirror again, he said, "You know how to read, Bobby?"

"Yes, pretty good."

"So, you know how to read a newspaper then."

"Sure I can. I used to read the paper to my ma and pa. And I also used to read the funnies to my little brother and sister."

"Okay then, young man, as long as you lay claim to the ability to read —you may as well read something."

He pointed to a newspaper lying on a small round marble topped table near the door. Bobby picked it up.

"Page one, column four, Bobby, might be of some interest."

Bobby looked at the newspaper headline and back to Garner, saying "Holy geez, Mister Garner, this is about you. You're in the newspaper, picture and all."

"Us, Bobby, us. You're my partner tonight, so it's about us."

Bobby held the newspaper and stood still, biting down on his lower lip to help him concentrate. It was magical, to read a person's name printed on a sheet of paper and then look over and see that same person standing there for real.

"Maybe you should read some more of it, Bobby, see what kind of program it's going to be."

"Yes sir," said the boy, as though about to carry out an important assignment. He sat in the chair next to the round table and began to read with great concentration:

**PROFESSOR GARNER RETURNS
WILL REVEAL APE CUSTOMS.
SECRETS EMERGE TO EXPLORER
AFTER LONG JUNGLE RESEARCH**

**GORILLAS SPEAK OF LOVE
AND OTHER AFFAIRS
TO PATIENT LISTENER**

**HIS THIRD VISIT TO KNOXVILLE
EXPLORER RETURNS TO AFRICA
VIA CUBA AFTER TALK**

Professor Richard Lynch Garner is
returning to Knoxville, bringing news
of his latest scientific discoveries
about the great apes living in French
Equatorial Africa ...

When he started reading the article, Bobby was reading in a barely audible way. Halfway through he was so excited he was reading out loud. When he finished he looked over at Garner who sat across the room.

"Well," Garner said, "they didn't muck it up too bad this time. They must have a new editor nowadays. They probably even put some punctuation into it."

"Oh, yes, sir," Bobby said proudly, "they've got lots of punctuation in it."

"Yes. Well ... wonders never cease."

Garner stood up and said "Now, Bobby, why don't you take your time and read about the other wonders of the world. I'm going down the hall to look in on Miss Talbot for a few moments. After that, I must talk to a newspaper reporter down in the lobby. Then you and I will have a quick supper before we go to the lecture hall."

"Okay, Mister Garner."

Garner adjusted his tie in the mirror near the door, turned his head to the side, examined his profile briefly, and then turned and went out the door. Bobby began at once to re-read the article, determined to know it by heart.

It just became that kind of day

About a quarter mile upriver from the police boat, Linder was rowing along with the current and looking over his shoulder every couple of pulls, watching for any jams up ahead. In the near dark, eerie silhouettes lined the riverbank. He lifted his oars when he saw some peculiar white spots skittering across the water down river, occasionally bouncing up to the underside of the trees, making them half bright, half dark, like a light held under a person's chin.

"We gotta get off the river, Eddie. They's lights ahead." He turned the sluggish boat towards shore, Eddie bailing this time without having to be told. At the bank they jumped out and splashed ashore. From up ahead light beams shot at them like spokes toward the hub. Linder knew he should hide the boat in the weeds, but it was too heavy to turn over or drag along the shallow bottom. He could hear a motor, now two motors, getting closer, and see the light beams broadening. They were going to have to run for it through the woods. "Oh man, don't let there be dogs," he mumbled. "This way, Eddie."

Linder forced his way through the thick brush of the hillside, sometimes climbing up and walking across the tops of the boulders. After only forty yards he needed to stop and catch his breath. Down at the river, the beams of light were already converging on the spot where they'd come ashore. Linder started up the hill again, hoping to find a logging road. A noise came from down below, and he stopped, dampening the sound of his strained breathing as he listened. Their pursuers had cut their engines so they could listen for him and the boy. Then muffled shouts. A beam of light suddenly swept under the tree canopy right near Linder, exposing the undersides of the leaves overhead. The jerking light passed by.

Linder laughed, "Must think they're huntin' coons, huh?" He couldn't see if Eddie smiled at that. Then it went dead quiet again down where the searchers were. Linder climbed up on a boulder and reached down to pull Eddie up. He didn't see any lights down there anymore. He turned and looked around. There was no way to go but up, and hope there'd be a road somewhere. They huffed along and, sure enough, half-way up, he saw a clearing ahead. When he emerged from the woods into the moonlit clearing, he sat down to wait for Eddie.

He noticed that nothing up here had started to grow back yet, meaning the logging was recent. They'd find a lumber road if they kept going. Eddie was in the clearing now, sitting against a stump. He let him rest for a minute and then told him they had to get going again. The hill was steeper up here and made his legs ache, but he kept going and finally stumbled through some brush out onto a rutted dirt road. Breathing heavily, he sat on a stump and caught his breath. Eddie sat on his own stump on the other side of the road.

Linder needed to decide whether they should follow the road up or down, there being no telling from where they were. He guessed downhill, mostly because he was tired. He looked over at Eddie. The boy looked pooped.

"How you holding out, okay?"

"Okay, I guess."

"Ya tired?"

"Little bit."

"Me too." Then after a pause, "We'll be outta here soon."

"Where we headin,' Linder?"

"Back to Knoxville."

"I'm hungry."

"Yeah, okay, I reckon eatin' wouldn't be a bad idea. We'll get ya somethin' soon. Less you see something out here I missed."

Eddie didn't laugh. "Linder, I ask you something?"

"Yeah, what?"

"What we been doin' all day?"

"What kind a question's that?"

"I'm not sure. I'd just like to know what's going on."

"Look here, Eddie, I'll answer ya like this: Do I ask you why you like blue chalk?"

"No."

"Do I ask you why everything that stands still for a minute you draw a picture on it?"

Eddie didn't answer.

Linder said, "No, I don't."

Eddie still was quiet.

Linder said, "And why don't I? Cause I don't tell you how to run your life and you don't tell me how t' run mine."

Eddie said, "Yeah, but how come I gotta run alongside you all day when it ain't my business?"

"You got me there kid. It didn't start out that way, it just became that kind a day. I wouldn't a drug ya into it if I'd known all this was gonna happen."

"But I'm here, ain't I?"

"Yeah, I guess you are."

Silence.

"Well, we ain't got no choice now but to stick together. Everybody else is against us."

"They are?"

"Today they are. Hell yeah."

"Why?"

"Why? Ain't your eyes been open? That woman jumped off the train and everybody and his cousin's gonna be blaming that on us."

"Who was she? Why'd we capture her?"

"We captured her 'cause she's got somethin' a mine."

"What?"

"Somethin' important, that's all."

"And you want it back?"

"Yeah, that's right."

Eddie was going to ask if that was why Linder took her locket, but that was a topic he knew he should avoid. Instead he said, "She take it with her when she jumped?"

"That she did."

"That why we're going to Knoxville again?"

"Right again."

"What about that boatman?"

"I shouldn't a hit him so hard. I never hit anybody with a rock before so I misjudged things a little."

"The law gonna lock you up?"

"Don't think so. Weren't no witnesses, nobody seen us take the boat."

"What if somebody seen us in it, like that farmer?"

"We say we found the boat driftin'. That's all we say."

"You gonna try to get that thing back the lady took from you?"

"That's one a the things I gotta do, yeah."

"Tonight?"

"That's right."

"What'm I supposed to do?"

"Stay out of it, that's all."

"There gonna be trouble?"

"Some, but you'll be okay."

"What if you ain't okay?"

"Just hang in there, junior. I need help you'll be the first to know."

"How will I know it?"

"Just you will, is all. You figured all this other stuff out didn't ya?"

Eddie was quiet.

Linder stood up and walked over to Eddie and tapped his cap brim." Time to move on," he said.

Eddie fixed his hat and got up and followed him down the winding road. They reach flatland in five minutes and found a road going away from the river and shortly came out of the woods onto a gravel road. Linder was happy to see this road. It even smelled good to him, dusty as it was. He closed his eyes and pictured the turns they'd made since they left the river and decided they should follow the road to the right.

He also decided that he was going first to the lecture hall, if he could get there in time. She might be leaving with that Garner man tomorrow and he couldn't count on her going home after his speech was over. If he was careful about it he could surprise the hell outta both of them, he thought. Beyond that, he couldn't predict what would happen, other than once he saw them together, he'd know what to do.

"Simple as that," he said.

"What?" said Eddie.

"Nothin,' watch where you're walking."

Clara asleep

Three rapid knocks on the door awakened Clara. She said, "Come in."

Garner entered, steely and determined, obviously needing to tell her something.

"May I sit down?" he said. She nodded. Garner pulled a wicker chair next to her bed and said, "I've just come from doing an interview in the hotel lobby. It never had time to actually turn into an interview because the moment I started to talk to the reporter, he told me some distressing news, which I came right up here to tell you."

"Oh my goodness, it's about Linder isn't it?"

"Yes, it is and it's not good news. What I was told is that as far as the police can tell, he made his way from where he jumped off the train to the river. He stole some trapper's skiff and may have killed the man. He then started making his way to the city here. The police were telephoned by a man he met on the river somewhere and they're now out looking for him in motorboats and flashlights. He might be captured any minute, if not already."

"And he might not be, is that right?" she said.

"I hate to admit that, but you're possibly right. It would be best for you in the meantime though, to stay in the hotel and keep the door locked until they catch him for sure. I'm going to ask that the house detective sit outside your door."

"Oh my goodness. They'll never catch him. He's too wily. He won't stop till he gets here and confronts both of us. You should not go to give your speech tonight until he's captured. You don't know what he's like."

"I'm not worried about myself, one little bit. I can handle twenty like him. I just want to be sure you'll be alright. Promise me you'll stay here."

"I will. But please don't go unto he's caught. Why even take a chance? He's probably really desperate by now. He's been building up to this for months. You see how he tracked me down to Lynchburg. Nothing stops him. Please don't you go."

"Too many people bought tickets. I have to go. And besides I wouldn't want to miss having a showdown with him if he does manage to get through the police net. I've got a score to settle with him."

"Please. You sound foolish talking like that, Richard."

They were both silent for a second, each surprised by her calling him "Richard," what that meant.

She spoke first, "If they don't catch him, you know he's heading for the lecture hall tonight. I have no doubt. I know his way of thinking and that's the only likely place he could find you if he's bold enough. Which he is."

"Well, it's not likely to happen anyway. He shouldn't be too hard to catch and when he's caught he'll get what he's got coming to him."

Clara looked down, as though she was considering Linder's capture, but what she remembered was how Linder looked when he was shaking her, as though his intense eyes had squeezed the world into a one straight line. And she could still hear his scream as she jumped from the train. He was going to the lecture hall first and if he didn't see her there he was going to her apartment. She was afraid of him, but she still wanted the locket and she'd strike a bargain if she could.

Garner used this quiet moment to say "I have something else to discuss with you, if you feel up to it."

"What is it?"

"It's of a more personal nature. I hesitate to introduce the topic on the heels of what I've just told you, but this matter greatly affects my immediate plans."

"I can listen for a little while."

Though his words were neither snappy nor breezy, nor said in the wise-cracking mode of the magazine writers she idolized, his speech was elegant and flattering in an old-fashioned, roundabout way and Clara was touched by its sweetness. His timing, however, could not have been worse. She tried to stop him from asking the question he was building toward by saying, "Well, needless to say, I am flattered that a man of your station, Mister Garner..."

"It would please me if you called me Richard."

"Thank you. Richard. As I said, I am flattered that you have an interest in me ..."

"And may I call you 'Clara'?"

That did it for her. She'd better get to the point at once. "Yes, if you like, but I am obliged to be straightforward and tell you that I can not reciprocate your feelings." He looked as though his stomach had just flipped. "Nor accept your intention to court me. That is what you are suggesting, is it not?"

"Yes, I suppose so. I might have chosen another way to say it, but, yes, that was the idea. I wanted to know you better." They were both silent. Clara was anxious to leave. Her bag was packed. She'd go downstairs and get a taxi to her apartment as soon as Garner left. She'd written to Mr. Allen last week and he'd agreed to have someone come in and freshen up the place for her return. She'd have her encounter with Linder there, rather than with Richard present. Linder would surely tell Richard about the baby they made together.

"Could you tell me why, Clara?"

Clara was distracted now, keyed up by the challenge of combating Linder again. She wished she owned a gun so she could shoot him dead out on the fire escape when he showed up. They'd give her a medal for that. But first she'd take her locket from his shirt pocket.

Richard sat next to her looking defeated and oh so sincere and she had to deal with him first. She felt rushed and was tempted to tell him the truth, but there was no need for that. She'd only met Garner today, he had no right to know her personal business. Too preoccupied to make up a fresh story and lacking the energy it would require to deny him an explanation, she gave him an allegorical version of the truth.

"I'm sorry, Richard. I very much enjoyed your company today, but the timing of our meeting is unfortunate. Someone important to me died recently and I am in mourning. It would be both unwise and disrespectful of me to embark on a new personal relationship under such circumstances. And I must also reveal, though I can't discuss the details, that some family entanglements and complications surrounding this death require my complete attention. I'm sorry."

She looked up after saying that, expecting Garner to look crushed, but saw instead that he wore the same dubious look he'd had when she'd told him the locket story this morning. The glint in his eye bothered her. Even though her story wasn't quite true, he had no reason to disbelieve her. It reminded her of how irritating he could be.

"Is there some way I could be of help to you with these problems?" he said.

She guessed he was trying to keep his foot in the door. She shook her head and looked away. "I'm sorry, Mister Garner." She thought she'd made things clear enough, but he was still sitting there and she was anxious to leave the hotel. She said, "I need to rest again. I'm very tired."

Garner took the cue. He rose and extended his card. "Should you change your mind, I'll be here for a few days. After that, you can reach me via this address. I'd very much enjoy it if you did. I've enjoyed meeting you and knowing you for this little while."

"Thank you, Mister Garner. The feelings are mutual." She extended her hand. He took it gently, held it, then squeezed it and let go. Neither of them said goodbye. When he left she brushed away the bother she'd started to feel from the smug smile he gave her, as though he knew she'd change her mind. She had too many other things on her mind.

Out on the river Captain Ward was getting ticked that he hadn't seen his officers yet. It was nearly dark and they should turn their lights on. Last year in May the light was good this time of day, but the politicians in Washington had repealed Daylight Savings Time almost as soon as they passed it. But they kept the Volstead. Nobody seemed to care that he had a job to do. He turned on the spotlight, then pointed toward the left bank and the motorman propelled them that way.

Back in the city, Bobby and Garner were in a taxi, headed for dinner at a restaurant on Gay Street near Mechanics' Hall. Garner was trying to keep his mood steady so his final speech of this road trip would be strong. He was sure Clara had lied to him again, but he couldn't get a grasp of why. He was certain though that if she didn't come tonight or contact him tomorrow, he'd find where she lived and pay her a visit. There couldn't be too many used bookstores in this city. In the seat behind him, Bobby had made up his mind to eat as much as he could tonight, despite his nervousness about operating the projection machine tonight. The way things looked, he'd be on the road again tomorrow.

Clara was still in the hotel. She'd felt dizzy when she first got out of bed and stood up, but had recovered enough to move over to the cane chair. She was trying to put her shoes on when Doctor Beaseley and Mister Helms returned.

"Ah, there's the patient," Beaseley said, "Looks like you're getting ready to go somewhere. How you feeling, young lady?"

"Much better, thank you," she said, wanting to be polite but determined to ignore whatever opinion he was about to render. She was leaving here as soon as they were gone. The doctor came over and started to examine her, though not as thoroughly as before. He smelled even more beery than this afternoon. She tried to breathe shallowly while he held her lids open and shined his little pen light into her eyes. He said, "By the way, Miss Talbot, did you know they caught that man, the one who was bothering you?"

She pulled back. "They did?"

"Yes, little lady, they sure did, out on the river. Dumb cluck was in a stolen rowboat and the police just drove up in their motor boats and arrested him."

"Well that's sure good to hear," she said, "that man was a menace."

"Not no more. He's a jailbird now."

In a few minutes Doctor Beaseley pronounced Clara fit to travel and said she could join him and Helms tonight, they had front row seats for Garner's talk. They told her to meet them in the lobby at fifteen minutes before eight if she wanted to come along. She had to fan the stinky air when they left.

And decide whether Linder's capture changed what she wanted or needed to do tonight.

Misinformation

Doc Beaseley had the story wrong and Linder was still a free man.

Captain Ward's mood hadn't improved. He still hadn't even found his deputies. He spotted lights up ahead near the east bank and told the driver to head toward them. Every once in a while a light from the other boat hit Ward right in the eyes. When he was close enough to be heard over the engine he told whoever it was to get that damn light out of his face. They pulled alongside the other boat and saw it was the two patrolmen he'd sent out earlier.

Motor troubles, they said, danged engine just quit on them. They'd been drifting because they forgot to take the oars in their hurry. Ward said "You lying sons of bitches ran out of gas, didn't you?" Each of them looked at the other. Before they could start bullshitting, he handed over the extra gas can he carried, saying, "Get that damned thing started or your sorry asses are gonna swim back." Five minutes later, both boats were heading upriver again, their lights bouncing off the water and onto the shore.

The White Man's Graveyard

The posters around town had promoted Garner's talk as **Entertaining and Enlightening** and Mechanics' Hall had filled with people from every aspect of Knoxville life, from farmers to bank presidents. At eight-thirty the houselights dimmed and Warren Hooper, the hall manager, came on stage to announce some future programs and settle people down before introducing Mayor Branch McKinney. The mayor declaimed for a while on the subject of "Progress and the Future in Knoxville," and then described Garner with fulsome praise. Then he stepped aside and flourished his arms as though he were introducing the Governor of Tennessee himself.

People applauded enthusiastically as Garner walked to the podium. Their greeting was loud and friendly, but boisterous enough underneath to warn Garner that a fair number of folks hadn't come to waste their Saturday night on mere enlightenment. Never mind, he was determined to get the upper hand right away. He stood at the lectern and swept his eyes over the crowd, keeping his silence until the crowd let him assume command.

Then he leaned forward and said, "Thank you, Mayor McKinney, and thank you, all you good folks here in Knoxville who care to enlighten themselves through learning. I'm here tonight to tell you about the new discoveries I've made this year in my travels and researches in Africa. I hope my unbridled enthusiasm for this subject is contagious.

He paused, anticipating some scattered applause, but there was none. Someone in the back whistled, provoking a murmur of disapproval. The crowd seemed anxious for him to get going.

"I've got to tell you folks right off that I've had a lot of adventures doing this kind of work, but I'm most certainly not a danger seeker. I've never been a tempter of fate. I am motivated by loftier notions about what's important and I have found that curiosity, pursued far enough, will provide all the adventure one can handle.

And, if I may, I'd also like to correct Mayor McKinney when he refers to me as an explorer. I do not believe that I deserve that title—let alone, being called a "great" explorer. I say that because I've done very little, if any, geographical exploring. It's true, only a very few white men have been to the places I've been, but they were there before me. I have discovered no new territories, have made no new squiggles on the old maps.

"My explorations, have been other than geographical. They went deep inside the minds of men and animals. I have see the inner workings of the primate mind, noted the wellsprings of contemplation, of manners, and morals. And, I must emphasize here that the key to doing this was my breakthrough in the understanding of their private languages. I have deciphered the code, the language, if you will, of these mysterious animals and I have come here tonight to tell you what they are really saying. Until my work came along, the rest of mankind listened to these creatures and thought that the gorillas and chimpanzees were merely babbling like a bunch of happy little infants who had discovered their toes and couldn't get over the glory of those finely placed appendages.

"In that sense, I will accept Mayor McKinney's description of me as an explorer—an explorer of the deepest fathoms of the primate brain!"

Garner said this last statement with enough flourish to provoke light applause, but it was faint enough to make him decide he'd better keep moving.

"Well now, ladies and gentlemen, I suppose I've stood here clearing my throat long enough. I now present to you: "Explorations The Minds of The Great Apes," the story of my newest scientific discoveries. May we have the house lights dimmed, please?"

The lights dimmed and a quick quiet came over the audience. Bobby Williams, seated in the midst of the audience behind a machine mounted on a projection table, was ready for action. He looked at Mister Garner standing at the podium, illuminated by a small, soft spotlight. He looked like a god. And sounded like one, too. Aside from a few preachers he'd been dragged along to hear when he was little, Bobby had never heard so many words spoken continuously by one person in his entire life. He was enthralled.

At the same moment he heard some latecomers arriving and turned his head to see the shaded silhouettes of two men and a woman going down the center aisle. Their shoulders were slightly bent in apology for interrupting and the older man held the woman's arm as though he were guiding an old, infirm aunt. Bobby noted with mixed feelings that the woman was Clara. He knew her presence would please Garner but also suspected that he'd just become the fifth wheel again.

Garner was saying, "I've brought some pictures to show you so you can see for yourselves what tent life was like in what is aptly called 'The White Man's Graveyard.'" If any of you cares to, you are cordially invited to go there and see for yourself."

The audience laughed.

"And I've also brought some pictures to show you what these amazing gorillas and chimpanzees look like, and they way they behave as they traipse about under the canopy of the great tropical rainforest."

In saying that, Garner left the podium and walked to his right, toward center stage, where a large projection screen had been set up. His action was unexpected by the spotlight man, so for a few seconds Garner was out of the light. While the light man worked the swiveling beam, Garner was no longer blinded and could see into the audience. To his instant and utter delight he saw Clara sitting in the first row. With her were Mayor McKinney, Tyree Helms, Doctor Beaseley and a number of other leading men of Knoxville. Garner put his heels together and bowed his head slightly towards Clara. They caught each other's eyes for a second and smiled. The spotlight caught up to Garner, blinding his ability to see the audience, so he continued his walk to center stage.

"And now...Ladies and Gentlemen... the first slide please."

Bobby had the first slide ready. He flicked the projection lamp switch and the screen beside Garner filled up with a black and white drawing of a large male gorilla drawn up to his full height as he beat his chest. His open mouth exposed two hideous fangs. He looked ready to roar and charge and into the audience.

The hum of excitement that ran through the audience took a few seconds to settle, like a flock of birds taking wing and settling again.

"As you can see," Garner said, "this image is not a photograph but a drawing that appears in the explorer Paul DuChaillu's book about gorillas. It is the best known picture of a gorilla in the world. When most people hear the word 'gorilla,' this is the image that comes to mind. DuChaillu's picture is responsible for making people worldwide believe that the gorilla is a bloodthirsty, ferocious beast who's constantly spoiling for a fight.

"Yes, always spoiling for a fight ... probably you know someone like that. But, I submit to you, ladies and gentlemen, submit to you with unflinching candor, that Mister DuChaillu's picture, the best known gorilla picture in the world, is a fraud. That's right, a fraud.

"You know, I believe that down here in Tennessee you folks don't go around using words like that lightly, so I want you to know I'm fully cognizant of my words when I repeat that Mr. DuChaillu's picture of a gorilla, the best known picture of a gorilla in the world, is a fraud. There. Have I made my opinion clear on this matter? Do I need to say it again?"

Murmurs, occasionally shouts, of approval came to Garner out of the darkened auditorium. "Work 'em preacher," one man yelled.

"Okay, then, we'll go on." In a quieter voice, "It's a fraud because the gorilla, seen undisturbed in his own habitat, living among his own kind, not harassed and chased by humans and their dogs, is among the gentlest and most fair-minded creatures on God's green earth. The male gorilla is impressively strong, but a gentle and benevolent patriarch to his brood.

"I am not engaging in armchair speculation here, ladies and gentlemen. I have been to their homeland and lived there amidst the squalor and danger in order to observe the gorilla, and to an extent, the chimpanzee, in their own worlds.

"I have witnessed their daily lives, their joys and their tragedies. I have listened to their speech also, and listened long enough and hard enough to finally gain the knowledge and confidence to speak to them in their own tongue. My long and silent hours of patient observation eventually paid off when they finally trusted me enough to speak back to me."

Clara, freed—or so she thought—by Linder's capture, sat in the front row marveling that Mr. Garner, Richard, was every bit as spellbinding as the newspapers had made him out to be. Her clothing changed, her body bathed, a touch of eau de toilette dabbed about her wrists and scarred neck, she was thrilled to be sitting at her first cultural event since coming to Knoxville. And to think she knew the evening's principal speaker, and that he wanted her company. The pains of the past months and the terrors of today all gave way, for this evening at least, to a nicer pleasure than any she'd ever known.

Garner was saying, "Although the apes and I had some intense dialogues, and they seemed honored that I would speak to them in their native tongue, they never spoke to me in any human language, at least not one I recognized.

"I was not insulted by this omission, however, because I truly believe it shows the glory of the human mind over the minds of these lower creatures. Only humans can bridge that great divide."

Clara wanted to absorb every sight and sound of this occasion. With the podium light off, Garner's voice came to her from the darkness, assured and learned, while she stared at the gorilla magically floating in the air. She was thrilled that such a man wanted her to be part of his exciting life. With both arms across her breasts, she sat absorbing the delicious feelings his speech aroused, her raised finger tracing slowly across her bottom lip.

"May I have the next slide, please?" Garner said. Bobby flicked it to the screen. "Here you see the tents we erected in a clearing as we set up our camp. That fierce-looking gentlemen in the helmet, rifle in hand, stands here before you tonight. In this picture, I am making ready to leave camp in the morning to go off to do my research. As you can see, tent life isn't very fancy, especially compared to the hotels of New York—but I can assure you it was a whole lot cleaner."

While the audience laughed at his Yankee snipe, Garner said, "Next slide, please."

The photo showed him walking cautiously up a narrow jungle trail, rifle at the ready, fire in his eyes. He looked the perfect image of the jungle action man who adorned the dust jackets of boys' adventure books. The audience applauded, some from familiarity with the picture, others because it was what they'd come to see.

Garner was giving them their money's worth.

A couple of bo's in the alley

Less than a mile away from Mechanics' Hall, Linder and Eddie were walking warily down an alley in town. They'd caught a ride outside town with a young farmer who was heading in to "get drunk's I can, boys."

After he let them off, they took through the back streets and alleyways towards their rendezvous with Garner and Clara. Linder knew they'd missed the beginning of Garner's talk and whatever chance he might have had of pulling Clara aside before it started. He wanted to get down there, soon as he could, and find his chance to get through to her. Eddie, though, had been complaining for the past hour that he was tired, cold and hungry. Linder gave in.

The alley ran beside a lunchroom that was still open. Up ahead, a screen door squealed open and then slammed shut quickly. Linder stood tight to the wall and listened to know whether whoever went through that door was now inside or outside. He heard a match strike. A few seconds later he saw, then smelled, a thin cloud of blue cigarette smoke curve around the corner toward them, staying low in the night air. A dishwasher or cook catching a smoke, he thought.

Linder stepped quietly around the corner into view. A big-bellied man wearing a sleeveless undershirt and a greasy apron was standing with his back and one foot against the dirty brick wall. The second he saw them, he jerked back, putting one hand on the door handle, saying, "What the ...! Watchoo want?"

"Sorry friend," Linder said. "Didn't know you was there."

"Jesus H Christ, I sure as hell didn't know you was. You didn't make a sound. Whatcha sneakin' up the alley fur?"

Linder took his cap off and grinned.

"Heck," he said, "we wasn't sneakin'. Our feets're killin us, so we're walkin' light."

"You tramps, you two?"

"Might be. Whatever we are, we're hungry Mister Cook."

"Hah. Never met a tramp that weren't. Where ya'll from?"

"Here 'n' there. Mostly Jellico, though."

"What's up there?"

"Not much, bud, ah'll tell you. Why we down here."

"Yeah, aint I heard that before? Hold on, Ah'll fix y'all wit' a lil' sumthin'."

The man went back in, this time easing the screen so it didn't slam. Linder looked at Eddie sitting with his back to the red brick wall. The boy had his pocket knife out, still trying to work the broken blade back in to the handle. The boy looked punchy, he was so tired. Linder felt sorry for him and wanted to say something nice, but couldn't think of anything. Who knew it would be such a long, crazy day? It seemed like today's every plan had collapsed and left him doing things that had been forced upon him. He had to get a better handle on what was happening, think things all the way through.

The cook was back, carrying two wrapped brown paper parcels which he handed over. Linder held them up to his nose one at a time and sniffed. He gave one to Eddie, who was still sitting.

"These smell real good," Linder said.

The kitchen man looked pleased. His cigarette was mostly ash now and dropped flakes when he spoke, "That's about all I can do fur you Bo's right now."

"That's plenty, we're much obliged," said Linder.

"Say fellas, no offense meant," said the man, "but I'd appreciate you eatin' them vittles somewhere's else so the Bossman don't get on me."

"No offense taken, Mister Cook, we're on our way."

"And one more thing, boys. The local dicks run Bo sweeps 'round here jest about every night, so look sharp."

"Okay, boss."

"And looky here," the man said, taking two quarters from his pocket and offering them to Linder, "The cops say a vagrant's any man passin' through that ain't got a dollar on him. So take this. Maybe they won't bother you."

Linder was getting edgy because the food was getting cold. He just said, "Much obliged."

"Don't mention it. I been a tramp. Might be one again. Never know 'bout that kind a thing."

Linder said, "Well, maybe we'll see you again, then. By the way, that boy's name is 'Lucky' and they call me 'Curly.' Be seein' ya."

As he was pulling Eddie up from his seat against the wall, the man said,

"Ho, that's a good one, Bo. You ain't got a curly hair on yer head."

"True enough," Linder said, "but they say I got the 'bility to make other people's hair curl."

The man laughed, then said, "I guess we all gotta git. Go on down this alley here inta the next block. There's a old barn there that's mostly fell down, but you'll find a place to flop. Keep away from the dicks. They're mean in this town."

These last words were said to Linder's and Eddie's backs because they were heading down the alley already. Linder heard the screen door snap shut behind them like the business end of a mouse trap. He looked down at Eddie who was holding the warm food sack against his cheek and patted the boy on the head.

"He was a nice man," said Eddie.

"Yeah," said Linder, "but he smoked. I hope you never get into doin' that. It's a dirty habit, Eddie."

Soon they were sitting in the shadows of the decrepit stable eating their handouts. Overcooked chicken wings seemed to be the major idea, along with three hard biscuits and a small slab of spare ribs. In Eddie's package, the ribs were short on meat and undercooked. The bones were thick and barely hollow. As he ate his own meal, Linder watched Eddie nibble what little meat there was away from the ribs and then heft each of the three bones as though it were a handle. He tossed two of them away and put beside him the one he was keeping while he started in on his biscuits.

He's found a new toy to play with, Linder thought. He ate slowly and returned to trying to find the plan behind all the running they'd done today—and had yet to do. Aside from getting into the lecture hall and seeing Clara and Garner together, he couldn't figure what he should do after that. He was puzzled that Garner bothered him so much since he'd never seen him, or even heard of him, before today.

A metallic tapping sound, only some faint clicks, caught his ears and he looked over to see Eddie sitting with his back to him, the boy's elbows moving as though he was working on something. He was going to hush him, but decided against it, because he didn't want to interrupt his own thoughts.

Yeah. His anger. Kept it in pretty good even though he hadn't been treated right. She had no cause to kick him out. And the baby. That was what bothered him most. What about the baby? Linder winced and thought, "That goes to show I can't go running around without a plan." He picked up one of the ribs he'd chewed at before and nibbled some tiny bits of meat still clinging to the bone.

She's linked up to Garner now, he thought. He'd known it in his bones even before she admitted it on the train. They did it by writing letters to one another and now he's come to claim her like a mail-order bride. She's wicked with that letter writing. Messed up my mind that way and now she's got a man that wears a necktie. That baby wasn't going in the scrap heap, that's all he knew. He couldn't allow that.

"Thought I had it all figured out," he said softly to himself, still sitting in the dark alley, amidst the chicken bones and spare ribs. Over in the corner Eddie was scraping something that made a metallic whetting noise.

Someone was coming down the alley. Cops, maybe. He didn't need to come this far and run into cops. He was alert and ready to run. Eddie had also gone still. They waited in silence to see who it was.

Two men talking quietly came through and were soon past. They didn't sound like cops, just a couple of drunks going home. Linder relaxed.

What in hell we doin,' sittin' here in a garbage-filled alley in Knoxville? he thought. No question those flashlights on the river were the law looking for them. Maybe they found that dead boatman or his boat. Maybe both. And they for sure would blame him because Clara jumped off the train. And he was also sure she'd claim he took her necklace, which he didn't even care about, except as trade bait for her telling him where the baby was.

He patted his shirt pocket to be sure the locket was still there and remembered again that it wasn't. He'd lost it under the railroad trestle. Clara wasn't going to tell him anything if he didn't have something to trade. What was he going to do? He should find a way to get back there, but that was impossible because he didn't know how to get back there except by retracing his route along the river, which might be crawling with cops. The locket was a dead issue now, he had to find some other means of getting her to tell him, appeal to her sense of what was fair and then use force when she laughed in his face. Where, when, and how were beyond him right now, he'd have to go down there and size it up with his own eyes.

"Dang," he said, "Eddie you sure you didn't see that locket somewheres?"

Eddie said, "Didn't see it." He couldn't tell if Linder was on to him. He put his hand in his pocket and began to squeeze the locket. The cool metal warmed as he held it, and in a little while Eddie could not tell the pulsing of his own fingers from the heartbeats of some tiny creature come to life within.

How their little friend got transmogrified

At Mechanics' Hall Bobby Williams was feeling like Roland to Garner's Oliver. Together they were winning the battle. Garner's wonderful voice was manly and still southern when he wanted it to be, despite his years in Yankeeland. He held the audience enthralled. Bobby had not missed a cue. But that didn't mean he could relax. He told himself "Halfway ain't done" and kept hurling his lightning bolts—such they seemed to him, towards the stage to collide and flatten on screen into wonderful pictures of a faraway natural world. Each new bolt produced a chorus of "ooohs" and "aaahs" from the audience. Then laughter, or applause filled the hall. Bobby felt more useful than ever before in his life, like a smoothly moving wheel within some grand machine.

Garner, too, was feeling good, very much at ease, at the top of his powers. From the very beginning he'd felt the audience gather about him like children in a parlor game, delighted to go wherever he took them. And since Clara's arrival he'd felt giddily enthused, maybe a bit show-offish in the way he moved the audience at will. A new slide image flashed, right on cue. He'd been right in his judgment of Bobby. The boy was quite reliable.

"Now, this slide and the next few that follow it may be difficult for those with delicate sensitivities to attend to, ladies and gentlemen. You see before you a female gorilla sitting at the edge of a clearing, holding a small, dark thing in her arms. A small, dark furry thing, I must add. That dried up scrap of fur she's holding is all that remains of her baby. This mother gorilla gave birth to him three months before this picture was taken.

"From the moment that baby was born, this young mother carried him everywhere she went. She nursed him. She held him. She looked at him. She picked at his fur to keep it clean and she kept the other members of her tribe from getting near him.

"And that little gorilla pup: he nursed and made cooing sounds and clung on for dear life whenever she had to go somewhere.

"And then, one day, he didn't seem able to cling so well. He kept falling from her chest onto the jungle floor. So, she helped him. She held him with one arm and went around on three limbs for the rest of the day.

"And the next day he wasn't any better. Still too weak to hang on. So she kept carrying him. She held him against her, but his arms and legs were weak and gave out. By the end of the day he was hanging limp as a rag doll.

"The next day he must have started to smell wrong, because she kept sniffing him. He was smaller and shriveled. She'd put him down whenever she was feeding herself and he just lay in the posture imposed by gravity. Even if she poked him with a finger he just lay there. Most peculiar, she must have thought.

"Next slide please."

The next slide showed a large male gorilla face glaring at the audience. He filled a third of the screen, just as he must have filled the photographer's camera lens. Behind him in the same picture, over his right shoulder, the mother gorilla sat before a scrap of fur. Three young gorillas stood close by, one leaning forward to smell the scrap. The male gorilla looked as though he wondered if his duty toward the mother and child would be to attack someone or something.

The audience seemed nervous.

"Here you see, ladies and gentlemen, what I call the "World's First Funeral Parlor." The three youngsters you see are calling to pay their respects to one of their associates who has died. But in the limited world of gorilla philosophy there is no word for death and hence, even if one of them made a deep mental breakthrough and figured it out, he'd have to know it all by himself because he'd have no way to communicate his insight to the others.

"Thus, they stand and stare in fascination, not knowing why their former companion no longer moves, just lies still in the dust. Nor can they explain to themselves how their little friend got transmogrified into a lifeless scrap of fur.

"What can they do, creatures of such limited understanding? Nothing really, except be like most people coming to a wake or a viewing: they bring along their sympathy and a great deal of curiosity. To my way of thinking, folks assembled at a wake are just as curious as they are sympathetic, but perhaps I do them an injustice."

The audience broke into an uneasy applause at that point and Garner used the moment to step over to the podium and take a small drink from the water glass he had there.

Just as Garner slipped out of his small spotlight, the rear door in the center pushed open and Linder stepped in, his eyes squinting while he adjusted to the shock of the bright screen with a gorilla picture hovering in the air. The shaft of lobby light Linder let in from behind distracted some of the audience sitting in the rear and they turned to see who it was. Linder was back lit, however, and could be seen only as a crude silhouette. At the same moment Garner returned from the podium and stepped back into the spotlight near the screen.

Linder wasn't sure but thought the man up on the stage had to be Garner, so he headed down to the front to get a better look, and maybe a seat, Eddie trailing. They walked pass the midpoint and through the projection lamp beam without bending over, thus causing two shadows to join the gorillas on screen. Garner saw the shadows and hesitated a moment until they walked out of the jungle clearing.

Bobby Williams knew who they were—the fellows that jumped off the train after Clara did. He was positive. He didn't think he should leave the projector though, so he stayed at his post, deciding he'd run down right after the last slide and tell Mr. Garner.

At the twelfth row, there was an aisle seat empty and Linder went to it and sat down, then gestured to Eddie to sit on the floor beside him. Eddie sat, staring unblinkingly into the eyes of the angry gorilla that was looking at him.

Garner continued, "Yes, ladies and gentlemen, those gorillas are trying to do the most difficult feat of imagination there is in this world, they are trying to learn something about the nature of their own death by staring at the dead body of one of their own kind."

The man next to Linder turned to him and whispered, "Sir, that seat's taken. My friend will be back in just a minute."

"What's that?" Linder said loudly.

Again in a whisper, the man said, "I said that seat's taken by someone."

"Finders keepers," said Linder in a louder voice than the first time.

"Ssssh," said several people who had turned around.

"Ssssh yourself," Linder said and settled in with his knees up on the back of the seat in front of him.

"Mister," said the man beside Linder.

"Lissen here," said Linder quietly, "you're gonna have t' settle down, friend. You're gettin' folks riled up."

The man stood up and pushed past the balky turnstile Linder had made of his knees.

Eddie took the man's seat and put his knees up on the back of the seat in front of him.

"You might also note, ladies and gentlemen, the baleful stare of that full-blooded male gorilla. He's probably the father of that dead baby boy gorilla and if he's making you nervous, imagine how I felt taking his picture."

The audience laughed nervously, but quickly settled, anxious to hear more.

"Not a lot is known about the role males play in gorilla family life, but I can tell you this much with no hesitation: Don't ever mess with one of the little ones because these adult males would rip you apart quick as look at you. They are extremely protective of their young ones."

Linder put his knees down and leaned forward to get a better look at the male gorilla, but just then Garner said, "Next slide, please."

Bobby swung the slide holder but it jammed halfway because of a warp. He calmed an impulse to panic as he pulled the slide out and gently pushed it across again. It stuck. He pulled it out, then across again. Half of the last scene and half of the next scene were projected on the screen. He pulled them out and then pushed firmly and evenly until the slide moved into place.

"Whew," he thought.

Garner went on, "There's little to see in this slide ladies and gentlemen. Just the jungle floor and a scrap of fur. It's ragged, scruffy and just a fragment of the boy gorilla it used to be.

"As I demonstrated to you in the previous pictures, this pup's mother carried him everywhere during his brief life, day in and day out, until days became weeks and weeks turned into months. Never was a mother more devoted. Never was a mother more driven by that tenderest of all emotions, the maternal instinct. She held him, cleaned him, and kept the morbidly curious away as the baby lost his hold on this world. He turned into a limp rag doll, then a shriveled mummy, and then to a scrap of fur, a mere scrap of fur. Only then did she give up, still unable to figure where her boy baby had gone and still unable to understand why all she got in exchange for the boy was a few pieces of fur. And, you might say, this picture you're looking at."

He let his words linger for a few silent seconds, then said, "Lights, please. We're through with the slides, Mister Williams. Ladies and gentlemen, before I conclude, I want you to know that I was ably assisted tonight by a fine and capable young man visiting us from Williamsburg, Virginia: Bobby Williams."

Many people turned to look as the audience gave Bobby a polite round of applause which took a sudden upturn when they got a look at his frail body and moony eyes. Bobby didn't smile or wave, but he felt good as he went about the business of putting the slides and trays away. As soon as Mister Garner was through he had to tell him that Linder was here.

"I'm not through quite yet, folks. I have some closing remarks. I told you this story, saved it for last as a matter of fact, because I wanted you to know that the gentler instincts of love and tenderness towards the small and the weak are not confined to our species alone.

"Mister Du Chaillu is wrong, folks, when he asserts that these beasts have no feelings other than the compulsion to dominate and destroy. We can learn much about how the strong should protect the weak by observing the sagacious and gentle behavior of this supposed brute, the gorilla.

"Please continue to support and encourage the scientific work that will make the natural world more understood. It will provide us mortals—the only species on earth that knows it's mortal—with moral examples of how we can better live our brief lives on this earth.

"Thank you."

The audience broke into loud applause that grew louder as Garner stood against the screen with both hands behind his back, rising up and down on his toes as he enjoyed the well-earned applause. Many in the audience, and not just women, had begun crying during his final slide, reminded possibly of some child who had passed through their lives on its way out of the world.

Clara had willed herself to sit numbly while Garner's told his final story about the gorilla baby. She'd think about it later, when she felt stronger. For now, she looked at Garner with open admiration, fat tears rolling over the brims of her eyes and across her cheeks. She was crying as quietly as it possible to cry, and wondering if what she was feeling towards Garner might be what people called love.

Linder was still sitting in the twelfth row, on the aisle, looking around, occasionally half standing, in a quest to see where Clara was sitting. "She's gotta be down front, I'll bet," he thought. The time for reckoning was near.

Finally, Garner raised his hands to ask for silence. Reluctantly, the applause subsided until it was finally quiet enough for Garner to say, "I have a little extra time tonight and I'll be glad to answer any questions you folks may have about tonight's remarks.

"Does anyone have a question?"

Linder stood up and raised his hand. "I do," he said.

That sad, sick part of his soul

People looked around to see the man who had a question and saw a tall man in overalls who stood grasping the back of the seat in front of him like he was about to testify. He said in a loud, confident voice, "Yessir. I got a question."

More people turned. Garner couldn't see him because of the stage lights. He said, "Go ahead, sir."

"Here's my question," Linder said, "What time's the second feature start?"

A surprised gasp went up from those who heard him. Linder had no idea he was going to say that. He couldn't attack Garner with all these people here, but he did want to say something to get Garner off his high horse. When Garner didn't reply, he added, "I didn't get here till late. When's the second feature start?" More of the audience turned to see him, sensing the question was so dumb it must be hostile. A few fellows laughed.

Garner put up his hand up to shield his eyes from the lights and stepped forward to see who was trying to provoke him. At the edge of the stage he leaned forward slightly and said, "That was an impertinent question, sir." Extending his arms to indicate the audience at large, he said, "Any of you other folks want to ask about the talk?"

Bobby Williams had pushed his way out of his row and was hurrying down to the stage to tell Garner who he had talked to. And he wasn't the only one there who'd recognized Linder. Earl Pettigrew, the Louisville Slugger man, had been sitting only a dozen rows away from Linder. As soon as Linder stood up, Earl recognized him and immediately got out of his seat and hurried toward the rear exit, to fetch the police. Earl and Bobby almost collided, going opposite directions.

"Hey there, wait a minute, not so fast," Linder yelled. Earl thought he was talking to him, but he just kept going anyway. He scuttled out the exit as Linder asked his second question, "Yeah, and I was also wonderin' where you got that baggy suit. You run a funery parlor by any chance?"

Some rowdies in the audience hooted and whistled to encourage him, but the majority told him to be quiet, some even saying "shut up" and threatening to silence him.

Bobby Williams got to the foot of the stage and motioned Garner to bend down. Then he told him it was Linder. Garner stood up and said, "May we have the houselights, please?" The lights came up. Just about everybody was turned toward Linder now, some folks even standing on their chairs so they could see him better. He just stood, planted, holding his ground, his body rigid, his arms folded, his eyes narrowed with cold, focused anger, no longer the loose-limbed country fool as he stared at Garner. He was only sorry he didn't break up this happy little shindig a whole lot sooner.

A few rows ahead and to his right, Clara was one of the few who had not turned to look at him. She didn't need to. She was trying to make herself small and unnoticeable and regretting that she'd come tonight. She should have known they didn't catch him. That Doctor Beaseley must have been drunker than he seemed. She hoped Linder would back off and say he was just joking, like he sometimes did.

Garner went to the center of the stage and looked into the audience until he saw Linder. Eddie was beside him, still staring at the blank screen. Garner broke his gaze for a second to look over at Clara and that brief glance told Linder where she was, down front, to the right.

He smiled and gave Garner a mocking look before leaning forward to get a look at Clara. All he could see was the back of her head. She had slunk down in her seat. He'd finally caught the fox in the hen house. It was satisfying for a second, but the pleasure quickly passed and left him stymied. He hadn't planned any further than this.

At the edge of the stage Garner said, "That's the end of the program, ladies and gentlemen. Thank you for coming." Part of the audience seemed reluctant to leave, the proceedings having ended so abruptly, but most of them rose and shuffled noisily toward the exits. Garner called to the back of the hall, "Could we have the house manager down here?" Then he sat and slid from the apron edge to the floor. He hurried over to Clara and took her hand. "Quick," he said. They headed for a door next to the stage steps, Bobby right behind them. Garner yanked the door open and motioned them ahead. Hand on the knob, he looked back but saw only the milling crowd. He followed Clara and Bobby through the doorway and closed the door behind them.

They went down six steps into a long, dimly lit corridor whose low, arched ceiling made Clara feel like a fleeing refugee. This narrow passage ran in a U shape beneath the stage and was lined on both sides with doors to various rooms, including Garner's dressing rooms, which they rushed into.

Linder had stood on two seat armrests and got a glimpse of them going through the door next to the stage. They seemed afraid and he liked that, after a day of running from train people and boatmen and farmers and cops with flashlights, it felt good to be the chaser now. It was a feeling he thought he'd like to remember someday, maybe sit down and tell someone about—Eddie, or the little fella maybe.

For now, though, he had to get out of there. Garner had called for the manager and the house dicks would be coming. He considered following Clara and them through the side door but knew it might be a trap. He walked toward the exit on the other side, near the stage, pushing through some well-dressed people down front. Right near the exit he saw a door stage right and knew it was the mirror image of the one Clara and Garner went through.

The knob turned and the door opened easily, a sign to him that luck was back showing him the way. He pulled Eddie in after him and closed the door and stood at the top of the steps waiting for his eyes to adjust to the darkness. This is good, he thought, the darkness would make it easier to sneak up on them. He had a plan again and it felt right so it had to be right.

Earl Pettigrew just then pushed his way through the front door of the police station. He huffed up to the counter and tried to catch his breath before speaking, his face flushed from the quarter-mile bustle to the station. The two policemen sitting at their desks behind the counter looked up long enough to see it was Earl and went back to their paperwork.

"Heads up fellas," Earl said, "I just seen the boys that killed Buddy Parker. Where's Bill Ward?"

One of the cops looked up, "Ya did, huh? Where's that?"

"Down at the hall. They come in late and started raisin' hell."

The cop closest to Earl said to the other, "Better get Wardie."

The other cop got up, grabbed some keys from the hook near the side door and went out. Earl went to the door and watched him go down the iron steps to the dock where he unmoored a small motor boat and started it, then buzzed his way upriver.

Earl returned to the counter and said, "Where is Ward?"

"Still upriver."

"Lookin' for them two ?"

"They found Buddy's boat."

"How far up?"

"Not far."

"Well, you think maybe we should go up t' the hall?"

"Don't reckon. Chief'll wanna run this."

"Those two boys be gone by then."

The deputy said nothing more. Earl drummed his fingers on the counter. Then he went out the front door, leaving it open, and walked to the edge of the sidewalk to look down the street toward the hall.

"Crowd's thinnin' out," he said when he came back.

The cop said nothing. Earl drummed on the counter some more and went out the door and came back again. "Hardly anyone on the street now," he said. When he went out the third time, the cop picked up his coffee and went into the back room. Shutting the door behind him, he went over to the window and looked upriver for the lights of the returning boats.

Linder and Eddie sat at the top of the steps under the stage while their eyes adjusted to the darkness. Linder wondered why luck never sent him traveling a smooth road, on an easygoing horse. "Ours is not to reason why," he heard in his head. A big old Georgia boy used to say that on the turpentine gang in North Carolina. There was more to it but that's all Linder remembered. The guy said it meant no matter how nasty the job was, some poor sucker was gonna have t' do it. That sure was true, he thought. True, true, true, but Clara hadn't left him much choice.

Tapping Eddie to get him alert, he found his hand and they eased down the steps on their butts and then stood up. He could see a little better, but not by much. He put Eddie's hand on the right wall and then his own and, taking the lead, started walking slowly down the corridor, feeling with his feet in case something on the floor might trip them.

On the other side of the squared U, an agitated Garner paced in his dressing room while Bobby and Clara sat in two small arm chairs placed on opposite sides of a large hooked rug. Small side tables with lamps next to each chair made the room look like the parlor of a small home.

Clara felt weak. She wanted to get up and pacify Richard, but every time she stood she felt dizzy and had to sit back down again. His pacing was making her nervous, making her feel that part of his anger was directed at her because of Linder. But that was silly, she thought. If she'd met Richard first, she never would have even talked to Linder. Richard was the kind of man she wanted to be with, not Linder.

The silence was broken by the noise of rapid footsteps out in the corridor. All three of them became alert. Garner went to the makeup table, reached into his valise, and pulled out his pistol. Then he stood to the side of the door. Clara gasped, shocked that the stakes had risen to such a dangerous level. Garner turned to look at her. She wondered if he might construe her alarm as concern for Linder, which it wasn't, she hoped he'd shoot Linder and end this nightmare. Someone knocked on the door.

"Garner? It's me, Dave Helms."

Garner opened the door. Helms was there with Warren Hooper, the house manager. They both looked relaxed, like they'd just shared a funny story on the way back.

"I'm glad you're here," Garner said.

Helms saw the pistol and said, "You expecting company?" He said it like a joke, but Garner didn't smile.

"Wasn't sure what to expect," Garner said. He walked over to a small table and started to put his weapon down, but turned instead and came over to stand at the edge of the rug near Clara's chair. His face was tight. "You catch that man yet?" he said.

The manager said, "Who? That country fool? No, one of the boys said he thought he saw him slip out the side door."

"What? You let him get away?"

"Well. yeah, I guess so."

"Did you call the police?"

"The police? For being drunk Saturday night on Gay Street?"

Garner was getting angry, "Don't you know who that man was?"

Hooper got defensive, "Look here. That hillbilly couldn't have been drunk like that when he came in. He must've brought in his own bottle."

Clara felt embarrassed and hoped no one would associate her with 'that hillbilly' they were talking about. She sat up straighter.

"You don't understand what I'm saying here," Garner said, "He's the man who pushed Miss Talbot here off the train today. And he also killed a man today, up on the Holston."

Helms jumped in, "What? That who he is? The police are looking for him."

"That's what I've been trying to tell you," Garner said.

Hooper said, "Oh cripes, I thought he was just a dumb drunk."

"He wasn't drunk," said Garner.

"No, just dumb," said Hooper.

Helms gave him a sarcastic smile instead of a laugh, then turned to Garner and asked, "What do you think we ought to do?"

"I think you two should stay here with Miss Talbot and Bobby while I go look for him. His name is Linder Charles. The boy's his son, name's Eddie."

"Hold on Garner," Helms said, "You shouldn't go, you're the one with the weapon. You should stay here and look out for these two. I'll go get the police."

"Okay, but get a move on. Wait. Maybe you two should go together. For all we know he might still be around."

"Might be a good idea. Think you'll be all right here?"

Garner bent his arm at the elbow to show the pistol, barrel up, at shoulder level.

Hooper said, "We'll go up to my office and call Riverfront Station. It'll be faster."

"Depends on who's on at Central," Helms said. His joke made Hooper laugh. "Watch yourself," Helms said to Garner. He turned to Clara and touched the brim of his hat to her. "Bye for now, Miss Talbot."

Out they went.

"Quite an evening we're having," Garner said to Bobby and Clara.

"Yes, quite an evening," said Clara.

Silence.

Then Clara said to Garner, "I'm sorry."

"Why should you be sorry?"

Silence again.

Before she answered, Bobby said, "Did I do the slides okay?"

"More than okay, Bobby, you were terrific. Nobody would ever know it was your first time doing that. You kept the show moving quite smoothly."

"Thank you, Mister Garner."

Another knock at the door. This time they hadn't heard the approach.

"Who's there?" Garner said. He made no move to open the door.

"Wayne Newhouse, the custodian. You Mister Garner?"

"State your business, Mister Newhouse."

"My boys wanna finish cleanin' up and yer slide trays and stuff're still out there. Can somebody come get them?"

Garner opened the door, hiding the pistol behind his leg. "Can't you clean around them?" he said.

"We don't wanna take responsibility if anything's missin'. Besides, the boys're anxious to get outta here and they can't go till the whole place's clean."

"The crowd all gone?"

"Oh yes, Mister Garner. We scooted 'em all out."

"You sure?"

"Cross mah heart and hope t' die," he said, smiling to make up for his impudence.

"All right," Garner said. He turned to Bobby. "Could you take care of that Bobby?"

"Sure thing, Mister Garner, I'm on it."

Garner turned to the custodian, "You mind walking the boy back out there, Newhouse?"

"Don't mind."

"And when they're loaded up, could one of your men help him bring the boxes back here?"

"Yeah, we can do that."

"Thank you. Don't forget, those slides are glass, they break."

"We'll be extra careful, Mister Garner," the man said.

Turning to Bobby, feeling that now was as good a time as ever, Garner said, "I was wondering if you could stick around this week."

"Sure could. Any particular reason, Mister Garner?"

"I want you to come to Africa with me, so we'll need to get some things for the journey. Think you'd be able to do that?"

"Are you kidding, Mister Garner?"

"No, I'm quite serious."

"You mean you want me to come work with you?"

"Yes, I'd like you to work with me, come on this trip we're taking. You willing to do that?"

The boy looked more suspicious than delighted. "Sure I'm willing."

"Yes. Now, if you're coming, please get busy and pack up those slides."

"Yessir," said Bobby, leaving quickly.

Garner locked the door again and turned to Clara. She sat in the green chair, a small smile of approval on her face, but looking ready to fall asleep. He sat in the chair across from her. She looked at him. He put his index finger to his lips as though to say, 'hush' and tell her it was all right to nod off. She gave him another weak smile and let her eyelids close.

What followed was the first peaceful moment he'd known since she entered his compartment outside Lynchburg this morning. He studied her face. She seemed prettier to him every time he saw her. She had beautiful eyelashes, he thought. And fine skin. He was glad he'd decided to stay in Knoxville an extra week and take a chance on knowing her better.

Garner was not one to analyze motives, but he knew at some vague level that his bond with Clara had been created by the ominous presence of Linder. He'd stepped in as her protector and the demands of that role had awakened emotions he hadn't felt since his son died. The need to protect was so intertwined with love for him that the presence of one was necessary to the other. Before his thoughts could go further, she stirred. He leaned forward and said, "Are you all right?"

Her eyes had opened, but she looked as though she were taking in her surroundings before admitting to being awake. She looked at Garner and smiled. Then she said, "Yes, I'm all right. It was the strangest feeling. I didn't know if I was falling asleep or fainting. I just slipped away."

"This has been a trying day."

Clara sat up and looked at him and said, "You were wonderful, Richard. I was so thrilled listening to you. I could have sat there forever. Your talk was so interesting. I've never had such an experience. When the audience applauded I looked at you and wanted to pinch myself. I couldn't believe I knew you."

"Well thank you. And I want to tell you that when I saw you in the audience I was delighted. I wanted to do my very best because you were there."

"Thank you, Richard, that makes me feel wonderful."

"You deserve to feel wonderful. You inspired me. What were you thinking when you sat there?"

"I was thinking that I couldn't believe this was happening to me. Nothing like this has ever happened to me before."

Garner was afraid to say anything more, for fear of sounding too sentimental. He smiled at her, stood up, and started pacing.

"Richard?"

"Yes, Clara?"

"Were you really willing to stay on here in Knoxville for a whole week just because of me?"

Garner paused in mid-stride and said, "Yes, I was. I still am. I told you at the train station and I meant it, and I told you again in your hotel room and I meant it, and I mean it again now. That is, if my staying would please you."

"Oh yes, of course it would. I'm very flattered."

Garner decided to be bold, "Well, then, let's look forward to a wonderful week together. And after that, who knows? Maybe we'll meet somewhere other than Knoxville. New York? Paris? London? Africa?"

"Oh Richard, that sounds wonderful. But you shouldn't tempt a country girl with such worldly things. What ever would we do in those places?"

"I'd like to tempt you with all the world has to offer. We'd eat in fine restaurants, go to the theater, take in the museums, see the great oceans of the world."

"But what about your work? It wouldn't be good if I distracted you from the important work you do."

"Perhaps if I had an assistant?" he teased.

Clara wanted to exclaim when he said that, but smiled instead and said, "I might consider that, if it's an offer, but I'd need to know more about the terms."

Linder heard their laughter and sweet talking as he sat with his back to the dressing room door, listening. Soft as their voices were, he could hear, and feel, every word, as their voice vibrations traveled through the door into his back.

Some sad, sick part of Linder's soul thrilled to hear and feel her betrayal. The void of his sinking spirits was filled with the comfort of knowing that his worst suspicions were true. Clara's pretty mouth was producing the same fluty tones and sensuous laugh, the same breathy, teasing questions that had looped him when he met her. Not until that moment had he realized she was a like a bell that always produced the same tones when struck a certain way, no matter who did the striking. It almost took his breath away, being robbed of his uniqueness.

Though he felt betrayed, he also felt the pleasure of certainty, after so much doubt. He wanted to hear more, everything they'd ever say.

Clara was talking again, "That was a nice gesture you made towards Bobby, Richard, offering him a job."

"It was more than a gesture. I can use him. He's very dedicated and wants to learn."

"I know, but he seems so frail."

"He is. But he also has a quality that's of absolute importance when you're living in the bush—he's loyal. I know I can count on him if there's trouble. There's much to be said for that.

"But he's so small. What could he do?"

"He'll think of something if the need arises." Then, with an ironic smile, Garner added, "He'll defend me if some jungle creature attacks me."

"Well, I'll have to respect that you know about such things, you're the world traveler. But what if he becomes more frail? Won't that handicap your work?"

"Perhaps, but I'll deal with that when it happens. I can't go away and leave him to get sicker until he dies all alone." Garner went on to explain more details of his expedition.

To his surprise, Linder became bored with their conversation when the flirtatious talk tailed off. He had prepared himself earlier to kick in the door as soon as it sounded like they were making love, but now they were just talking stupid stuff.

He wasn't sure what to do next. He had come this far and probably would get caught if he stayed much longer. A showdown was needed. He had to go in there and demand that she tell him where his son was hidden. Otherwise the months of enduring her rejection were wasted. His vigilance was wasted. Following her to Lynchburg, stealing the locket, killing the boatman, all his actions were wasted. And so was the shame of seeing his crazy footprints in the snow, eating in dark alleys, being kept from his baby, sitting here right now listening like a kid with his ear to his parents' bedroom wall.

Shameful. Meaningless. His whole stinking life was nothing if he walked away from the trouble that was coming. That would not do. He was going through that door. It was clear now. There was no other choice. He stood up and took the two steps to the corridor wall opposite the dressing room door. He was confident he could break through there. It had three hinges but looked like it was made of a light wood. Should he kick it, or use his shoulder? He liked the idea of putting his entire body into the collision. Lifting up on his toes, he bundled his shoulder into a battering ram and charged the door.

The exchange

The door gave so easily that Linder's momentum carried him into the room and he fell to the floor near the chair where Clara sat. She screamed and jumped up and hid behind Garner. Linder was on his feet already and stood gripping the back of the chair Clara had moved away from.

She yelled, "Linder!"

Garner had moved in front of the chair facing Linder, standing sideways, his right arm at his side concealing the loaded revolver. Linder stepped back from the chair and to the right to see Clara. Garner countered his move, so Linder stepped to the right again, still charged with energy, Clara his focus.

Just then Eddie hurried between Linder and Garner, like he'd arrived late for a picture show, and sat in the chair between the men.

"What are you doing here?" Clara asked again.

"You know why I'm here."

"Yes, to create more trouble."

Before Linder said another word, Garner brought the revolver from behind his leg and held it up to be seen, and though he wanted to, he did not point it at Linder.

"Sir," Garner said, "you are under arrest. Do what I tell you or I'll shoot you dead."

Well, here we are, Linder thought, at the end, the final wall. After this, no more running and hiding, and no shame. He was ready for whatever happened, but not until he was sure they understood what he was willing to kill or die for. He didn't want his death remembered from anybody's point of view but his own.

"You better stop waving that cap gun at me, Professor. This ain't yer business."

"Tell that to the judge, mister, just get over in that corner before I shoot you."

"This is between me and Clara. I come here to get something that's mine and I ain't leaving without it."

Clara panicked at the thought of what Linder was about to reveal. She was convinced that Garner would feel misled and leave her. She said, "Make him stop. Oh, please. Get him out of here."

Garner said, "You've got no claim here, mister. Get a move on."

"Clara, I want my baby boy. You tell me where you put 'im, so I can go get 'im."

"You're crazy, Linder," Clara shrieked. "He's crazy." She was trembling and could feel the blood draining from her face.

Garner suddenly realized from the intensity of their emotions that these two had more history than he'd known.

"I ain't crazy," Linder shouted at Clara. Turning to Garner, he said in a calm voice, "You know she had a baby in Lynchburg, Mister Bigshot?"

That sounded so nonsensical Garner could only think to say, "I've already warned you. I'm going to shoot you if you don't move over to that corner."

Linder held his ground, his arms open, exposing his chest, and said, "Go ahead. She tell you I was the father of the baby she had in Lynchburg? The baby she left there in the Crittenton home? The baby I want to raise and she won't tell me where it is?"

Garner thought of the scrolled certificate that had rolled out of Clara's luggage. Domestic Science. This was not the time to ask. He looked at Clara to know what he should do next.

Clara was crying. She said, "You're crazy, Linder."

"Oh yeah?" he said, "To me, crazy is havin' a baby and givin' it away to a bunch of strangers. I ain't crazy for wanting my own son."

Enough of what Linder was saying was getting through to Garner that he felt he was about to slip down a listing deck. He had a gun in his hand and was keeping a murderer at bay. A gear kicked forward within him. He hoped Linder would provoke him enough that he could shoot him.

Garner said, "Go stand over there. It's your last warning."

"Go ahead and shoot me. I ain't leavin' till she tells me where my son is."

Eddie mumbled. Everyone's eyes briefly flicked to him as he sat rubbing blue chalk on a bone he held in his lap.

Clara broke. "I'll never tell you where that child is. Never. That baby's being adopted and will live in a good home with good people. And neither of us is going to ruin that for him."

To Garner that sounded like an admission.

Linder shouted, "Just tell me where he is and I'll leave." He moved back to his left, trying to get a clear line at Clara. Garner raised his gun and pointed it at him saying, "I told you. Get in that corner. The sheriff'll be here any minute."

"Just tell me where the baby is!"

"Linder," Clara said, "listen to him, don't make everything worse."

Looking at Garner, Linder said, "Garner, either shoot me now or get out of my way."

Garner said, "I will. I'll shoot you dead. I've warned you for the last time."

"Clara," Linder said, "someone's gonna die here if you don't tell me how I can get my baby boy back."

"That's your choice," Clara said, "I'm not giving that child up to be raised by a petty criminal like you."

Linder stopped, suddenly as relaxed as though they were arguing under the willow tree back in Greeneville. He said, "Yeah, well, if I was so petty, why'd you make a father out a me?" He looked back at Garner to tell him with his eyes, 'I was there first, mister.'

Clara said, "You're as petty as they come. And if you weren't such a small time sneak thief you'd give me back my locket with the baby's picture in it."

It was not until this moment that Garner realized why the locket had been so important to her. He felt like he was caught between two arguing parents and wondered what he was doing there, pistol in hand, ready to kill a man and not sure why.

Although Linder didn't have the locket any more, he kept up the pretense that he did. "That's my boy's picture and I'm keepin' it."

"Give it to me," Clara shrieked, "It's all I have."

"Tell me where the boy is and I'll give you the picture."

"I want my baby's picture," Clara wailed. She was crying heavily, her face filling with tears, her nose running.

Linder said, "Well, there ya go, then. There's the difference between you and me. I want the baby, you want the picture. Some mother you are."

"Oh Linder," she sobbed, "that's so unfair. He's better off where he is."

"Speak for yourself, woman. I want my son."

And then Clara really burst. While crying uncontrollably, she sobbed, "The baby died, Linder. He died. He only lived three days. It was a little boy, and he died. I couldn't help him. He just died."

Linder stood with his mouth half open, his face frozen between thinking he knew all along this was going to happen and a suspicion she was lying to him again. He was about to start questioning her, when she said, barely managing through her tears and sobs, "That picture's all I have of him. I want my baby's picture."

She staggered away from Garner, moaning and choked with sobs, bent over. She reached the mantle by the fireplace and started to brace herself against it but then dropped to her knees and then lay down, curled into a shaking, sobbing ball.

"Clara," Linder yelled, and started toward her.

"Get back," yelled Garner, moving in front of the chair where Eddie sat, his pistol aimed at Linder's heart and about to shoot. He stepped too close, though. Linder grabbed for the pistol, but missed, the effort turning his body as Garner fired the pistol. The bullet hit Linder in the left shoulder, breaking his clavicle and spinning him around.

"Son of a bitch," he yelled as he fell to the floor.

Garner started to step to his side to fire a second shot into the fallen Linder and end the troubles between them once and for all. A small blur rose beneath him and for a second he considered shooting it but realized it was Eddie and held his fire. In the same motion the felt punched in the chest. It staggered him. Took the wind out of him. He was instantly weak and reached to touch the spot where he'd been punched and felt something sticking in his chest. He looked down. It was a bone. Sudden fear went through him and he felt something vital gathering to leave his body.

Linder had struggled up again, next to him, hunched over, holding his bent arm like he'd found it in an alley. He looked for Clara. Eddie was standing over her. What for?

Garner asked himself that same question. He felt as though he was standing outside himself looking around. He looked again at the bone in his chest. Perhaps that was the problem. He touched the edge of it with his fingertips. His knees gave and he went down, like an elephant he'd seen shot one day. His lay on his back with one knee bent up, the other one under him, still holding his revolver, clutching his heart. He remembered the truck the train had hit this morning and now pictured himself inside with the man who didn't get out in time when the train came bearing down. He grabbed the man's arm to help him.

Then he was in the great lake, falling slowly through to the bottom ... to see Harry. Harry. He needs help. He'll be glad to see me.

His fall had distracted Linder. He looked at Garner lying on his back, a bone sticking in his chest. That's Eddie's, he thought. He moved over to Garner to pull the shiv out and keep Eddie from getting in trouble. Bending over made him faint, though, and he fell across Garner's body. Garner gripped his arm as though guiding him.

While Clara's two suitors lay spent on the dressing room rug, Eddie stood over the sobbing Clara and took the locket from his pocket and opened each side. He pinched up the hair, then the picture, and knelt beside Clara. Forcing open her hand, he put the hair and the photograph in it. She didn't stop crying. He looked at her, his brother's mother, and then got up and ran out the broken door, down the dark corridor they had entered through, and got away.

The man who was supposed to help him never showed up, so Bobby Williams dragged the two heavy boxes of slides, one at a time, across the auditorium floor to the stage door. Tilting the boxes on their sides he was able to slide them on edge down the steps to the narrow corridor. Then he dragged Box One half the distance to Garner's dressing room and went back for Box Two. The boxes were heavy, and awkward to handle, but Bobby was glad for the opportunity to be useful.

When he got to Garner's door, it was splintered and sprawled open as though something inside had exploded. Only the upper hinge, badly bent, kept the door attached. He leaned against the wall next to the doorway and listened. From inside the room he heard a woman sobbing and under that a man's muffled moaning. He looked around the corner of the doorway and saw two sets of men's legs sticking out past the green chair, Garner's on the bottom. Bobby entered and went around the chair and looked. A moaning, bloody Linder lay over a motionless Mister Garner who had his revolver in his hand, but looked dead.

Mister Garner's body frightened him. He pulled Linder off of him. Linder cried in pain when he was pulled, doubling up and cradling his shoulder as though tenderly holding a newborn. Bobby went to Mister Garner's other side and knelt down. When he bent to put his ear to Garner's chest he saw the bone sticking in it. That made no sense. Garner's gaping mouth and wide-open eyes were full of expression and empty of content. He had gone off somewhere by himself.

Bobby sat back on his heels. He nearly wanted to slap Mister Garner's face.

Why'd he have to chase after that crazy woman? Because she was pretty? Because she played him like a fiddle? Why'd he have to get between her and Linder? It had nothing to do with him. He wanted to curse Mister Garner for having given him hope and then leaving. Then his heart swelled with regret and he cursed himself. He reached over and gently closed Mister Garner's eyes the way he'd done when his father died two years ago. His hand rested a while on Mister Garner's brow.

Then he turned his head to the side. Garner's pistol was too close to Linder. Bobby got up and worked the pistol from Garner's hand and moved away from Linder. He saw Clara over near the fireplace, lying on her side, crying lightly. He walked over to her.

"You okay, Miss Clara?"

She seemed to want to respond, but could only roll over and face him, wiping her nose and mouth on her sleeve in the same movement.

"You okay?" Bobby said again. "You hurt?"

Clara sat up, braced by one arm still on the floor.

"What happened?" Bobby said.

"I don't know. I heard a shot."

"Mister Garner shot Linder, I think."

"He did? He shot Linder?"

"Yes, but he's alive."

"Oh."

"It's worse than that, though. Linder killed Mister Garner."

"Oh no, no, don't tell me." She grabbed Bobby. "It can't be true."

"He killed him, Miss Clara. He stabbed him with a bone or something. Right in the heart."

"Oooh," Clara moaned. She braced herself against the wall, noticing for the first time there was something, hair or something, in her hand. She opened her hand: her baby's picture and some tiny pieces of damp hair. How? Who returned them? Where was the locket?

Linder moaned again. She followed Bobby over, a few tiny, clipped strands of baby hair stuck to her eyelids, nose, and cheeks where she'd touched her face when she was crying.

She walked over to where Garner and Linder lay and sat down beside Garner and took his hand away from the bone in his chest and held it in her hands, uncomfortably conscious that some baby hairs were still on her palm but not wanting to wipe her hand clean even though some of the pieces were getting on Garner's fingers.

She looked at Garner's face. Without the leaven of life in him, devoid of his powerful gestures, his confident voice, and his penetrating eyes, he looked old, as though a lifted veil revealed his true age and tired spirit. A Man of the World, Clara thought, too good a man to be brought low by such common folk. She bent and kissed his cold lips and realized as their lips met that she was experiencing alone their first and only kiss.

Linder groaned behind her. She turned and looked. He was sitting up. She got up and moved away from him. Bobby came and stood beside her as they watched Linder rise, a look of disgusted fascination on their faces as though they were watching a snake emerge from an egg.

"Keep that gun on him, Bobby," Clara said.

"My shoulder hurts," Linder said, "I need a doctor."

"You need another bullet in you, that's what you need. How could you do that to Professor Garner?"

'Whoa. Easy gal. I got enough bullets in me for now."

"That's your opinion. Why'd you kill Professor Garner?"

"He shot me."

"Why'd you stab him?"

"He needed it."

"You should have stayed away from here. Professor Garner had nothing to do with your grudges against me."

"He shouldn't a messed in family business."

"There never was any family. There was never any family business for you to defend. You're just a cold-blooded murderer."

"He shot me."

"He warned you first."

"He should have stayed out of it." Just then, Linder's arm spasmed and he had to keep still. He decided to shut up until he could think of what to do next. He looked at Garner lying on his back with the bone sticking in his chest. That's some kid, Linder thought with pride.

"Wipe that stupid smile off your face," Clara said, "Or I'll tell Bobby to shoot you. He'd like to, you know."

Holding his arm, looking defenseless, Linder said, "Aaah Honey-bee, watta ya wanna talk that way for?"

"Shoot him," Clara said, and she meant it. Bobby fired, shooting high on purpose, but close enough and loud enough to make Linder flinch. Flinching caused him more shoulder pain and he gritted his teeth and rocked as he held his arm.

Captain Bill Ward, Hooper, Helms, and two policemen were rushing through the corridor towards them when Bobby fired the warning shot at Linder. They too flinched, and flattened themselves against the wall. Captain Ward knew a gunfight here in the corridor would be a disaster and he considered pulling everyone, himself included, out of the tunnel. He and the men froze where they were.

After a few seconds of silence, Ward whispered to the two cops, "Let's rush 'em." They drew their guns and ran the last twenty feet of the corridor before the first policeman tripped on the slides boxes Bobby had left there and fell over. Ward and the other policeman almost collided with him, but jumped over him and rushed into the room, guns drawn.

"Drop the gun," Ward yelled, his pistol aimed at Bobby, who immediately bent and put the gun on the floor.

"What's goin' on here? Who you people?"

"That one there's the man you've been looking for," said Helms, pointing at Linder. The two policemen hustled over and grabbed him, one to an arm, jerking his arm down so they could cuff him.

"Easy boys, I been shot. Right where you're grabbin me."

They pulled Linder by the arms over to the other side of the room. Linder was trying to double up from the pain, but they jerked him back up every time he tried to bend.

"Ah, man, go easy boys. I ain't resistin'. My shoulder's killin' me."

"Stand up, ya bum," said the policeman who'd tripped on the slide case.

"I'm up," Linder yelled.

In the meantime, the chief had gone over to Garner and knelt down.

"What the hell's this sposed to be?" he said, indicating the bone in Garner's chest. He looked the body up and down, and seeing no other signs of a scuffle, went to examine the knife. He pulled at the bone, but it was slippery from Eddie's blue chalk and Linder's blood and wouldn't come out. Wrapping a handkerchief around it, and using two hands, he worked the bone shaft away. The blade still stuck in Garner's chest.

"Prison knife," said Ward.

"What's that?" said Helms.

"It's a prison knife ... a shiv, homemade ... prisoners make 'em to settle grudges. Whoever stabbed this man, I'll betcha he done time."

Everyone turned to look at Linder whose arms were now cuffed before him. He was tilted to one side, his head practically bent enough to touch his wounded shoulder. His moment had arrived.

"Self-defense. That man Garner there shot me and said he was gonna shoot me again. It was self-defense."

There. He was a family man now, let's see what Honeybunch had to say about that.

While Linder spoke, the younger policeman was patting him down for more weapons. "Looky here," the policeman said, drawing everyone's attention to a pant leg he'd pulled up over Linder's boot. A short hunting knife was held in place by a rag Linder had tied around his calf.

Ward stood up from Garner and came over to look. "Two knives," he said. "Watcha come inta my town with two knives for? Expectin' trouble?"

"Self-defense," Linder said through gritted teeth. It felt good to say that, like saying 'God and country' or something.

Ward walked closer to Linder. He put his arm on the mantle like they were two friends having a drink near the fireplace during a house party. Then Ward leaned forward and put his face near Linder's and said under his breath, "Watcha kill Buddy Parker for? Ya just want his boat?"

"Don't know nobody by that name, Captain."

Ward swung hard and slapped Linder across the face, leaving a red mark. The suddenness and the noise of the slap made everyone jump.

Ward turned and looked at them. "Just askin' 'im about a mutual acquaintance," he said.

Blood ran from Linder's nose over his upper lip and dripped onto his overall pocket where he'd kept the hanky and the locket with the picture and hair of his youngest son earlier today. The sting of the slap forced tears from his eyes which made him, in the middle of all his other problems, resent that the others would think he was crying.

"Didn't know him, Captain," Linder said.

"We'll stick for now with the one we know you did. That gentleman there you put the jungle knife in," said Ward.

"Self-defense, Captain," Linder said, hoping Eddie was on his way back home by now.

Final Dispositions

Garner had shattered Linder's shoulder and Linder had filleted Garner's heart. So everyone concluded. Linder never actually admitted to stabbing Garner, just said, "self-defense," or, "he shot me," to every question he was asked, even though that earned him more bloody noses.

The evidence amounted to each man having the other's blood on himself, to Linder's being in the room at the time Garner died, and to the presence of such a unique murder weapon. It didn't help Linder that he'd been to county jail before, entitling Captain Ward to testify that the knife was a "prison shank" (Out of court he called it a 'jungle knife' to add cop irony to Garner's demise).

Of course, Clara had been in the room too, but she could only testify that she'd seen Garner point his weapon at Linder and threaten to "shoot him dead." After that, she said, the weight of the day overwhelmed her and she collapsed in the corner. She couldn't even recall hearing a gunshot. She did, however, have a vague memory of Eddie in the dressing room. The prosecutors considered calling the boy to testify, but let the notion drop after everyone agreed that the boy was too feebleminded to have killed Mister Garner.

One thing arose in Linder's defense that the prosecutor hadn't anticipated. Linder's publicly appointed attorney argued to the jury that all the case amounted to, really, was just a simple country quarrel. A slick and sophisticated Man From The Big City (Garner) tried to get between a Country Boy and His Woman, right after the two of them Just Made A Baby Together. To make matters worse, the City Man shot the New Father in a jealousy fit. Plenty of heads nodded after that was said.

In the end, though, self-defense or no, the twelve good men of the Knoxville jury knew that Linder had to be punished for something.

After all, Mister Garner was from out of town and a popular visitor, a high class man. They convicted Linder of involuntary manslaughter and the judge gave him fifteen to twenty with time off for good behavior. Many people thought the sentence harsh for a country boy defending his family's honor.

Neither Buddy Parker nor his boat were mentioned in court. Captain Ward, and a few other men who liked to see blood coming from other men's noses, interrogated Linder from every direction with both hands. But he stuck to his story that he and Eddie had found the boat drifting and 'borrowed' it to get to town in time to hear Professor Garner speak. There were no witnesses to contradict that story and nobody liked Buddy Parker anyway because, although he was secretly rich, he died owing nearly everybody.

When the time came, Linder entered prison quietly. In that environment he was much respected as a man who had stood up for the honor of his family. Though his shoulder never healed enough to regain full use, he spent his days planning the fishing guide business he wanted to operate some day with Eddie.

Every once in a while he was tempted to tell some inmate that was getting out about the locket under the railroad trestle and ask the man to fetch it for him. But he knew he couldn't trust any of them. As for the 'little guy' that had died, Linder was sorry he never got to know him, but whenever he started to get sentimental about it, he quoted his father: "You can't miss what you never had." Besides, he wasn't entirely convinced that Clara had told him the truth. That baby could still be alive. He was going to look into that as soon as he was released.

On the night Garner died, Clara told Bobby he could stay at her place for a while, she'd look after him. Bobby thanked her but wasn't interested. He felt something was not right about her, ever since his first good look at her in the railroad car. Numb as a rock, he went back to the hotel and packed his bag and put it by the door. Then he went down to the hotel restaurant, a speakeasy made possible by the friendship of Mister Helms, Mayor McKinney, and Captain Ward.

He opened the door and went to the darkest corner to watch. Young farmers, salesmen stuck here for the weekend, local Mechanics', even some men he recognized from the train ride today. Or was it yesterday? It was after midnight, so yeah, it was yesterday. He was right back where he was this time yesterday, only he'd had something yanked from him.

An eruption of laughter came from the bar. A man in dungarees and a green flannel shirt was acting out some story. Bobby recognized him from the train, the beetle-browed man who got cinders in his chin bringing Clara up from the marsh. The other men threw enough jeering wisecracks you could tell they thought he wasn't just funny but foolish.

The man started across the room again, arms chugging, yelling, "Follow me men." The crowd laughed. He walked on, and then did a nifty turnaround to walk backwards without losing his rhythm, saying, "She's down here somewhere, men," and then turned without a hitch to marching forward again. The other men laughed again. The man was pretty good at the maneuver and you could tell he had respect for Garner in the way he imitated him.

Still, the man was drunk and once was enough. And it bothered Bobby to see Garner's memory on its way to becoming a cheap barroom legend. The man must have enjoyed doing it, because he started again with hardly a pause. This time the others didn't watch him as much. He got most of the way through, but then misjudged his distances and tripped over a chair leg, crashing across several chairs and falling to the floor, a chair upside down on top of him. The other fellows turned when they heard that and a cheer went up. A couple of them whistled and applauded this new twist. One of them, his brother if you could judge by appearances, helped him up and led him back to the bar.

Things settled down for a while, but the clowning started again whenever a newcomer arrived. "Hey, Ray, tell Billy here what happened on the train today." And this fellow, Ray, would get up and tell about how this girl, pretty girl too, got pushed off—maybe jumped off —the train today and this man Garner stopped the train and led a search party to find her and then … well, then, he acted out Garner's walk down the railroad tracks, including his turnaround-and-back-again maneuver, and then, this time, deliberately crashed into some chairs and fell down. Up went the roar of laughter that built during his performance. Then Ray's maybe-brother helped him up and led him back to the bunch and they all talked for a while until another new fella arrived. Then they'd all get that gleam of enthusiasm in their eyes and ask Ray, like he was a trained monkey, to do his little novelty act again, and so on.

After a while, even if a new fellow joined them, nobody asked Ray to act out the story anymore. That didn't stop him, though. He got up and staggered through a reenactment that only Bobby watched and then fell to the floor. A few men turned to look, more relieved than concerned, and let him lie there. Bobby crawled under the table and went through the man's pockets and took his money and then slipped out of the saloon.

Back in the hotel room, he didn't turn the lights on, it was awful enough being in a place that felt like a graveyard. His bag was packed, but he wasn't ready to leave. He got into the soft bed he'd tried yesterday afternoon, still fully dressed in the new clothes, including the shoes, Mister Garner had bought him. He'd lain there yesterday fighting the luxury of it all while Garner washed up before his big talk.

Garner was dead, he thought. "Dead" didn't seem like a nice word to use about a friend, but he couldn't think of any other that was as true. In the dark, feeling like he was floating, he could smell the last traces of soap and shaving cream and hair tonic mingled in the pleasant mannish smell Garner left behind. Bobby went deep into his will and shut down his ache for a father. No tears, he thought. I'm lucky I got what I got.

In the morning, he took his bag and left and was never seen again by anyone who'd taken the train from Lynchburg, Virginia to Knoxville, Tennessee that day, May 13, 1920.

Clara went back to Mister Allen's used book store and began to live in her apartment again. As luck would have it, Aunt Polly died and left her another inheritance, bigger than the trust fund her parents had bequested her, this at the same time Mister Allen wanted to retire. She bought his business and enjoyed it enormously. Over the years, she achieved a reputation among the town's book people for being well-read and she occasionally gave talks to local cultural and literary groups. She also met many literate and interesting men, but never one she would call a *homme du monde*, as she'd learned to think of Richard Garner.

She thought about Richard often and how he'd gallantly defended her on one of the most difficult, but splendid, days of her life. She'd learned from her brief romance with him that she had what it takes to attract a man of quality and that it might happen again if luck sent such a man her way again.

The day after she returned to the book store she went to a jewelry store and bought another locket. She put the baby's few remaining pieces of hair and the photograph in it and wore it for a while around her neck. It swung and dangled when she worked though, which bothered her, so one day she took it off and hung it over the finial of her bedroom bureau. That's where it stayed. She kept the baby's memory alive in her mind, but she could not bear to look at his picture anymore.

It took Eddie a lot of walking, a few hitched rides in farmers' wagons, and three days to get back home from Knoxville on his own. His life then returned to normal, such as it was—sitting in the backyard chalking designs on bark-stripped logs and carving designs in everything else.

Sometimes he thought about the time he hurt the man who shot Linder. He didn't feel bad about doing it, though, because Linder had told him in the woods that night that he'd know if Linder needed his help. Linder had even written him a note from jail a year later and told him he was sorry he told that man he was not his son. He appreciated Eddie helping him with that "problem" he was having that night and he wanted to say he was proud to have a son such as him. Eddie rolled the note up and kept in a match safe, just like he'd seen Linder do when they were on the river that day.

One day, his mother was sitting on the porch crying. Eddie went up to her and said, "Linder got this for you when we was away." The locket was quite plain, but nice.

"Open it," Eddie said. "This side first."

She opened it slowly, curious to know what was in there. It contained a small lock of brown hair. "Yours?" she said. Eddie nodded yes. "Shall I open the other side too?"

"Yes," he said.

"What's this, a drawing you did? It looks like you."

"It is me."

Some other time, he'd tell her how he did it, tell her he made a pencil drawing of himself and kept practicing it, reducing it in size until it was just right. And then he got a piece of tin and cut it oval-shaped and painted it glossy white. And then he copied onto the tin what he'd looked like while he stood on tiptoes seeing his own image in his father's shaving mirror.

"Here, put it around my neck for me."

Eddie went behind her and fastened the repaired clasp.

Later, on bad days, when the suspicions returned, she would be tempted to throw away the locket and keep only the hair and picture. She had a sense of where it had come from and it made her jealous and angry. But she kept it because she sensed that Eddie had gone through a lot to get it for her and she didn't want to hurt his feelings.

As a labor of love, Hiller James, the Knoxville journalist whom Garner had stood up that day, wrote a seventy-eight page indictment of Garner's work as fraudulent. No publisher was interested, not even in Europe. The consensus seemed to be that Garner was a pioneer in his field and need not be judged by the same exacting standards as the new crop of professional animal behavior scientists that now proliferated the world's tropical rain forests. Since it was no longer fashionable to study animals as prototypes for human behavioral evolution, Mister James had excited himself over a matter of little worth.

A diorama of a gorilla family may be seen on exhibit at the United States Museum of Natural History in Washington, the nation's first stuffed gorilla social group. The Great Explorer and Scientist, Richard Lynch Garner, had shot them all on behalf of the Smithsonian Institution. Though the gorillas were shot in various places at different times, they are presented as a "family" group in the nation's diorama, not unlike the group assembled on the Southern Railways train that went from Lynchburg to Knoxville on the fateful day narrated in this book.

Although their skins are getting up in years now, the family group endures and can be found behind glass on the first floor in the East Wing of the museum.

The End

About the Author

Hugh Gilmore lives in Philadelphia, where he owns and operates an old and rare book business. He also appears weekly in The Chestnut Hill Local newspaper, writing a column called "The Enemies of Reading." Before moving back to his native Philadelphia twenty years ago he worked as an anthropologist, specializing in primate behavior, especially vocalizations. He has long been fascinated by the life and work of Richard Lynch Garner, one of the subjects/characters of this story.

Acknowledgements

Last Night on the Gorilla Tour went through many drafts during the twelve years of its composition. In that time my work has benefitted from several close and sensitive readings from a few people. In the early days, my sister, Kathy Gilmore, read the entire "first" draft and helped me shape the story. In its "final" draft, Carol Coffin generously gave the book a close reading, several valuable suggestions for improvement, and the final encouragement I needed to bring the book to press. I am also grateful to the novelist and poet Lynn Hoffman, who offered me much sane and useful artistic advice.

I should also mention that in the year 2001 a chapter of this book, now called "Linder and Eddie in the Swamp," won a First Place Award in the Philadelphia Writers Conference's annual Novel Writing competition. I was greatly encouraged by that experience.

Through it all, my wife and best editor, Janet Gilmore, always put her finger on the pulse of the story and kept it running smoothly. Nothing can ever match the fun of coming home from my bookshop office each day to read her the daily installment.

Made in the USA
Lexington, KY
20 February 2013